W9-ANI-585

tmi

tmi

SARAH QUIGLEY

dutton children's books

DUTTON CHILDREN'S BOOKS | A division of Penguin Young Readers Group

Published by the Penguin Group | Penguin Group (USA) Inc., 375 Hudson Street, New York, New York 10014, U.S.A. | Penguin Group (Canada), 90 Eglinton Avenue East, Suite 700, Toronto, Ontario M4P 2Y3, Canada (a division of Pearson Penguin Canada Inc.) | Penguin Books Ltd, 80 Strand, London WC2R 0RL, England | Penguin Ireland, 25 St Stephen's Green, Dublin 2, Ireland (a division of Penguin Books Ltd) | Penguin Group (Australia), 250 Camberwell Road, Camberwell, Victoria 3124, Australia (a division of Pearson Australia Group Pty Ltd) | Penguin Books India Pvt Ltd, 11 Community Centre, Panchsheel Park, New Delhi - 110 017, India | Penguin Group (NZ), 67 Apollo Drive, Rosedale, North Shore 0632, New Zealand (a division of Pearson New Zealand Ltd.) | Penguin Books (South Africa) (Pty) Ltd, 24 Sturdee Avenue, Rosebank, Johannesburg 2196, South Africa | Penguin Books Ltd, Registered Offices: 80 Strand, London WC2R 0RL, England

Library of Congress Cataloging-in-Publication Data
Quigley, Sarah.
Too much information / by Sarah Quigley.—1st ed.
p. cm.
Summary: Fifteen-year-old Becca has the habit of revealing too much personal information about herself and her friends, but when her boyfriend breaks up with her and she vows to stop "oversharing," she does not realize that her blog postings are not nearly as anonymous as she thought.
ISBN 978-0-525-47908-6
[1. Self-control—Fiction. 2. Interpersonal relations—Fiction. 3. Dating (Social customs)—Fiction. 4. Blogs—Fiction. 5. High schools—Fiction. 6. Schools—Fiction.] I. Title.
PZ7.Q4158To 2009
[Fic]—dc 22   2008014607

Published in the United States by Dutton Children's Books,
a division of Penguin Young Readers Group
345 Hudson Street, New York, New York 10014
www.penguin.com/youngreaders

Designed by Irene Vandervoort

Printed in USA | First Edition

10 9 8 7 6 5 4 3 2 1

We all need to do something
Try to keep the truth from showing up.

—The White Stripes

*To my family, for putting up with so many of my TMI moments,
and
in memory of Wayne Brix*

ACKNOWLEDGMENTS

TMI: thanking many individuals

Sarah Shumway, my brilliant editor, found my blog by chance and then contacted me about writing a book, which has to be about the coolest thing that has ever happened to me. I would totally buy Sarah a pony if I could.

My awesome parents constantly told me that I should write a book (they were right, as usual) and have cheered on a lifetime of writing efforts. I also owe big thanks to super dad-in-law Harry, fab sis-in-law Erica, and favorite sister Anna for giving me feedback on early drafts. My statuesque brothers, Robert and Michael, told me what teenage boys like to read and inspired some of the best lines in the book.

Wayne Brix, English teacher extraordinaire, fueled my passion for writing and encouraged me to keep doing it, always. I miss him and think of him often.

Charlotte, my wonderful daughter, literally kicked me (gently, with her tiny fetal feet) to finish the book and had sense enough to be born after the manuscript was done.

Finally, I must spoon a huge dollop of gratitude on my rockin' husband, David, for his support, patience, love, ideas, shoulder rubs, and mad editing skills. And for letting me overshare, again and again.

tmi

Becca's diary:

NO ELECTRONIC VERSION AVAILABLE

Friday, February 20

None of this would have happened if it hadn't been for Evan Johnson's tongue.

When we were making out in my basement, our yearning physiques silhouetted against the soft glow of a Mafia movie, everything would start out really nicely. There'd be a romantically chaste lip-lock like the one between Anne and Gilbert at the end of *Anne of Avonlea*. I'd feel a ripple of electricity run down my spine, bounce off my toes, and ricochet through the roof of my mouth. Things would get all tingly. I wished we could have kissed that way forever.

And then, the tongue.

It slithered in slowly, the way I imagine that snake entered the Garden of Eden and totally messed things up between Adam and Eve. In a way, Evan and I were like Adam and Eve, although we wore more than fig leaves for the practical reason that it was December in Minnesota, so we had to fend off frostbite. I was Evan's first girlfriend, and he was my first boyfriend. We were each other's make-out guinea pigs. Our relationship was an example of the blind leading the blind. It was truly beautiful.

Except for the tongue.

Making out with him set off this crazy chain of events. If I'd just stayed at home watching Molly Ringwald movies with Katie like a good little girl, or if Jai had never entrusted me with his biggest secret, I could have spared everyone some major angst.

But that's not what happened. Katie and I met Jai, one of the best things ever to happen to us in this one-horse town. I dated Evan, who opened his mouth and slipped me the tongue, and I turned around and opened my mouth and had many subsequent slips of the tongue. And after all the drama that went down, I've more than learned my lesson. I will never kiss and tell again.

A lot of people think that what happened was all my fault and that I'm this terrible person for what I did, but those people don't know the whole story. And I'm not blaming Evan, really. He's just a nice boy who needed some kissing lessons.

All of that seems very far away now. In fact, if I go back to the beginning, I can't believe what a different person I was. At least, I hope I am different than I was. That's why I'm starting this diary today, on the morning of my sixteenth birthday. I got up half an hour early, just so I'd have time to write the first entry.

It's time to turn over a new leaf. I hope the old leaves stay buried under the February snow and disintegrate before the spring thaw comes.

1

So there was this gigantic bag of prunes sitting on the counter, right?" I say. "I don't know why my mom bought them, since I've always associated prunes with constipated old ladies, you know? But there they were."

It's December 1, and I'm eating lunch with my best and only friend, Katie Eidsvaag.

"So the prunes were on the counter, and then what?" Katie asks.

"Well, I figured if my mom bought them, they couldn't be that gross because she's always going on about the gross things that other people eat, like hash browns covered in ranch dressing and Funyuns and stuff."

Katie nods and picks a stray fuzzy out of her waist-length auburn hair and smoothes out her broomstick skirt. Katie has big, gorgeous brown eyes, a heart-shaped face, and a long, sloping nose. She's never worn a drop of makeup, which fits in with her effortless bohemian fashion sense.

"Anyway," I continue, "I decided to try a prune. And you know what? It was really good—totally sweet and much better than a raisin. Plus, I could really bite into it, as opposed to trying to bite into raisins, which have always reminded me of little rabbit turds—"

"Eating. I'm eating, Becca."

"Well, you may not like the next part, then, but I'm going to tell you anyway."

Katie puts her sandwich down and sighs. "What? You ate too many prunes and had to run to the bathroom every half an hour?"

"It was frickin' terrible! Really gross and a little painful. But I won't say anything more about it now."

Katie gives me a look that says, *I totally don't believe you.*

We eat in silence for a few moments, but I need closure on the trauma of the prune incident. Plus, I want Katie to learn from the error of my ways. "Let's just say that a prune binge is a mistake a person only makes once—"

"Look, cool new boy!" Katie exclaims, pointing at the lunch-line checkout. I'm prepared to get all pissy at Katie for interrupting me, which she knows I absolutely hate, but I'm struck speechless by the sight in front of me.

Cool New Boy (CNB) is a few feet away from us, clutching his tray and looking as lost as a marooned pirate. Even more striking than his vulnerability is his outfit: a black Ramones T-shirt with pink lettering, black pleather pants, and wingtips. CNB has molded his sandy brown hair into a faux hawk.

I notice Rod Knutson, Lance Tucker, and the Schwermer twins, Dustin and Justin, aka the Rod and Gun Club, staring at him in utter confusion. It usually takes the proximity of a dance-liner's firm little booty to draw them out of their world of monster truck rallies and demolition derbies, but the presence of CNB distracts them.

Lance shouts, "Halloween was in October, Screw Boy!"

"Yeah," adds Rod. "Those pants scream, 'I drop the soap on purpose.'"

Poor CNB's mouth drops open. I know I should stay out of this, but the Rod and Gun Club boys always make me so mad.

"Thanks for that glimpse into your future, Rod," I say. "Because really, if anyone around here is going to end up in prison, it's you."

It's true. Rod was suspended a couple of months ago for setting off a stink bomb in the boys' room. He clearly has criminal tendencies.

"Shove it, Farrell," Rod shoots back. "And while you're at it, go make out with the Franklin What's-His-Butt Roosevelt poster in your bedroom."

"It was *Theodore* Roosevelt," I correct Rod, which only makes him and his friends burst out laughing. I can't believe those guys haven't let go of last week's Teddy Roosevelt incident in American history class. Mr. Huhn asked us what we knew about Roosevelt, and when I saw a picture of Teddy in our textbook, all I could say was that I thought he was pretty sexy, despite the mustache. The Rod and Gun Club went crazy concocting these perverted fantasies involving me and the twenty-sixth president. I never should have said anything, but I just couldn't help it.

CNB is obviously confused by this exchange because, I mean, who wouldn't be? He's most likely thinking, *What planet spawned this mutant? And does she really have a thing for Teddy Roosevelt?*

To my utter surprise, CNB smiles at me, so I beckon for him

to join us. He rushes toward Katie and me like he's drawn by a magnetic force, his spine arrow straight and his legs propelling him like a duck.

"Teddy Roosevelt, huh?" says CNB. "What was that all about?"

"Oh, they think I have a crush on him."

CNB squints. "*Do* you?"

"No!" I say a little too loudly as CNB sits down. "Whatever. Forget it. And don't listen to them. They're just a bunch of tools who like to murder squirrels while they chew Skoal."

"The Rod and Gun Club. Blech," declares Katie solemnly.

CNB looks puzzled. "The Rod and Gun Club?"

"Yeah," I say. "Katie and I call them that because the guy who just made that charming comment to you about the soap is Rod Knutson, and he and the rest of his redneck cousins think they're these big hunting-and-fishing studs. They're mean to everyone except for girls who are willing to climb into their pickup trucks and touch their crusty—"

"Yeah, I can smell a redneck from miles off," CNB says quickly, looking vaguely ill. I'm too charmed by his deep voice to be very mad that he just cut me off. "I'm Jai, by the way. Jai spelled with an *i* instead of a *y* at the end."

"Why do you spell your name with an *i*?" Katie asks.

"Well, my full name is James Andrew Irving, so my initials spell *J-A-I*."

"God, that is *so* cool," I declare, not caring how lame I probably sound. "Much cooler than my initials. I'm Becca. Rebecca Olivia Farrell. *Rof!*"

Katie gives Jai a weak smile that says, *Yes, she's* always *like this*. Fortunately, Katie is too nice to say anything so direct. She leaves that to me.

"Nice to meet you, Becca." He turns to Katie. "And you are?"

"Oh, this is Katie Eidsvaag," I volunteer. "Actually, her real name is Kathleen, and she doesn't even have a middle name. Isn't that crazy? Anyway, she's really quiet and shy, so that's why she's not talking, but don't worry, Katie's totally fun once she gets to know someone. She just takes a while to open up. I'm not sure why, but she has major trust issues."

"Um, Becca," Katie says slowly. "If I had trust issues, I certainly wouldn't be hanging out with you."

"Ouch," I say. "But true enough."

I turn back to Jai. "Obviously, I'm not like Katie at all. In fact, I really have the opposite problem. People are always telling me to shut up, but I can't help it. Katie seems to get a kick out of me, though. So does my boyfriend, Evan Johnson. We've been dating for two weeks."

Jai wets his lips. "A boyfriend, huh? Wow."

"Yeah, I know. I thought no guy would ever like me. In fact, I was starting to wonder if I'd have to resort to becoming a slut to get any attention from guys. Not that I want attention from guys who like slutty girls."

"Like the Rod and Gun Club?" Jai volunteers.

"Exactly," I reply. "And since Evan asked me out, I didn't have to turn into a slut."

"Close call," remarks Jai.

"Um, so because I've never had a boyfriend, does that mean that I'm on the road to Slut City?" asks Katie.

"Of course not," I assure her. "Besides, one of these days, Luke Kleinschmidt is going to come to his senses."

"Becca!" Katie whimpers, covering her face with her hands. "Don't!"

"Don't what?" I ask. "Tell Jai about your big crush on Luke? He seems trustworthy."

Jai purses his lips and knits his brow. "Do you spill *all* of your friends' secrets?"

"Of course not," I say quickly. "I don't have any other friends. So whatever we talk about here stays in the circle. That's the rule."

"Or it is now," remarks Katie. She turns to Jai. "Yeah, I have a crush on the captain of the hockey team. He's a senior, but we have an art elective together. He only talks to me when he wants to borrow my paintbrushes, and he always calls me Kelly."

"Sounds like the beginning of something beautiful." Jai chuckles. Katie's face falls, and I see Jai quickly trying to think of a way to cover up his unintentional dis.

"You're a doll," Jai says to Katie. "The boys will come to their senses soon."

Katie's eyes widen, as if this is a true revelation. "Really?"

"I've told her that a thousand times, Jai," I say. "She never believes me." I'm a little jealous that Jai just called Katie a doll because I doubt anyone would ever say that about me. Unless they were referring to one of those dolls that tells you it just wet itself.

Jai just looks at Katie, who shrugs and finishes her sandwich. Jai digs back into his food.

I decide to change the subject. "I adore your outfit, Jai. You look like a rock star."

Jai looks up from his lunch and grins. "I guess the faux hawk worked. And I just got the Ramones T-shirt last week."

"So cool," I remark.

Jai leans toward me conspiratorially. "So, Becca, you seem like a girl in the know, and since I'm the new boy in town, what dirty little secrets can you tell me about this place?"

"Pine Prairie?" I squeak. "If this town has any dirty little secrets, I'm certainly not aware of them. Living here is totally boring. I mean, yeah, the theater finally started showing first-run movies, and you can even get espresso here now, thanks to my mom. She owns Prairie Perks, the only coffee shop. But in this tiny town, everyone sticks their cold, sniffling noses in each other's business. It's lame, lame, lame."

Jai nods in amusement. "Sounds familiar. Go on."

"Go on?" I repeat incredulously.

"Becca meets very few people who actually encourage her to talk more," Katie explains.

"I see," says Jai, turning back to me. "So what else?"

"Well, the newspaper here comes out once a week, and people even advertise their Tupperware parties. The crime report includes things like, 'Gang of nine-year-olds caught riding their bikes after eight P.M.' I guess that tells you something about how little there is to do. It's a pretty big problem, to tell you the truth. It's like an *After School Special* script. Kids wind up drinking and doing it. Here at the high school, someone's always pregnant. Even my mom had me when she was in high school—the condom totally broke after junior prom."

Jai blinks.

"Anyway, most people stay here their whole lives. But not me—I'm dying to get out of here. I'm going to college in New York. I've already started looking into the application requirements for NYU and Columbia."

"Becca has big plans," Katie adds. "She's always reading blogs by people who live in big cities and claim to have glamorous lives."

"Right," I remark. "I mean, I have to be prepared for life outside of Pine Prairie. I have to know what's going on if I'm going to be glamorous."

Jai nods. "Makes sense. What's the point of a life without glamour?"

"Totally!" I exclaim. "Jai, you're a gem."

"Oh, stop," Jai protests, but he doesn't look embarrassed by my compliment.

"So what's your story, Jai?" Katie asks.

"Um, well, I moved here from Northfield. You know it? The town with two colleges?" I nod and Katie shakes her head.

"Not your typical small Minnesota town with a bar, a church, and a gas station," he says. "It's pretty cool actually. There are lots of coffee shops and thrift stores and stuff."

"You must miss it," I say.

Jai contemplates this. "Kind of. It's too soon to say, really."

"So what else can you tell us?" I snap my fingers. "Quick! Five amazing facts about James Andrew Irving right now!"

Jai looks a bit startled by my request, but he grins. "Okay, I'm an only child, a Sagittarius, I like to draw, I'm learning how to silk-screen my own T-shirts, and I think you two should come over to my house after school to bake cupcakes and watch *Hairspray,* the greatest movie ever made."

Katie and I exchange awestruck grins.

"It's like you dropped out of the sky from Planet Awesome," I remark. Seriously, I didn't know they even *made* boys like Jai.

"Oh, *stop* already!" Jai says again, rolling his eyes in mock embarrassment.

"So you said *Hairspray,* right?" asks Katie. "The new one or the old one?"

Jai clutches his chest. "I love that you even know about the old one. I'm impressed."

"I know about it, too," I say.

"Of course you know about it," Jai says. "I could tell you two were clued in."

"So which one do you prefer?" Katie asks.

"Well, the original does have some very fine moments," Jai answers, "but I'm a sucker for musicals, so the new one is more my speed."

"If you like musicals, then you have to try out for *Grease* next month with me," I say.

Jai's face brightens. "This school is doing *Grease?*" He leans back in his chair. "Hmm, a musical. Maybe Pine Prairie won't be so bad after all."

2

Later in the afternoon, I'm standing in Jai's kitchen. There are moving boxes stacked against the wall by the refrigerator, and Jai has to fish the electric mixer out of the pile of boxes before we can start making cupcakes.

While Jai is rummaging, I go to find the bathroom, wandering down the hall of the Irvings' split-level home and tripping over more boxes as I go. I find the bathroom on the left, but instead I turn to the door on my right and open it. It must be Jai's room, since he's an only child and I'm guessing that his parents don't sleep in a twin bed.

The room is immaculate. The black-and-red-striped bedspread is tucked tightly over the bed, and books are already in neat rows on their shelves. A line of half a dozen hats, from fedoras to plaid golf caps, rests on the top shelf. A poster for the Broadway version of *Hairspray* is tacked up above Jai's desk, upon which rests a framed photo of Jai and a very hot boy with black hair, bronze skin, and a wide smile. I wonder who he is.

By the time I get back from the bathroom, Jai has successfully extracted the mixer. Newspaper, dishes, and utensils are scattered throughout the kitchen, and I'm surprised that someone with such a tidy room would just tear through the boxes in the kitchen.

"Of course it had to be at the bottom of the very last box I looked in," Jai says.

"Figures," I agree. "I bet you'll be happy when all of this stuff is put away."

"Oh yeah," says Jai, raising his eyebrows. "I'm a total neat freak."

Katie and I exchange a wary look as we glance around at the mess he's just made in the kitchen.

"Except when it comes to urgent matters like making cupcakes," Jai adds quickly. "Let's get these going."

After the cupcakes are in the oven, we go into the living room and start watching *Hairspray*. After a while, Jai pauses the movie to pull the cupcakes out of the oven, and when the movie is over, we go into the kitchen to start making the frosting, gushing about our favorite scenes and characters and who we'd want to play if a stage version of *Hairspray* ever made it to Pine Prairie.

"So tell me some more about your boyfriend, Becca," says Jai, frosting a cupcake. "I'm fascinated. I mean, I don't have any experience in the romance department, so I need a vicarious thrill. If you don't mind, of course."

"Mind?" Katie snorts. "You're talking to Becca, who will tell you everything. For example, she is widely known as the worst Truth or Dare player on the planet. I had a slumber party in sixth grade, and we had to make a rule that Becca could only do dares because we already knew all of her secrets."

"Wow," responds Jai. "So I guess you'll tell me whatever I want to know?"

"Sure. I have no shame," I admit. "And anyway, the girls that Katie invited to that slumber party were *boring*. They could barely talk about which movie stars they thought were hot. I, on the other hand, was game to talk about anything: my new body hairs, the date of my last bed-wetting experience, you name it. But nobody wanted to hear it. They all shouted, 'Too much information, Becca!'"

"She hates that," adds Katie.

"What, TMI?" asks Jai. "Why?"

"Let's just say I've heard it one too many times," I answer, swiping a fingerful of frosting from the bowl on the counter. "Anyway, what would you like to know, Jai?"

"More about your boyfriend."

"Hmm, let's see, what can I say about Evan? Well, he's a freshman, and I don't have to tell you that it's slightly embarrassing and scandalous to be dating a younger man, but he's awesome, so I don't care. The Rod and Gun Club makes fun of Evan and me whenever they see us together, but I usually just tell them to choke on their Skoal."

"Okay; younger man," says Jai, as if he's got a mental checklist. "And?"

"Um, he has a ponytail and plays the bassoon and—"

"Have you made out with him yet?" Jai interrupts. I draw in a breath. It's a shock to have the tables turned on me like this. Usually I'm the one asking the juicy questions.

Katie giggles. "I think you've met your match, Becca."

I lean against the counter. "I can handle it, Katie." I turn to Jai. "No, we haven't made out yet. We're both a little shy about that sort of thing, and there also hasn't been a very good opportunity, you know, away from prying eyes. Namely the prying eyes of my mother, who freaked when I told her that I had a date in the first place."

"So how did you two get together?" Jai asks.

"We met during the fall theater production. *Our Town.*"

"Good play," says Jai. "What part did you have?"

"I was Emily."

"Wow," remarks Jai. "The lead. That's pretty impressive."

"I was surprised to get it," I say. "Especially since I was only in the chorus of *Fiddler on the Roof* last year."

"Were you in the play, Katie?" Jai asks.

Katie shakes her head and peels the baking paper off a cupcake. "Not me. I'd have a nervous breakdown if I had to get up in front of so many people and sing and dance and stuff."

"Although you'd be really good at it," I remark. "Seriously, Jai, you should hear her sing sometime. Katie has an amazing voice."

"I don't know about that," counters Katie. "But it doesn't matter anyway. I like to be part of the theater crowd, but I stay strictly behind the scenes. I do set design and props."

"Nothing wrong with that," Jai remarks. He turns back to me. "So how was *Our Town?*"

I pause, smoothing back a wisp into my ponytail. "It was sort of fun, but sometimes not, because of Jamie."

"Who's Jamie?"

"Jamie Whitaker? She dates Rod Knutson."

"That's gross," Jai remarks. "She must have very poor taste."

"Oh yes. Jamie is someone with severe likability issues," volunteers Katie, her doe eyes narrowing.

I jump in. "That's saying a lot, coming from Katie, because she hardly ever bad-mouths anyone. Anyway, Jamie was totally bitter because she had to be Mrs. Soames. She kept saying that she would have made a much better Emily than me."

"And she threw a fit when she had to wear this big baggy dress, saying that it made her look all dumpy," adds Katie. "When someone said her character was supposed to look that way, she actually cried and threatened to drop out of the play."

"Unfortunately, Ms. Miller, our director, convinced her not to."

"Yikes," says Jai. "Can anyone say *prima donna*?"

"Totally. So I was distracted by that and also by Matt Wooderson."

"Who's that?" asks Jai.

"Just this boy that Becca's been drooling over since middle school," volunteers Katie. She knows I don't care who hears about this. Except for maybe Matt. That would be a little embarrassing.

"I'll point him out tomorrow at lunch," I say.

✳✳✳

"See that table full of jocks over there?" I tilt my head to the right.

"Yeah?" says Jai, his voice laced with suspicion.

"Your favorite people, I'm sure," I say, because let's face it:

any high school boy who wears pleather pants isn't exactly looking for an invitation to hang with the football crowd. "Anyway, Matt is sitting on the end. The one with the really good hair?"

"Yeah, I definitely see him," replies Jai, biting his lower lip. "Is he a complete jackass?"

"That's the thing, he's not at all!" I say, not taking my eyes off Matt and his thick, wavy hair, long limbs, and pecs that are visible through his sweater. Matt takes a long sip of milk and scratches his head. I draw in a shuddering breath. "He's a sweetheart. And a really good singer and dancer. He played Perchik in *Fiddler*. He's popular, too, but not in an I-crush-beer-cans-on-my-forehead sort of way. Matt is the kind of guy who's friendly with everyone, even freaks like me."

Jai laughs. "So basically, as far as high school guys go, Matt is a unicorn."

We all crack up.

"Pretty much," I say. "So you can imagine what it was like to be in the play with him. He played Mr. Webb, my character's dad. At least he wasn't George, Emily's fiancé. That was Derrick Hansen, who's pretty nice but has a girlfriend. He doesn't inspire any hot and heavy feelings in me, anyway."

"Hot and heavy?" Jai repeats, smirking. "That's a choice phrase. Is that how you feel about Evan? Or maybe Teddy Roosevelt?"

"Shut up! You know what I mean. And anyway, I'm not sure how I'd describe my feelings for Matt, but whenever we were onstage together, I could totally smell his neck. It smelled so good that I just wanted to lick it. I had to stay in character, so I'd tell myself, 'This guy is supposed to be your *dad*. You wouldn't want to lick your dad's neck, would you? That's messed up.' But I couldn't help myself from thinking it because his neck smelled so awesome. Sort of like campfire smoke and Ivory soap. If someone bottled that scent, I would pay big money for it."

Jai chuckles. "You're an overshare artist, Becca," he says. "I like the way you marinate your words in the tiniest details. It makes everything you say even juicier."

"Jai, that is literally the nicest thing anyone has ever said to me," I say.

"So, um, getting back to Magically Scented Matt," Jai says, and Katie and I can't help laughing. "If you were so hot for him, then how did you end up with Evan? You haven't even mentioned him yet."

"Right. I just wanted you to understand why I didn't even notice Evan until later. He was up in the lighting booth."

"Oh, a techie. Is he here? Can you point him out?" Jai glances over his shoulder.

"Oh, no. Like I said, Evan's a freshman, and they have their lunch period before the sophomores. I'm actually kind of thankful for that because otherwise I'd feel obligated to sit with him, which would be fine if it were just Evan, but Josh is unbearable."

"Josh?" asks Jai.

"Evan's sidekick. He's the kind of guy who says crap like, 'Peachy keen, jelly bean' when anyone asks him how he's doing."

"Good God," Jai declares with disgust. "That's pitiful."

"Yeah, I know. But anyway, I was leaving rehearsal one day, and Evan just stepped out of the lighting booth and told me he thought I was doing a really good job in the play. And that's when I noticed how cute he was."

"Describe," begs Jai.

"Um, well, he's tall and skinny and has a ponytail and pierced ears."

"Oh, a little fourteen-year-old badass, huh?"

"He just turned fifteen," I say. "Anyway, he's not conventionally handsome, mainly because of his nose. It's kind of like Gonzo's from the Muppets. Still, there's something about him that tells me there's a man hidden beneath the adolescent shield of acne and the nose that his face hasn't grown into."

Jai glances over at Katie knowingly. "Okay, Matt may be a standard-issue hottie, but Becca is clearly way into Evan."

"Yeah, she is," Katie agrees, smirking. "Even though he hasn't grown into his face yet."

Jai raises his eyebrow. "I just grew into my face a couple of months ago, so there's still hope for the kid." We have a good laugh over this, and then Jai's face is serious again. "So what happened next?"

"Well, after that, Evan started coming down from the lighting booth and asking me about my hobbies and stuff. It turned out that we like a lot of the same bands. He even burned me a CD of his favorite songs and I really liked it, so I burned him a CD, and we talked about the songs a bunch, and I just looked forward to seeing him after rehearsals. So when the play wrapped up two weeks ago, I was really surprised when Evan came up to me after the cast party and asked me if I wanted to go to Pizza Hut to cure our postplay depression. I was like, 'Sure! Pizza is an excellent cure for a number of ailments. Depression, starvation, constipation, PMS, menstrual cramps, erectile dysfunction. Anything, really.' And I just kept rambling on like that, like a total dork, until Josh walked up and said, 'Let's go.'"

"Oh," Jai says, blinking. "So Josh went with you guys?"

"Yeah, and I was way disappointed, but then before we were about to leave, Josh was like, 'Dude, I have to run to the can'"— I roll my eyes—"and Evan actually stroked my hand under the table and laced his fingers through mine. It really surprised me that he was totally taking charge of the situation in such a, um, *manly* way." I blush as I say this.

"Okay, so what did Mr. Manly do next?" Jai prods, as if I need prodding.

"Well, he squeezed my hand and asked me if I wanted to go out with him!" I bounce triumphantly in my chair.

"So of course you said yes, right?" Jai asks.

"Naturally." I nod. "So last weekend, we went to the movies, and I could tell that Evan was totally nervous, because he kept spilling popcorn and laughing in this really high-pitched way at parts of the movie that weren't even funny and I was so embarrassed for him. I was kind of expecting him to hold my hand like he did in Pizza Hut, but I guess he was just too shy this time. But then, as we were waiting outside the theater for his mom to pick us up, he did touch my shoulder and smile at me."

"Hmm." Jai looks pensively at the ceiling. "Well, that's something."

"So what do you think?" I ask breathlessly. "Do you think he really likes me? I mean, what do you do when you like a girl?"

Jai pauses for a moment. "Um, well, first, I think he definitely likes you. If he didn't, he wouldn't have been so nervous. And a dark movie theater is kind of a high-pressure environment for a guy because of the hand-holding and whole fake-yawn thing." Jai covers his mouth in a pretend yawn and drapes his hand over Katie's shoulder. She looks alarmed, and Jai quickly brings his arm back to his side. "Just demonstrating. Sorry, Katie."

"It's okay," she replies softly, staring at her lap.

Jai straightens and studies my face intently. "You're Evan's first girlfriend, right?"

"Oh yeah," I say.

"Then this is unknown territory. Give the boy a little time. He'll make a move eventually."

"You're probably right."

"So what's on for your next date?"

Three days later, on Friday evening, Evan and I are sitting in my basement watching *Goodfellas*, which he insisted I see after I told him I'd never heard of it. I chatter throughout the beginning of the movie about how weird it is that the police can't just control the Mafia and stop them from committing crimes. I'm struck with silent awe for a few moments when we get to the scene in which Ray Liotta leads Lorraine Bracco through the back entrance of a restaurant on their date. They wind their way down a hall, through the kitchen, and into the dining room, where waiters set up their VIP table.

"God, that's an amazing shot," Evan remarks.

"Yeah," I agree. "And it's very romantic the way he just takes control of the situation. I bet she's really turned on by that. He looks superhot in his suit, too. They'll probably do it later, don't you think? I mean, I doubt he's going to all this trouble because he hopes she'll kiss him on the cheek at the end of the night." Oops, did that just come out of my mouth? And will Evan take it as some sort of hint? I didn't really mean it as a hint, though I wouldn't mind if he tried to kiss me. This *is* a perfect opportunity with us here alone in the dark basement, although I definitely couldn't handle more than a kiss, and certainly not *sex*. My God. I don't know what Evan expects, but now I'm worried that I've confused him.

Evan coughs, and the cough turns into a laugh. "I, ah, I don't know what happens at the end of their date because the movie doesn't show that. And not to give too much away, but they do end up, you know, um, making love, because they get married."

I'm impressed with the way Evan rolls with my overshare but suddenly a little embarrassed that he just said "making love." Plus, he might be thinking about doing that. *Yikes.*

I shift on the couch. "Well, they're a cute couple, anyway."

"I think *you're* cute," Evan remarks. I look at him and smile shyly. All of a sudden I don't have *anything* to say.

Evan gently takes my hands in his and kisses me on the

cheek. I look at him intently, the blood rushing through my body so fast, I'm pretty sure it's going to squirt out of my nose.

✳ ✳ ✳

"So then what?" asks Jai the next afternoon. We're at his house making snickerdoodles.

"Drumroll, please," I say, tapping a wooden spoon on the countertop. "Evan kissed me on the lips! And I was like, 'Oh my God, my first kiss. It's really happening!'"

"What did it feel like?" Katie asks.

"Well, I was kind of surprised by how smooshy Evan's lips felt. They were almost like a ripe banana that's ready to be all mashed up and made into banana bread." Jai and Katie nod knowingly. Baking analogies totally work with these two. "So then our spit mixed together, and I finally understood why people use the word *mushy* to mean affectionate. It's like we weren't humans but more like fish or insects in a mating ritual on a nature show. And even as I was thinking about how bizarre the whole thing was, there was this crazy energy rippling through me. Like an electric shock. Anyway, it was really weird and cool at the same time."

"Wow! That sounds so exciting, Becca!" Jai's eyes are glowing.

"And then, the tongue," I declare solemnly. The glow swiftly fades from Jai's eyes.

"He slipped you the tongue?!" cries Katie incredulously, dropping a measuring cup on the counter. "Really? Like how?"

"Well, it started slowly and crept into my mouth. Before I knew it, I was practically choking on his tongue because it just filled up my mouth. And I was like, 'Holy cow, this boy has a ginormous tongue!' And instead of pulling his tongue back after a few seconds, Evan just let it hang out in my mouth while I tried to figure out what to do with it," I say, flattening dough balls on a cookie sheet.

"Ew!" shrieks Katie. "That's soooo gross."

"Tell me about it," I say glumly. It *was* gross. I shudder as I recall how slimy it felt.

"So what did you do?" Jai asks.

"I pulled away from his face and snuggled into his shoulder. We sat like that for a while, and then he started stroking my hair. He hit a snag, which hurt a little, but I decided that was better than dealing with his tongue again."

"No doubt," concedes Katie as she puts the cookie sheet in the oven.

"Still, you had your virgin lips deflowered," Jai marvels.

Katie adopts a concerned expression. "Are your lips sore? Or like, does your mouth feel weird or anything?"

I pause to consider this and run my finger over my lips, then rub them together.

"No, not really," I reply. Katie and Jai just stare at me. "Jeez, you guys are looking at me like I'm some sort of flippin' medical curiosity."

"Well, you are," Jai states plainly. "And if that's a problem, then maybe you need to hang out with bigger sluts than Katie and me."

"Like who?" I ask. "Jamie Whitaker? I think I'd rather put up with you two."

"Oh, thank you, Becca!" cries Jai suddenly, dropping to his knees. "Thank you for stooping to be friends with a couple of antisluts like Katie and me! We are forever in your debt, Overshare Queen!"

"All hail!" I shout, picking up a wooden spoon and holding it regally like a scepter.

"May your reign be long and prosperous!" declares Katie.

We all collapse into a fit of laughter and eat snickerdoodles until it hurts.

3

I can't take the tongue anymore," I say glumly to Katie and Jai at lunch two weeks later, two days before Christmas break starts. "I may have to dump Evan."

"You're thinking of dumping Evan because of *that?*" Katie asks. "I know it grosses you out, but can't you look past it or train him or something? I thought you were crazy about him."

"Yeah," echoes Jai. "I thought you were all psyched to finally be getting some action."

"I was. I am. Oh God, I don't know anymore," I whine. "It was really bad this weekend. I mean, I know you said I should give him another chance, Jai, so that's what I decided to do. So we were at his place on Saturday night, right? And I'd been reading about kissing in *CosmoGIRL!*, so I was all ready to be like, 'Here's how I like to be kissed. Let me show you.'"

"Yeah, you mentioned that strategy at lunch the other day," says Jai.

"I did?" I ask. "Oh, right, of course."

"So did it work?" Katie asks eagerly.

"I was hoping it would," I reply. "We were watching *The Godfather* in Evan's living room, and we were practically alone because his parents were out having dinner and his little brother,

Joey, was in his room, probably playing with himself the way seventh-grade boys do—"

"Becca!" Jai puts his hand up. "That's a little more information than we need."

I stare at Jai in horror. I can't believe he just said that to me, especially after I told him how much I hate being talked to that way. I glance over at Katie, who is staring at her lunch tray.

Jai frowns in confusion. "What? What's the problem?"

I take a deep breath. How can Jai be so oblivious to the foul he's just committed?

"Jai, you just TMI'd me," I announce, trying hard to mask the tension in my voice.

Jai wads up his napkin and tosses it on his tray. "No, I didn't. I said, 'That's a little more information—'"

"I know what you said," I say flatly. "And it was darn close to my least favorite phrase."

"She really hates that," Katie adds.

Jai raises his palms. "Wow, sorry. I had no idea that the effect was so severe. However, Becca, you have to admit that Katie and I don't really need to know the details of what young Joey Johnson was doing in his bedroom on Saturday night. It's not really relevant to what happened between you and Evan."

Hmm. Jai has a point.

Jai touches my shoulder. "Hey, Becca, you look like you're ready to cry or something."

"I'm okay," I say, and Jai smiles. "And you're right," I add. "The Joey Johnson detail isn't important. I'm sorry I brought it up."

"It's not a big deal," Jai answers, rubbing my shoulder. "So you were in Evan's living room watching *The Godfather* and thinking about the make-out techniques you read about in one of your girlie mags, and then?"

Katie looks like she's about to bubble over with excitement.

"Then I leaned over and kissed him." I pause dramatically.

"And?" presses Katie. "Vicarious-thrill time!"

"Well, I hate to disappoint you, but there was nothing thrilling about it. It was okay at first, and Evan even kept his tongue in his own mouth for a little while, and then—"

"Duh-dunt, duh-dunt, duh-dunt, duh-dunt," sings Jai in his velvety bass, doing the theme song from *Jaws*.

"Thanks for the sound track," I say. "Anyway, this time, it wasn't even gradual. Evan just shoved the whole thing in my mouth, and I was practically choking. I was like, 'Ick, ick, ick.' I mean, how can somebody be so cute and so vile at the same time?"

"I'm telling you," remarks Jai, "he's not vile. He's just new at this. He'll get the hang of it. And in the meantime, you can just imagine that it's like a big brownie or something."

"A brownie?" I ask. "That thing is *no* brownie. Katie?" I turn to her for some kind of validation about the lameness of Jai's brownie comment.

"I don't know. I mean, it sounds nasty, but you have to be enjoying the fact that a boy finally likes you," Katie points out. "Evan practically follows you around like a puppy."

"A puppy?" I repeat. "He is *not* a puppy. Although now I have this image of Evan wearing a collar and me leading him on a leash down the hallway. Sick. Thanks a lot, Katie."

Katie doubles over with laughter.

Jai snickers. "Wait, he's not a puppy, but maybe he's more like a full-grown Saint Bernard. They have huge tongues, after all. Dripping with drool. Yum."

I shoot Jai a look. "Why must you make this grosser than it already is?"

"Oh, come on, you're the one who told us all of that in the first place," he retorts. "And anyway, you should be grateful that Evan doesn't have chronic halitosis or a desire to chew your lips off or something."

"You may be right, but since you've never made out with anybody, I don't think that you're in a position to judge," I reply smugly.

Jai gives me a look of faux disapproval and brushes cookie crumbs off his gray blazer. "What about you, Katie? Any sage tidbits for Miss Becca, High Priestess of the Make-Out?"

Katie smirks. "Um, well, I'm kind of in the same boat as Jai, I guess, although I'd like to eventually get out there to do a bit of my own fieldwork."

Jai smiles. "It's a lucky boy who gets to be your research assistant, darling."

"Are you offering yourself to me for experimental make-out purposes, Jai?" Katie asks.

"Ashli Berg will be so hurt," I point out, failing to conceal a giggle. Ashli is a junior with three obsessions: German Club (she's the president), her stuffed panda collection, and our boy Jai. And yes, she dots the *i* at the end of her name with a heart.

A week after Jai arrived in Pine Prairie, he found a note in his locker from Ashli, asking him to prom. As in *next May*. Jai wrote her back saying that he didn't typically make plans that far in advance and hoped that was enough of a hint. It wasn't. Now Ashli makes a point of shouting and waving frantically whenever she spots him. He usually tells her that he really has to pee and ducks into the boys' room.

Jai shakes his head. "She told me the other day that she's planning to try out for *Grease* so that we can spend some more time together. I hate to disappoint her, but I'm holding out for Audrey Hepburn."

"Isn't Audrey Hepburn dead?" Katie asks.

"Yes," answers Jai.

"Oh, so you're going for a more realistic prospect," I say. "That'll work out well once you bring her back from the grave. And since things don't seem to be working out with Evan, would you and Audrey be up for a double wedding with Teddy Roosevelt and me?"

✳✳✳

The next morning, Evan comes up to my locker with a huge smile on his face. "Hey, Becca," he says. "How's it going?"

"I'm good," I say, smiling back at him, "even though Ms. Sommerfeld wants us to turn in this huge essay right after we get back from break. It's like she wants to ruin the holidays. I bet she does it because she hates her own life. She's such a crab. Maybe she isn't getting any sex."

"Oh," Evan replies, staring at the floor. Damn, why do I

keep mentioning sex in front of him? I can barely stand kissing him. I need to stop talking about doing it, otherwise he's going to get the wrong idea.

"So," I say brightly. "What's up with you?"

Evan looks up from the floor and clears his throat. He doesn't seem too freaked out. "Well, I've got something for you. Because you know, I'm leaving school early today. Right after history, actually."

"Right," I say. "You're going to Wisconsin?"

"Yeah." Evan rolls his eyes. "And I won't be back until New Year's Day. That's a long time to be without my girl."

Despite the fact that Evan is a repulsive kisser, I blush when I hear him call me his girl. It's sweet in a 1950s, he-gave-me-his-letter-sweater-at-the-malt-shop sort of way.

"Yeah, it's a long time," I agree.

Evan opens his backpack, pulls out a red envelope, which has *For My Beautiful Rebecca* written on it, and hands it to me.

"A Christmas card?" I ask.

"Just read it somewhere private," Evan says, leaning toward me. Whoa, it looks like he's going for it, right here in the hallway. I turn my head to see if anyone is spying on us, not that I'm all that embarrassed for someone to see Evan macking on me. In fact, it would be kind of cool for people to know that my boyfriend is so into me. I'm so caught up in this thought that I jump when Evan plants a kiss near my ear. Then he straightens and starts playing with his ponytail nervously.

"Oh," I say. "Um, thanks. I mean, for the card or whatever it is." I should have gotten something for him.

"Merry Christmas, Becca," Evan says sweetly. "I'll call you soon."

"Okay," I say. "Have fun in Wisconsin."

"Well, I'll be missing you, so I don't know how much fun I'll actually have. Bye." Evan turns and rushes down the hall to his first-period class. I feel warmth spread to my cheeks as I watch his lanky frame weave through the sea of students. He really likes me. Still, I wonder if it's mainly because I've basically given him the impression that I have sex on the brain.

I stare down at the envelope in my hands and then look up at the clock in the hallway. I have exactly two minutes until the bell rings. I run to the girls' room, lock myself in a stall, and tear open the envelope. Inside, instead of a card, I find a piece of notebook paper, the spiral edges carefully trimmed off. I unfold the paper, and my eyes widen.

> *Kiss My Soul*
> *Your voice is like an ale all too strong for me*
> *It flows into my ears so mellifluously*
> *Your ears are petals of a delicate flower*
> *Blooming softly, with such startling power*
> *When you're in my arms, I know*
> *That this is the way life's supposed to go*
> *I touch your face, and I feel whole*
> *I kiss your lips, you kiss my soul.*

An original love poem by Evan Johnson. *Whoa.* I was totally not prepared for that.

✳✳✳

"So show it to us already!" Jai demands at lunch.

"Okay," I say, "but you have to brace yourself. It's pretty cheesy."

"Just let me see it, Becca," Jai says, holding out his hand. I pull it out of my bag and give it to him. Katie scoots her chair closer to Jai's, and they both stare at the envelope.

"'For My Beautiful Rebecca,'" Jai reads. "That's cute."

"Wow, he thinks you're beautiful!" exclaims Katie. "What a romantic thing to write!"

"I can do him one better," Jai says, a mischievous gleam in his eye. He pulls a pen out of his back pocket and writes something on the envelope.

"Jai," I begin warily. "What are you doing?"

Jai puts the pen down and looks at the envelope with satisfaction. "There. Now it's perfect." He holds up the envelope for Katie and me to see. Below the original inscription he's written, *Love, Evan the Wonder Tongue.*

"Jai!" I shriek. "Give me that!" I yank the envelope from Jai's hand. I'm surprised. I mean, it is kind of funny, but Jai's just vandalized the only love poem I've ever received. Well, he vandalized the *envelope* it came in, but that's still not very nice.

Suddenly Katie is pulling at my sleeve. "Becca," she hisses. "Evan is *here*!" She gestures in the direction of the north cafeteria entrance.

Crap.

35

I slip the envelope under Katie's lunch tray in time to look up and see Evan striding across the cafeteria. He stops when he reaches our table.

I search his face for a clue about whether he saw me stash the envelope. "Evan! What are you doing here?" I ask. "Why aren't you in history class?"

"I told Ms. Holtz that I had a bad headache, so she gave me a pass to the nurse's office." Evan shoves his hand deep into his pocket and pulls out a slightly squashed minibag of Hershey's Kisses. "These are for you. I thought they'd go well with that, um, that other thing I gave you this morning," he says, deliberately avoiding the stares of Katie, Jai, and the Rod and Gun Club.

"Hey, Johnson," Lance Tucker calls out. "Way to scam on the older woman!"

Evan straightens but doesn't look over at Lance. It's like he's above their teasing. Evan's confidence is kind of hot. Maybe I should try making out with him one more time after he gets back from Wisconsin.

I grab Evan's hand, and notice that Jai and Katie exchange surprised looks. I'll have to explain my change of heart to them when Evan leaves.

"Evan," I say softly, "it's so sweet of you to bring me chocolate. Do you really have a headache? I have some ibuprofen in my bag. You know, for cramps." Evan shifts uncomfortably. Oops. I guess he can't handle *all* of my overshares. "Or whatever."

Evan holds up the chocolate. "I'm cool. I was just getting really bored with Holtz's lecture on checks and balances, so I

left. And you mentioned the other day that you liked Kisses."
Jai snorts in amusement, and Evan's face goes pink. "Chocolate
ones, I mean. Chocolate Kisses." He gestures for me to take
them. I lean forward and hold out my hand. "So I thought I'd
just—"

As I move to take the chocolate, my elbow accidentally
bumps Katie's tray, which shifts a few inches to reveal the red
envelope.

Double crap.

Evan looks at me with confusion and horror in his eyes. "Is
that," he begins cautiously, "what I think it is?" Before I can
answer, Evan swipes the envelope from the table. His eyes practically pop out of his head as he reads what Jai wrote. Jai shifts
uncomfortably in his seat and glances at Evan, whose face is
rapidly draining of all color. He opens his eyes and clears his
throat, like he's about to launch his lunch.

Before I can say anything, Jai opens up his yap. "Listen,
man, Katie and I didn't even read your poem. We know nothing
about it, honestly."

Jai is not helping.

Evan swivels his head around at me, shooting me a look that
would wilt a dozen long-stemmed red roses. "Becca, I should
have called this poem 'Kiss My Ass.' See ya." And with that,
Evan tosses the envelope on the table and makes a beeline for
the cafeteria exit.

Katie, Jai, and I just sit there for a moment, and I'm sure that
they're thinking what I'm thinking: I am *so* getting dumped. I
mean, Evan told me to read the poem in private, which I did,

but then I had to go and be all dumb and show it to my friends. God, what is my problem? Why can't I have just an eensy bit of self-control? It's no wonder I have only two friends.

Finally, Katie timidly whispers, "Can I still read the poem, Becca?"

I let out a burst of exasperated air. "Sure. I don't see what difference it makes now."

4

There is only one thing worse than Evan instructing me to kiss his bony ass: the knowledge that I've hurt him. I don't want him to break up with me, even if he practically has an eel living inside his mouth. I'll deal with the eel.

Evan doesn't call me that night, and I can't call Evan because he doesn't have a cell phone, and I don't know the number of his relatives in Wisconsin. All I can do is wait. And it sucks.

I'm sure Evan knows that I'm thinking about him, and I imagine he's thinking about me, though I also imagine he might need some time to cool off. I mean, my worries this afternoon about being dumped could have been a tad premature. Evan's already proven he's tolerant and forgiving where some of my previous overshares are concerned. He can get over this, right?

I crossed a line, and Evan has a right to be pissed. On the other hand, if he likes me as much as his poem implies, then he shouldn't be too hasty to drop me, should he?

The next day, Christmas Eve, Evan still hasn't called, so I decide to send him an e-mail. Evan is an active member of the Pine Prairie High Computer Club, so he needs the Internet the way other people need oxygen. I'm sure he'll see my message minutes after I send it.

Dear Evan,

I am SO sorry for what happened in the cafeteria. I had no right to go blabbing about our relationship to my friends. If it's any consolation, I know that they won't tell anyone else. And more importantly, neither will I. Promise. I hope you can forgive me. Please give me a call. I want to talk about this.

Merry Christmas,

Becca

I decide to wait by the computer. I alternate between checking my e-mail and reading a few of my favorite blogs. I discovered the wonderful world of blogs about a year ago when I Googled myself and found that another Becca Farrell lives in New York City. She writes a blog called "Bex and the City," which chronicles her fabulous life as a single sex kitten who prowls Manhattan for love. Bex has links to blogs by other New Yorkers, and I'm hooked on a few of them. These bloggers have shown me that there's a whole exciting world outside the cornfields of Minnesota, and I am totally moving to the Big Apple when I grow up.

Two hours, four blogs, and twenty-two Hotmail log-ins later, I'm called into the kitchen to help my stepfather, Dale, get dinner ready. I spend the rest of the evening involved in our holiday family traditions of eating mass quantities of barbecued ribs, singing carols by the tree, and helping my three-year-old brother, Nathan, put out Santa's snack.

Our house, which is a five-bedroom Dutch Colonial that

seemed huge when we moved in after my mom and Dale's wedding four years ago, feels particularly cozy tonight. The windows are steamed up from the heat of the oven and fireplace, and the Christmas tree is giving off that wonderful piney scent that makes me think of the presents I'll unwrap tomorrow morning. Mom and Dale are curled up on the couch together, and Nathan is showing me the pictures in *How the Grinch Stole Christmas* and retelling it in his own words.

I log onto my e-mail account one more time before bed, but I have no new messages.

I spend Christmas Day with my parents and brother, and it's nice but boring. Both Katie and Jai are out of town for the whole break, so I mainly just sit in the basement, knitting and watching *Footloose*, which Santa brought me, on DVD.

I check my e-mail fifty-six times.

This has to stop. The day after Christmas, I decide to limit myself to only checking once an hour. Still nothing. So either Evan has no reliable Internet access (which I'm sure would be Evan's idea of hell), or he's ignoring me. Both are distinct possibilities, but I decide to send him another e-mail just in case:

> Hi Handsome,
> I've been thinking a lot about us. I want to be a
> better girlfriend to you. Did you get my last e-mail?
> I'd really like to hear from you. Please write back or
> call me as soon as you read this.
> Your girlfriend,
> Becca

P.S. You looked really cute the last time I saw you.

I hope that by kicking the flirtatiousness up a notch, I'll get his attention.

There's still nothing by New Year's Eve, which I spend alone in the basement watching the countdown special on TV. The rest of my family has already gone to bed, so it's just me, my latest knitting project, a large bowl of peanut M&M's, and a distant crowd of Manhattan party people. *Woo-frickin'-hoo.*

I feel even more pathetic as I watch the ball drop in Times Square. Hundreds of couples start kissing away, and I check very closely to see whether or not their tongues are twirling around. It's hard to tell, but everyone looks pretty chaste. Probably because they're so cold.

I can't wait to be part of this crowd, living a chic life in New York and dating a make-out expert. It's just my luck to be stuck here in Pine Prairie with a boy who can probably do push-ups with his tongue.

Still, I would give anything to be kissing Evan right now. Then I would know that he still likes me, a possibility that grows more distant with each passing minute, making this the longest, most unbearable Christmas vacation ever. I need an answer.

I finally get one late in the afternoon of January 4, just as the sky is turning pink and the temperature is dropping into the frigid depths of evening. I'm in the basement rewatching *Footloose* when my mom calls out, "Becca! Phone!"

I jump off the couch, not bothering to pause the movie, and run for the phone, which is at the bottom of the basement stairs.

I can still see the TV screen, and Kevin Bacon is finally moving in for his first kiss with Lori Singer. No tongue, as far as I can tell. I envy Lori Singer.

"Hey, Becca, it's Josh." Josh? Josh Cheeseball Retzlaff? What alternate universe have I stepped into?

"Oh, hi," I say, trying to sound casual. My heart starts to race, and I sit down on the bottom stair. "How are you doing, Josh?"

"Everything's good in the hood," he singsongs in typical Josh fashion. "But anyway, I'm not calling to talk about myself. It's about my man Evan."

"Evan?" I squeak. Did Evan and his family get into a car accident on the way back from Wisconsin? They might have hit a deer or gotten sideswiped by a semi on the interstate. Oh, this is horrible. I suddenly picture Evan in the hospital all bandaged up, weakly rasping out my name as the puzzled nurses try to figure out who "My Beautiful Rebecca" is and how they can get in touch with her.

Josh must hear my heavy breathing over the phone because he says, "Relax, Becca. Evan's okay. But, um, well—"

"But what?"

"Well," begins Josh, "he wanted me to tell you that he's breaking up with you."

I bite my quivering lower lip. I have to keep calm. I can go die later.

"I see," I say flatly.

There's a ten-second pause, and I consider hanging up. Josh coughs.

"Oh yeah," Josh continues. "Evan wanted me to tell you that he thinks you're a loudmouthed pseudo-intellect who isn't—" I hear Josh muffle the receiver. "Okay, okay, I got it. Who isn't nearly as alluring as she thinks she is."

"Ouch," I say. Evan is really trying to hit where it hurts. And he's standing there scripting the breakup to Josh. Could this be more humiliating? I dig into my skull with my nails. "So I guess it doesn't make any difference that I'm sorry? Evan got my e-mails, right?"

"Yeah, he got them."

"And?"

"And what?"

"He knows that I'm fully willing to change, right?" My voice is starting to waver.

"People don't really change, Becca. That's a direct quote from Evan." I can just imagine Evan dictating all of my weak points to Josh as he scribbles them all down on an index card. Or maybe a whole package of index cards.

I feel like someone is winding a rubber band around my throat.

"Is there any way you could put Evan on the phone for me?"

"He, um, he isn't here."

"Yeah, I'm sure that's true, Josh. You are *such* a rodeo clown. And I'm not as dumb as I look, you know, despite my tragic status as an unalluring, loudmouthed pseudo-intellect."

"Hey!" Josh shouts. "I am *not* a flippin' rodeo clown!"

"Yes, you are!" My courage is mounting. I refuse to let myself be jerked around by a couple of ninth graders who are probably going to blow things up on Evan's Xbox after I hang up. "And you can tell Evan that I think he's a total coward for making you do his dirty work. You both suck!" I slam the receiver down and immediately burst into tears.

I cry because I know Evan is completely justified in dumping me. I betrayed his trust by showing my friends his poem and telling them all about his tongue. On the other hand, he knew exactly who he was dating, so what did he expect?

Besides, my friends egged me on. Jai and Katie were totally entranced by my make-out misadventures, so I felt obligated to tell them everything. I just didn't think that Evan would have a problem with this, especially since he wasn't officially supposed to know that I spilled all of this stuff to my friends, anyway. But really, he knew me well enough to assume that I would do that, didn't he?

Five minutes after the fateful phone call, I trudge upstairs, go into the kitchen, and pour myself a glass of orange juice. As I blow my nose and wipe my eyes, Nathan dashes through the kitchen butt naked.

"Faster than a speeding bullet!" he shouts, waving his arms frantically in the air. His peach-colored curls bounce as he runs. The only stitch of clothing on his body is a red baby blanket that he tied around his neck to serve as a cape. His milky-white skin glows in the light streaming into the kitchen from the dining room. My brother, the nude superhero, is here to save the day.

"Mom!" I yell, trying to mask my sniffles. "Nathan's naked again."

No response.

"Mom! Your son is running through the house in his birth-day suit again. He could flash the mailman, who would hold you responsible. Do you really want to be slapped with an indecent-exposure lawsuit?"

I hear my mother sigh from the bathroom. "Yes, I'm sure that Vern would press charges if he saw Nathan in all his glory. I have more important matters to deal with at the moment, though," she answers. "Can you come in here and give me a hand with this?"

"Where's Dale?" I ask.

"Grocery shopping," Mom replies.

"Well then, shouldn't I watch Nathan?" I inquire hopefully. After all, I'm trying to mend a broken heart, and the last thing I want to do is stand in the tub handing her tools as she sways on the stepladder.

"Rebecca, he's fine," my mother shoots back, exasperation welling up in her voice. "Now will you get in here, please?"

My mother is wallpapering the bathroom today, an endeavor that seems pointless to me, since the paper is just going to get steamed off from all of our showers.

I walk into the bathroom, and bits of sticky, cut-up wallpaper immediately cling to my socks. My mom is smoothing out an air bubble on a freshly hung sheet. Her shoulder-length red hair is covered with a blue bandanna, and her short, curvy figure is hidden beneath a pair of Dale's paint-splattered overalls. There are bits of wallpaper paste clinging to her hair and arms. I marvel at how beautiful my mother can look even when totally slobbed out. We look nothing alike. That's not to say that I'm a dog or anything, but I inherited my father's long limbs, dark hair, and round face, although my eyes are the exact shade of emerald as my mother's. People are always asking us if we wear colored contacts; they can't believe our eyes are really that green.

"Okay, I'm here," I say, making an attempt to sound cheerful. I'm in no mood to explain what has just happened. My mom disapproved of my relationship with Evan, anyway. She thought that our status as boyfriend and girlfriend was all a bit silly, which was why I withheld certain details about our activities together, such as the Great Saliva Exchange. Having gotten pregnant with me in high school, my mother tends to be a bit down on the whole concept of teenage dating, and she would have lectured me sternly about the evils of getting physically intimate with boys before I turn thirty or receive my Ph.D., whichever comes first. I heard the lecture first when I was six and told her that I wanted to marry Timmy Wightman, my elementary school crush.

My mom looks down at me from the stepladder and I smile, doing my best to look like someone who didn't just get dumped.

It doesn't work. My mother puts down her putty knife. "What's wrong?"

"Nothing, nothing at all." I try to keep the pitch of my voice even and low, since my mother once informed me that I tend to squeak when I lie.

My mother wrinkles her brow and blows a stray hair out of her eyes. "It looks like you've been crying."

Ugh. Busted.

I know it's futile to try to make up some story about a fight with Katie or a C-minus on a math test or something. My mother will eventually (and happily) notice that Evan isn't calling or hanging around the house, so it's best to come clean sooner rather than later.

"Yeah, well, Evan just broke up with me," I admit, picking at the crusties on a patch of scraped, unpapered wall.

My mother takes a seat on the stepladder. "Why did he break up with you?" she asks, failing to conceal her smug little smile. My mother has been praying for this moment ever since I asked for permission to go to the movies with Evan the first time. She reluctantly agreed to let me go, although the number of rules and terms attached to the whole outing were so elaborate that I was surprised Evan didn't have to submit blood and urine samples.

"I don't know," I lie. The tears are starting to form at the corners of my eyes again.

My mother straightens and climbs back up the stepladder. "I'm sorry that you're sad, but this is for the best. You and Evan should both be concentrating on school."

"I knew you'd say that," I retort, unable to stop myself from crying again. "But Evan and I weren't doing anything wrong, just hanging out together and talking on the phone."

My mother snorts. "You made out with him. I could tell."

"How could you tell?" I ask cautiously. It's not like Evan left any incriminating evidence behind, like a hickey.

"I just could," she replies in an all-knowing tone that really gets under my skin. I wouldn't put it past my mother to have hired a detective to sneak into my bedroom at night, swab the inside of my mouth with a Q-tip, and take the saliva sample to the crime lab for investigation. Or maybe she just rigged security cameras in the basement.

"Fine," I admit. "We made out a couple of times. Actually, it was disgusting, but whatever. We were *dating*, Mom. Evan was my *boyfriend*. It's normal for girls my age to make out with their boyfriends." She just stares at me, and I can tell that my mother doesn't care whether I'm normal or not.

She starts scraping at the wall again, harder than she really needs to. "I'm all too familiar with the phenomenon of high school dating, Rebecca, and you're living proof of that. I know what happens when two kids hang out in a dark basement, and I want you to have more options than I did at eighteen."

My anger gets the better of me. "You're assuming that I'm going to do the same things that you did. Well, guess what? I won't! I've never done anything past kissing a boy and don't plan to go any further for quite some time."

My mom turns to me, disappointment in her eyes.

"Jeez, Mom, you're looking at me like I've really let you down. I said *kissing*, not *screwing*!" My mother's mouth drops open in shock, but I keep going. "And the last time I checked, it's semen that causes pregnancy, not saliva."

"That's enough!" my mother snaps. "There's no need to be vulgar."

"I'm sorry," I say, my voice shaking, "but I wish you'd just trust me. And anyway, it's not like your life has been some horrible tragedy. Sure, you and Dad didn't live happily ever after, and he flaked on the whole parenting thing, but I think things have worked out, anyway."

Her eyes well up with tears.

"Listen, I know that I have a good life now, and you helped to make it that way. I know that you, my beautiful, intelligent daughter, have so much to offer the world. You should be able to do anything you want and not have to deal with the constraints that I did. You deserve that." My mother grabs some toilet paper and dabs at her eyes.

I walk over and give her a hug. "I know, Mom. I know you only want the best for me. But can you understand that I'm disappointed that a boy I like doesn't like me back? Can you at least see that my feelings are hurt right now?"

My mother nods. "Of course I can. Now, let's hang this next sheet of wallpaper. You stand over there."

❉❉❉

Dale has cooked his famous homemade chicken fingers with hash browns this evening, and we all sit around the table eating ravenously.

"More juice, Mama!" Nathan shouts. He shakes his sippy cup above his head.

My mom gives him the eye. "More juice, what?"

"Please!"

"Way to remember the magic word, buddy!" Dale chimes in.

I peer over at my brother, who is still in his superhero costume. "Am I the only one in this family who finds it disturbing that Nathan's privates are in full view?"

My mother continues eating, and Dale chuckles softly, rubbing the top of his hairless skull. He shaved his head last summer when he realized that the hair he had been losing since his early twenties was never coming back. My mom loves it, especially since, paired with his little square glasses and blond goatee, he has a groovy alternative look that she's always been into. Throw in the wardrobe of flannel shirts and corduroy pants, and Dale is a former grunge groupie's dream.

Dale is from Portland, Oregon, but he came to Pine Prairie to help out his sister, my aunt Susan, for a few months when her husband, Jeff, died, leaving her with my cousins, two-year-old Jacob and an unborn Madison. For some reason, he liked Pine Prairie so much that he decided to stay. Even after five years in this town, Dale never fails to get a kick out of how little actually happens here. But today, I have a major news flash.

"Evan dumped me," I blurt out.

Dale looks over at Mom, who nods knowingly.

"So what can I do?" Dale asks, adopting his best Concerned Dad tone.

I roll my eyes. "Nothing. Why do you always try to be Mr. Fix-It?"

Dale looks slightly wounded.

Mom puts down her fork. "Becca, cut Dale some slack. He's just trying to help."

"Yeah, Mom, I get it, but there's nothing to be done. I screwed up and it's over. End of story." I will myself not to cry again.

Nathan jumps out of his booster seat and starts sprinting around the table. "Becca got dumped! She screwed up and it's over! Cut Dale some slack! He's Mr. Fix-It! Dumped, dumped,

dumped!" Nathan does a little hop as he pronounces these final words, each one stinging my ears more sharply than the one before. His boy parts jiggle freely beneath his cape.

My mother catches Nathan by one arm. "Get back in your chair and finish your superhero chicken, buster."

"No! Cut me some slack! I'm just trying to help!" Nathan shouts vehemently.

"That's right," Dale says. "So if you want to fight the forces of evil, you need the power of chicken on your side. Two more bites, please. Then you can go play."

Nathan takes two microscopic bites and bounds out of the dining room, cape flying behind him.

"Did you tell your friends much about your relationship with Evan?" Mom asks.

Who, *moi*? I give her my best shocked stare. "Of course not. Why would you ask me that?"

"Because we know you too well," Dale remarks, adjusting his glasses. "You told your friends everything, didn't you?"

I feel like I'm in a prison interrogation room. What are they going to do next, start pressing lit cigars into my forearms?

"There wasn't much to tell," I respond. "And anyway, telling my friends about him isn't a good reason for Evan to break up with me. Maybe he broke up with me because he's just a stupid high school freshman who realized that he was out of his league." My face is flushed with indignation. "Obviously, Evan wasn't ready for a real girlfriend. After all, his breakup technique positively *reeked* of middle school. I'm surprised he didn't originally ask me out with a note that required me to say yes by checking a box."

Dale considers my statement. "Okay, maybe that's true, but you might want to consider the possibility that your lack of boundaries had something to do with this."

"Unbelievable," I squawk. How do they know all of this stuff? "Dale, you don't know anything about Evan or what our relationship was like." I follow Nathan out of the dining room and go to my room.

✳✳✳

Lying on my bed, I gaze out the window and admire the snow falling gently in flat, heavy flakes. A snowplow cruises by, the only traffic our street is likely to see until morning. The family of snowmen that Nathan and I made earlier this week marches across the front yard, sparkling under a dusting of fresh snow. It's beautiful, but I can't appreciate it.

The thing is, Dale knew why Evan broke up with me without even having to ask. What a slam on my character. Is that how he sees me, as some sort of immature blabbermouth? And my mother didn't say much of anything in my defense, which meant that she probably agreed with Dale. Ugh, this is all too depressing to contemplate.

I need to change, but how? I'm incapable of going through life all bottled up and inhibited. I need to be free to express myself on matters both big and small. Prune overdoses. Boyfriends with wayward tongues. Sexually frustrated English teachers. Menstrual cramps. These thoughts must be unloaded. If I don't talk about everything, I know I'll suffocate. I'll explode. The problem is, talking gets me into trouble lately. What else can I do?

I head down to the computer room, still deep in thought, and check my e-mail. There is a message from my cousin Tricia in Oregon and a few pieces of spam. Nothing from Evan, of course. I log out of my account and click over to "Bex and the City." The other Becca Farrell is in fine form today:

> *Bex had no idea that she still had so much innocence to lose until this weekend. The bachelorette party that she was so looking forward to in her previous post went smashingly on Friday, and the bride-to-be in particular had a killer time. A group of six lovely ladies, including Bex, made their way to the Slipper Room on the Lower East Side to catch the Hot Box burlesque show. In addition to spectacular performances by Ms. Tickle and Anita Cookie, Bex and the rest of the audience were treated to a display of filth so unspeakably shocking and vulgar, she can only insinuate what happened.*

Of course Bex is a girl after my own heart, and she always provides more than just an insinuation. The fact that she writes about these things in the third person just makes them even funnier. As I scroll down the screen to find out more about this display of filth, I'm suddenly hit with a brilliant revelation.

I could start my own blog.

The blog would be the perfect platform to cater to my oversharing needs. I could freely dole out too much information while sparing my parents, friends, and any future boyfriends

I might be lucky enough to have the obvious burden of listening. What's more, the blog would give me a chance to reinvent myself as someone far more sophisticated than the real Becca Farrell. Who would my alter ego be? Certainly not a girl who lamely shoves red envelopes under her friend's lunch tray when her boyfriend approaches her in the cafeteria. And definitely not someone who would be at a loss for words when the boyfriend's lackey delivers a breakup dispatch.

No, this improved version of me would be a girl entirely confident in herself, a girl with the perfect retorts to accusations of her pseudo-intellectualism and illusions of allure. Her name would be Bella, and she would speak the truth in eloquent, measured tones. And like Bex, she would also write in the third person, to add an extra layer of mystique to her persona.

I waste no time. I go to Blogger, set up an account, and begin typing in my first entry. I decide to name the blog after the phrase I hate the most. I will embrace it.

Too Much Information
Sunday, January 4, 8:35 PM

Bella, bodacious Queen of the Overshare, is making a New Year's resolution. A big one. Bella is the proprietor of many a fascinating and juicy story, but it seems that everyone around her is too uptight, self-absorbed, judgmental, clueless, or out-and-out lame to handle said stories. She's not sure why; maybe there's something in the water here.

But whatever the reason, Bella knows this: the world obviously isn't ready for her in concentrated form, so she's going to have to dilute her personality. Bella hopes that by doing so, she'll make her friends and family happier, and maybe even attract a boy who actually knows how to kiss. This transformation will be tricky, not to mention hugely stressful for a girl who has trouble holding back. It's not that Bella doesn't *want* to share anymore; it's that she fears the consequences of doing so.

Bella's greatest worry is that if she doesn't confess her deepest desires and choicest bits of gossip, she may explode, leaving her parents to clean up the gory mess while mourning her death and keeping tabs on her three-year-old brother, who has a tendency to run around nude. Even though Bella's parents nag her and make her scrub too many pots and pans, she loves them enough to do whatever it takes to prevent such a disgusting tragedy.

Speaking of tragedies, Bella recently experienced one. Her boyfriend, E. Jector, broke up with her, a mistake that will surely haunt him until the end of his days. Bella can picture it now:

In the master bedroom of a large lakeside home, E. Jector, age ninety-eight, lies on his deathbed. He is skinny and shriveled and *still* hasn't grown into his face. A priest is administering the last rites in Latin. E. Jector's wife and two gray-haired children weep silently by his side. E. Jector looks up at his wife. She sniffles and takes his hand in hers. "E., I've had such a good life with you. You are the love of my life." She gazes at him expectantly through her tears.

All E. Jector can say is, "That's nice, honey, and I've enjoyed your company as well, but you're no Bella. She was the one that got away."

And then he croaks.

5

On Monday morning, I sit at the dining-room table eating my breakfast when Nathan whizzes past minus his pants. All attempts to keep him clothed have failed—even bribes of ice cream, new coloring books, and a pony ride at the county fair.

"I think we need to take more drastic measures to cure Nathan's nudity habit," I say as Dale sits down across from me with a plateful of toast.

"What did you have in mind, Becca?" he asks.

"Well, what about a padlock belt or some duct-tape wristbands? You know, something to make it harder for him to take his clothes off."

Dale chuckles. I want to tell him that I'm not saying these things for his amusement, but I doubt he'll really listen. He never takes my suggestions about how to deal with Nathan seriously.

"I think you're worrying too much about it," Dale says. "Nathan will outgrow this eventually."

"He better. I can just see him when he's like thirty, lurking around a park or public restroom ready to flash an innocent passerby. Then he'll get charged with indecent exposure, and he'll go to jail. Is that the kind of future you want for your son?" I ask. There's no way I'm going to fly out from New York to visit my hapless younger brother in prison.

Dale laughs again and unfolds the newspaper. I can tell that this conversation is over.

Why doesn't Dale see what a dire situation this is? At least my aunt Susan recognizes that something needs to be done. In fact, she's the only person who has had any success getting Nathan to keep his clothes on. He is only allowed to play with our cousins, Madison and Jacob, if he has a top and bottom on. And given that Nathan is a very social kid, that tactic usually works.

I might not care as much about Nathan's penchant for running around au naturel if he only did it in the presence of blood relatives, but he does it in front of my friends, too. I was a wreck the first time Jai came over to visit because I didn't know what he'd think of my freaky little brother. Fortunately, Jai thought the whole thing was funny. Katie, of course, was already used to Nathan greeting her at the front door wearing only socks. Both she and Jai find it hilarious when my brother refers to his male member as his peanut, a mistake so endearing (and startlingly accurate) that my parents can't bring themselves to correct it.

Sitting in front of my empty cereal bowl, I'm struck by the realization that my brother and I might have something in common. Nathan enjoys showing his peanut to the world, and I specialize in unfiltered, uncensored monologues. Maybe that's why my parents don't see Nathan's behavior as a problem—I've already set an example as a nutty exhibitionist in my own right.

Nathan is simultaneously my hero and nemesis, a reminder that my oversharing urges are always swirling right below the surface, eager to pop up at the slightest provocation. Since I am no longer three years old, maybe I need to display some restraint. I'm jealous that Nathan still has years of wackiness in front of him, but I hope that, unlike me, he has the sense to change before he makes a huge mistake.

✳✳✳

The one and only hall of Pine Prairie High is awash with its five hundred students, resplendent in their new Christmas sweaters and jeans. I pass Lance Tucker on my way to my locker and overhear him talking to Dustin Schwermer.

"That Jamie Whitaker chick is hot. And she just dumped Rod because he wouldn't spit out his Skoal when they were kissing, so she's a free woman. God, Rod is so stupid. If a girl is going to give me some action, I'll definitely give up dippin' and chewin'."

"Yeah, man. My brother told me that she fully put out this summer," says Dustin.

"Sweet! And I'm going to audition for *Grease* this week because I think Jamie would dig that. And if by some crazy chance she's not into me, one of those other drama chicks will be, right? 'Cause hey—the ladies love Lance."

I can't begin to imagine which ladies Lance is referring to, as I've never known him to have a girlfriend.

I feel a tap on my right shoulder. I whirl around to see Jai standing to my left.

"Hey, Jai," I say, motioning for him to come closer. "I just heard Lance talking about how he's going to try out for *Grease* so that he can seduce Jamie Whitaker."

Jai's sticks his finger in his mouth and pretends to gag. "That's the most repulsive thing I've heard in weeks."

Which is saying a lot, considering that Jai hangs out with me. Of course that's all going to change.

I survey Jai's carefully calculated New Year's outfit. Wow. He must have hit the thrift shops hard when he was back in Northfield over the holidays. The Scottish-plaid golf pants, black-and-white wingtips, black cardigan, and yellow T-shirt leave me with only one comment. "Are we channeling Duckie from *Pretty in Pink* today?"

Jai shoves his hands into his pockets, purses his lips, and gives me a long once-over. What could he possibly say about my fetching wool houndstooth miniskirt, black knee-high boots, red turtleneck, and matching red headband?

"And what are we doing?" He snickers. "Putting the latest spin on a tired Catholic schoolgirl fantasy in hopes that it will make a certain ponytailed freshman come a-howlin'?"

The very mention of Evan makes my heart sink. How am I going to hold myself together when the embarrassment of being dumped is still so raw? And how am I going stop myself from telling Jai every last excruciating detail?

I decide to play dumb. "Why, Mr. Irving, I have no idea what you are referring to."

Of course I put together this outfit carefully, with the hope that Evan would instantly notice me and inwardly weep over his decision to break up with me. The only thing that bums me out about my outfit is how transparent it is to Jai. Not that he can see *through* my clothes or anything (can we say awkward?), but he knows what I'm trying to do. Such is the curse of having befriended Pine Prairie High's most fierce fashionista. Or is it fashionisto when it's a guy?

"Speak of the devil," murmurs Jai. "There's your boy now." He flicks his eyebrows to the right, where Evan has entered the hall.

Great. This is just what I need right now. Still, I have to at least attempt to act like I'm doing fine. I shake my hair like a model in a shampoo commercial, hoping that I'll cause Evan's head to turn. He strides past sporting a new T-shirt that reads JUST ANOTHER SEXY BALD GUY. His face is as stony and solemn as a pallbearer's. He doesn't so much as glance my way.

Jai lets out a small cough. "Ooh, that was cold. What happened between you guys over the holidays? Are you still together?"

"Um," is all I can say as I nervously shift my weight from one foot to the other.

"What happened?" Jai squawks. "I'm *dying* here."

"Can we just talk about it later?" I beg, adopting my best wounded-kitty expression.

The first bell rings. Jai checks his watch. "Damn. I have to go now, but promise that you'll tell me all about it at lunch, okay?" Jai takes off down the hall before I have time to reply.

And so the first challenge is on. If I'm going to be the new, improved Becca Farrell, who refrains from doling out too much information, I have to quickly devise a strategy for how to deal with my friends, who have come to expect me to dish as surely as the sun rises and sets. Even though my relationship with Evan is officially over, I want to stay true to my resolution. Since I was dumped by a nerdy freshman via his even nerdier sidekick, I'd actually prefer if they didn't know.

How does a reformed Overshare Queen avoid rehashing a breakup with her best friends? I don't have a clue. And with T minus four hours and counting until lunch, I have to get one fast.

✳✳✳

In the lunch line, my heart starts to pound. With trembling hands, I dish up chili, a homemade cinnamon roll, and salad, which is normally my favorite school lunch but today holds no appeal. I grab some milk and make my way over to my friends, who are already attacking their lunches the way only hormone-infested, growth-spurting adolescents can.

When I arrive at the table, Jai and Katie both say "hey" before plunging back into their food. I inhale deeply, plaster a smile across my face, and plunk down next to Katie.

"Ooh, cute sweater, Katie," I begin. "Is that a hint of shoulder I see peeking out there?" I brush Katie's hair away to reveal a freckled patch of skin.

Katie swallows her bite of cinnamon roll. "Um, yeah. So?"

Jai laughs. "What do you mean, 'so'? It's a pretty risqué choice for you, madame."

Katie presses a napkin to her lips. "This sweater was actually a gift from Santa."

Jai smirks. "Was someone very good this year?"

"Stop it!" Katie protests. "Why are you concentrating on my clothes when we need to find out what happened with Becca and Evan?"

Jai looks at me expectantly as I tuck my hair behind my ears. My only defense is to shovel a huge spoonful of chili into my mouth and take a generous bite of my cinnamon roll. I try to smile, but my cheeks are too stuffed with food to pull it off successfully.

Jai squints in disgust. "Jeez, Rebecca, what's with the Charlie Bucket impersonation? Were you fasting over the holidays or something?"

I nod, my mouth still full. Jai and Katie just sit there staring at me.

As the new, improved, nonoversharing Becca Farrell, the girl who doesn't kiss and tell *or* get dumped and tell, I realize that this is the moment of truth. What am I going to do? Lie? Run away screaming and crying? Distract everyone by taking my turtleneck off and wrapping it around Jai's head like a bonnet?

None of these options appeal to me. And Jai would be furious if I messed up his hair.

I decide to play it cool, finally swallowing my huge mouthful of food. "Well, if you really want to know, Evan broke up with me," I state with no more emotion than if I had just announced that one of my own hairs was floating in my chili.

Katie gasps. Jai's eyebrows shoot to his hairline.

"I'm fine," I lie.

"Liar," purrs Jai.

He's right, of course. I am a dorky, oversharing, freshman-dumped liar.

Katie draws her sweater up over her shoulders and opens her mouth, then closes it.

I reposition my hair behind my ears, smoothing it with false composure. "Can we please change the subject? I don't want to make this into a big deal that you expect me to rehash again and again. And besides," I add coyly, "I'm holding out for Lloyd Dobler." Lloyd Dobler, played by a delicious young John Cusack in Katie's favorite movie, *Say Anything*, is the sweetest boyfriend in the history of film.

Katie's eyes brighten. "I just watched *Say Anything* again last night. That movie gives me major goose bumps, especially when Lloyd stands outside Diane's bedroom window with the boom box blasting 'In Your Eyes.'"

I stand up. "I'm glad you understand, Katie. And I need to get going. I'll see you guys later." I pick up my tray, which still contains most of my lunch, deposit it at the dishwashing station, and hightail it out of the cafeteria. My relief is short-lived as I rush to my locker. Evan is standing at the drinking fountain. I can feel my palms ooze sweat as I near him. He eyes me for a millisecond, then becomes intensely interested in his hall pass.

I decide to take the high road. "Hi, Evan. How's it going?"

Evan glares straight at me. If looks could maim, I would be missing an ear or one of my more crucial fingers. Evan turns on one heel and lumbers down the hall. I make it to the bathroom and lock myself in a stall before the tears start.

Too Much Information

Monday, January 5, 7:21 PM

Confidential to E. Jector

Although she already apologized via e-mail, Bella wants her ex-boyfriend E. Jector to know that she really is sorry for hurting his feelings and betraying his trust. If Bella had her way, things would have ended very differently.

Picture a majestic house with a sprawling lawn, much like the ones in *Dangerous Liaisons,* or *Cruel Intentions* for those who prefer the contemporary version. Bella stands on the terrace in a stunning black prom dress with pink accents selected by her personal shopper, Dr. J, who detests monochrome ensembles. E. Jector appears in the doorway clad in a James Bond tuxedo, his long chestnut locks blowing softly in the breeze. He walks toward Bella with doglike devotion in his eyes. Bella turns toward him, and before she can protest, E. Jector enfolds her in his finely muscled arms and gently kisses her bejeweled ear.

"I forgive you, Bella," he whispers. "I know that you never meant to hurt me, and I'd like to give you another chance." Although his voice is like honey, Bella puts a finger to E. Jector's lips.

"No, don't," she breathes. "You don't deserve me."

And with that, Bella untangles herself from E. Jector's embrace, kicking off her pink kitten heels. She hikes up her gown and dashes across the lawn to find another boy,

Mr. Wonderful, waiting for her behind one of the hedges. Mr. Wonderful's dark curls fall around his face, which is filled with love for Bella. He breaks into one of his heart-melting smiles and extends his arms toward Bella, who isn't even the least bit out of breath after sprinting like a hundred yards.

Bella finally reaches Mr. Wonderful and falls into his arms, nuzzling her face into his totally buff chest. He gently cups her chin in his palm and guides her face toward his. Their lips lock and Mr. Wonderful waits a respectable amount of time before slipping Bella the tongue, just a little bit, and then he takes it out again. He knows exactly what to do. Mr. Wonderful leads Bella behind a high, sculpted hedge, where a large chaise longue sits, piled high with pillows. Bella falls onto the pillows and Mr. Wonderful tumbles after her. They dissolve in the ecstasy of the moment.

After making out on the chaise longue for several hours, Bella gazes adoringly into Mr. Wonderful's eyes and brushes a stray curl off his forehead.

"I learned my lesson with my first boyfriend. I promise you that I will never tell anyone about our tryst, not even my best friends."

Mr. Wonderful stares at Bella, startled. "Why, my darling, I don't care who knows about our activities. Tell the whole world if you like." He smiles at her again, and the glow of love on his face washes over her like a million perfumed bubbles.

6

Even though it's a smaller role, I think that Frenchy suits you better than Sandy," says Jai, taking a bite of his tuna sandwich.

"Hmm, maybe," I say absently, looking across the cafeteria at Matt Wooderson as he takes a swig from his milk carton. Damn, that boy is gorgeous. While I was dating Evan, I tried not to let myself think about that sort of thing too much. And even now that I'm unattached again, there probably isn't much point in torturing myself by pining over something I can never have.

"I thought you wanted to be Sandy," Katie says, stirring her applesauce.

"What?" I ask, tearing my eyes away from Matt. "Um, yeah. I do."

"I think it's a boring part," says Jai, turning up the collars on his layered Izod polos. He doesn't seem to have noticed me staring at Matt. Too busy attending to his fashion needs, I guess.

"I think it's a great part," I say. "Sandy starts out as a goody-goody, but she transforms herself during the course of the story. By the end, she's sex on toast."

Jai laughs. "Nice. I know why Becca is interested in being Sandy, since a certain junior whose initials are Matt Wooderson is pretty much a shoo-in to play Danny."

Damn. Jai *did* notice.

"So . . ." Jai's voice is laced with amusement. "Do you think Matt's presence will provide enough distraction to help you mend your broken heart? Evan will be safely tucked away in the lighting booth, so—"

"Why don't you quit picking on Becca already?" Katie protests. "Jai, she needs some time to grieve her failed romance with Evan, and there you go bringing up another guy."

I know Katie's just trying to help, but the words *failed romance* are particularly acidic to my ears. I need to take charge of this situation before I melt into a pile of tears and call an emergency cupcake-baking summit where I confess all.

"Listen, you guys," I begin, keeping my voice even. "I've had just about enough of all this boy talk. If you can't think of anything more interesting to discuss, maybe I'll just eat my lunch in a bathroom stall. I expect that by tomorrow you will have dropped this." And for the second time in as many days, I pick up my lunch tray and flee the scene. I stroll down the hallway, wondering what I'll say to Evan if I see him again today. Maybe, "Hey, what's happening, Evan? Did you flex your tongue with any Wisconsin hotties over the holidays? How *was* that for you?" Then again, I shouldn't ask Evan questions if I don't really want to know the answers.

✳︎✳︎✳︎

"I have a few announcements before we start the auditions, so everyone listen up!" shouts Ms. Miller with more force than one might expect from her petite frame. Ms. Miller is Pine Prairie High's choir director and fearless leader of all things dramatic.

As Ms. Miller goes over some of the rules for the auditions and hands out scripts, I fidget in the front row of the auditorium next to Jai, who is sitting utterly still and chill. I don't understand how he can be so calm when I know how excited he is about this.

I look to my right and see Matt Wooderson a few seats away, studiously reading through some lines in the script. He looks gorgeous as usual, and I notice that he's slicked his wavy hair back with gel, and he's wearing dark navy jeans, a plain white T-shirt, and black Converse high-tops. Matt is definitely prepared to transform himself into a 1950s greaser. He hunches forward and rests his elbows on his knees, and I see a black plastic comb sticking out of his back pocket. I really envy that comb for being so close to such a fine butt.

Matt sits up again and turns his head toward me, the corners of his mouth twitching upward. I quickly open up my own script and pretend to stare intently at the words on the page. I certainly don't need Matt to catch me drooling over him the way every other girl in school does. Even though he's really nice, he'd probably think it was pathetic.

I'm startled by a kick on the back of my seat and turn around to see Jamie Whitaker, sitting between her best friends, Haley Matheson and Melissa Stromwell, poring over her script.

I don't say anything to Jamie because I know she'll just pretend that she didn't kick my seat. That's the sort of middle school game she likes to play. She did crap like that all the time when were in *Our Town* together.

After rehearsals for *Our Town* began, Jamie would stand backstage and laugh at me if I forgot a line. A few minutes before the curtain went up on opening night, she stepped on the hem of my costume, and there was no time to mend it. Jamie claimed that the whole thing was an accident, but she never apologized.

And here she is now, flanked by two assistants.

As far as I can tell, Melissa and Haley are totally interchangeable. Like Jamie, they both frequent the tanning booth and highlight the crap out of their hair. Whenever I see them in the girls' room, they're always reapplying lip gloss and talking about their latest weight-loss strategies. Once, in the locker room, I overheard Jamie convince Haley and Melissa that she had subsisted for a week on Diet Coke and gummi worms alone. That's one explanation for why she's so unpleasant most of the time.

They're the kind of girls that most people think are pretty because they spend so much time grooming themselves, but if you really look at any of them closely, they're not that stunning. It seems a bit unfair that someone as beautiful and sweet as Katie gets overlooked by guys while these three are considered the hottest girls in our class.

I'm shaken from these thoughts as Ashli Berg plunks herself down next to Jai and me.

"Whew!" she says breathlessly. "I thought that German Club meeting was never going to end. I almost didn't make it here!"

Ah, Ashli, the girl who undoubtedly scribbles *Mrs. James Andrew Irving* in her notebook. She's decked out in a sweatshirt that hollers GUTEN TAG, FREUND! Her wavy blond hair is pulled back in a high ponytail, and her blue eyes shine like sapphires. She's actually kind of cute. I guess I hadn't noticed this before because her yippy skippy personality pretty much overwhelms everything else about her.

"Oh, hey, Ashli," Jai says casually.

She grins and rubs her hands together. "Isn't this exciting? I've always wanted to be in a musical. Maybe we'll both be the stars!"

Jai gives Ashli a small smile. "You never know."

Ashli leans over and waves at me. "Break a leg, Becca!"

"Thanks," I say. "You, too." I'm too nervous to chat. Weird.

"The real talent has arrived!" a voice bellows from the back of the auditorium. Everyone turns to see who has made this cocky declaration.

Lance Tucker strides down the aisle of the auditorium, flipping his Minnesota Twins cap backward. He's loudly chewing on a huge wad of gum, perhaps in an attempt to wean himself off Skoal so that Jamie will go for him.

Ms. Miller eyes him warily and thrusts a script into his hands. "Take a seat, Lance. And lose the gum."

Lance parks himself in the row behind me, a couple of seats away from Jamie, Haley, and Melissa, who immediately start whispering and giggling. I don't understand how they can be excited about someone like Lance when Matt, who is much hotter and *way* nicer, is sitting right in front of them. Then again, I'd like to think that in a just world, Matt wouldn't be interested in these girls either. He'd be interested in me, of course.

If he didn't mind dating a girl who got dumped by her last boyfriend because she couldn't shut up about his tongue, that is.

Speaking of the tongue, I see Evan and Josh walk up to Ms. Miller. They talk quietly for a moment, and Ms. Miller hands Evan a set of keys. Then he and Josh stride up the aisle to the lighting booth and let themselves in.

"Thanks for taking care of the lights, guys," Ms. Miller calls as they shut the door behind them.

Evan and Josh's presence really makes the circle complete. Now I have my biggest enemies, my crush, my ex, and his breakup messenger all in the same space, plus about forty other kids just waiting for me to screw up. Well, maybe Matt isn't, but I don't want to screw up in front of him just the same.

Jai must sense my anxiety because he pats me on the shoulder. "Hey, relax. You're going to be awesome. Don't worry about who's watching." Jai's reassurance reminds me that I've also got a friend here, which is comforting. He's totally rooting for me.

I feel another kick on the back of my seat and turn around. Jamie and her friends are still studying their scripts, but Lance looks right at me with dead-fish eyes. He opens his mouth slightly and lets his tongue flick his lower lip.

I quickly face forward, now certain that I'm going to hurl right here. Ew.

"All right!" bellows Ms. Miller. "Let's get this started. Doris, are you ready?" Doris, an adorable grandma figure who serves as the accompanist for all Pine Prairie Players productions, nods and poises herself at the piano resting stage right.

"Rebecca Farrell, you're up first."

Me? Why me first? I feel my legs lift me up out of my seat and I walk toward the stage.

"Hi, honey," says Doris.

I nod and whisper, "Hi."

Evan shines the spotlight straight into my eyes, and the audience becomes invisible.

Too Much Information

Tuesday, January 6, 6:12 PM

MOST CRINGE-INDUCING MOMENTS
OF THE WINTER MUSICAL AUDITIONS

1. When Bella forgot the first line of the first verse of "Hopelessly Devoted to You"

2. When Lord Terrible, famed Skoal-chewin' ladies' man, crawled on top of the baby grand as he belted out "Beauty School Dropout"

3. When Janie Wickeder, Bella's archnemesis, claimed to be "too damn hot" under the spotlights and flung her cardigan at Lord Terrible, who was salivating in the front row

4. When Bella forgot the first line of the first verse of "Hopelessly Devoted to You"

5. When Alli Bubbles, Dr. J's would-be prom date, dedicated her rendition of "Hopelessly Devoted to You" to "someone very special" and winked at Dr. J

6. When Bella realized that she was in no position to judge Alli Bubbles because at least Alli remembered the first line of the first verse of the frickin' song

7. When E. Jector walked past Bella after the auditions were over and totally ignored her. Again.

8. When Bella forgot the first line of the first verse of "Hopelessly Devoted to You"

MOST THRILLING MOMENTS
OF THE WINTER MUSICAL AUDITIONS

1. When Bella got through her audition and didn't throw up. Not even a little bit in her mouth.

2. When Dr. J took to the stage and blew everyone away with "Beauty School Dropout" (without resorting to climbing on the baby grand, thank you)

3. When Mr. Wonderful followed this tough act with a rockin' rendition of "Greased Lightnin'"

4. And slicked back his hair with the comb in his back pocket (aka the Luckiest Comb on the Planet)

5. When Dr. J told Bella that her voice soared like a butterfly and was way less nasal than Janie Wickeder's

6. When Mr. Wonderful told Bella she sounded "really good"

7. And smiled at Bella

8. Sigh

7

After writing about the audition on my blog, I collapse on the couch. I can hear Dale puttering around in the kitchen, Nathan singing along to a Disney video, and my mom swearing at the bathroom walls, which are still only halfway papered. I know that it won't be long before I'm summoned to help in either the bathroom or the kitchen. I take out my iPod so that I can tune out the rest of the world.

The next thing I know, Nathan's voice is cutting through the music. I must have dozed off. "Time for dinner, Becca! I'll race you to the table."

"Mark, get set, go," I respond groggily, removing my earbuds. The clock on the mantel says it's 6:15. I was only asleep for about twenty minutes. I stumble into the dining room, where Nathan is hopping around Dale as he tosses the salad.

"I won, I won, I won!" Nathan shouts. He screws up his flushed little face and puts his hands on his hips. "You're so slow, Becca. You're too old to win a race against me."

"Don't I know it," I answer as I drift into the kitchen for a glass of orange juice. I wonder where my brother gets all of his energy. I suddenly have a vision of several tiny gerbils racing on a wheel in his stomach. Captain Nathan: the rodent-powered superhero. When I enter the dining room, Dale is already dicing up Nathan's pork chop. I sit down and spoon some roasted potatoes onto my plate. I hear a crash from the bathroom, and cursing follows.

Dale takes a step toward the noise but stops. "Annie, come and eat. The wallpaper will still hate you after dinner."

My mother stomps into the kitchen, brushing bits of paste off her arms and wearing a frown typically reserved for the customer-service line at Target on the day after Christmas.

Dale piles salad on his plate. "So, Becca, how were the auditions today?"

I spear a pork chop from the platter. "I don't know. I kind of screwed up my song, but Ms. Miller didn't yell, 'Cut!' or kick me out of the auditorium or anything." I know I'm overdramatizing my audition gaffe, but I still feel terrible about it. I don't even really want to tell my parents what happened. For once.

"It couldn't have been that bad," Dale reassures me.

"I sure hope not," I reply. "We'll have to see."

Mom remains quiet, an indication that she still hasn't gotten over whatever trauma she experienced with the wallpaper.

Suddenly Nathan lobs a carrot coin at my mom. "Why are you so quiet, Mama?"

My mom's sneer intensifies. "Don't throw food, Nathan. That's not nice."

"Hey, buddy," Dale adds, "superheroes who throw their carrots instead of eating them don't get any superhero ice cream for dessert."

Nathan hurls a carrot at Dale, who stands up.

"That's it. You're going in the corner for two minutes. One

minute for each carrot you threw. Come on." Dale picks up Nathan and goes into the living room, where his Seat of Shame stands in the corner. My mother and I eat in silence while Dale disciplines Nathan. When they return to the table, Dale squats down and addresses Nathan sternly. "Are you going to act like a superhero now, bud? No more carrot wars?"

Nathan purses his lips.

"Eat your meat, Captain," my mom orders.

"So catch me up on the auditions," says Dale as he settles himself back down in his chair.

"Well, most of the best singers in choir were there, like Jamie Whitaker." I hate to admit it, but she *does* have a good voice. Not to mention a serious flair for the dramatic. And despite what Jai said about her voice sounding nasal, she did a great job singing "Hopelessly Devoted to You." I wouldn't be surprised if Ms. Miller cast her as Sandy. Maybe if Jamie gets Sandy, she'll stop picking on me the way she did during *Our Town*. I doubt it.

"There were a few random people there, too," I continue. "Like Lance Tucker."

"Lance? Wasn't he one of the guys that egged my windows last year?" my mom asks.

"The one and only," I answer. The Rod and Gun Club was actually caught by the police lobbing eggs at the Prairie Perks storefront around midnight on Halloween my freshman year. This was not only vandalism, but a violation of city curfew, which is 11 P.M. The Schwermer twins were benched for the first half of the wrestling season, and Rod and Lance, neither of whom plays a winter sport, were suspended from the Taxidermy Club for the rest of the year.

"Mmm," replies my mother, her mouth full of carrots. "Lance. Why would a guy like that be interested in drama?" she asks.

Since I no longer overshare, I decide not to tell her that he sees it as an opportunity to hook up with Jamie Whitaker. "Who knows," I offer instead.

"So who else tried out?" Dale asks.

"Well, Jai was awesome. He totally blew everyone away with his singing. But I'm not sure that he'll get the lead, since Matt Wooderson was also very good."

Mmm. Very, very good. Delicious, in fact.

"Matt?" my mother says. "Tall guy? With wavy hair? Really polite?"

I'd like to add to my mother's string of identification questions. Oh-so-firm pecs? Killer smile? Amazing ass? Instead, I just say, "Yeah, that would be him." My mother would probably be horrified to hear me admit that I notice guys' asses. I'll have to write about it on my blog.

"Oh, I know Matt. He comes into Prairie Perks a lot. Always orders double iced lattes, even when it's really cold out," my mom says. She prides herself on knowing the beverage preferences of everyone in town.

"Oh, and I almost forgot," I say, giggling. "Mom, you remember that I told you about that girl Ashli Berg, the one who is totally in love with Jai?"

My mom looks at the ceiling. "The one who already asked him to prom?"

"Yep," I say. "She tried out, too. Jai is really hoping that she doesn't get into the play, though. He's so embarrassed by the way she fawns all over him."

"Why?" asks Dale. "She likes him. He should be flattered."

"Dale, you don't know who this girl is. She's *president* of the German Club. What's dorkier than that?"

Dale scoops some more carrots onto his plate. "Excuse *me*, I guess not everyone can be as cool as you."

"Guess not," I reply. Yeah, I'm so cool, it boggles the mind. I suddenly feel bad for dissing Ashli. I'll have to remember to keep those thoughts to myself, too. Man, this resolution is going to require even more discipline than I thought.

"So when will the cast list be posted?" Dale asks.

"Friday after school."

"Well, give me a call as soon as you find out," he says. "If celebrations are in order, I want sufficient notice. Chicken cacciatore, perhaps?"

"Great," I say, wiggling nervously in my chair and fiddling with my ponytail. "But it might be a consolation meal." I'm not too optimistic about this. Jai told me I sounded fantastic, but he was probably just saying that to help me feel better about messing up.

"I doubt that!" my mother chirps, but I have to wonder if she only said that because she gave birth to me.

"I'm sure you'll steal the show, no matter what part you get," adds Dale. His cautious optimism is a bit more believable.

"Thanks for the vote of confidence, you guys," I say.

After dinner, I know that I should tackle my algebra homework, but I'm too wound up to concentrate. I wander into the computer room and log onto my blog account, but my mind goes blank. I hear my mom upstairs trying to negotiate a bath with Nathan, a surprisingly difficult proposition considering his usual willingness to get naked. Dale is out for a postdinner grocery run, presumably to retrieve the celebratory cacciatore ingredients.

I pick up the phone to call Katie but fear that she'll ask me some pointed question about Matt Wooderson or worse, Evan. And if I call Jai, he'll just want to talk more about the auditions, and I need to get them off my mind right now.

I finally decide that my only sensible option is to veg. I head to the basement TV room, unearth the sweater I'm knitting for my mother's birthday in March from behind the couch, and pop *Napoleon Dynamite* into the DVD player. Nothing relieves stress like knitting while watching some hapless, dancing dork whose love life and social status are even more pathetic than mine.

✳✳✳

By 2:56 on Friday afternoon, my hands are shaking so badly that I can't take proper notes as Ms. Larson, my health teacher, lectures on hallucinogenic drugs. I can only think of the cast list, which Ms. Miller is probably taping to the theater door at this very moment.

2:57: What if I didn't get The Lead? And even if I get it, what if someone awful like Lance Tucker is cast as Danny? I'd probably throw up in my mouth if I had to do a stage kiss with him.

2:58: On the other hand, if I did get The Lead, Jamie's never going to stop torturing me. So maybe having a bit part or landing in the chorus would be a blessing in disguise.

2:59: I probably didn't get in the play at all. Not even the chorus. I suck.

When the bell rings, I slowly get up from my seat, collect my books, and walk out of the room. Suddenly a drowsy sense of calm comes over me. I've resigned myself to bad news, so I'm merely going to confirm those suspicions. The prospect is almost liberating.

The hallway is flooded with the usual suspects. Derrick Hansen and Brookie Deutsch are making out against the backdrop of the state-championship trophy case, and a wave of envy shoots through me. I simultaneously miss Evan and lust after Matt more than ever. I'm sure Brookie would never show a love poem from Derrick to a living soul. And as a reward, she gets her tongue caught in his braces and her pores clogged with the grease from his shiny nose every day after school. Okay, maybe I'm not as jealous as I thought.

Our principal, Mr. Bredeson, makes a beeline toward Derrick and Brookie, presumably to break up the action. A squad of wrestlers stands in line at the candy machine for some pre-practice sustenance. And to the right I see my people: the thespians of Pine Prairie High, in mass exodus from the classrooms to check out the cast list for *Grease*.

I feel a tap on my shoulder and turn around. It's Jai.

"Well, you're taking your sweet time getting to the theater door, aren't you?" Jai snaps his suspenders playfully and waits for my scathing comeback. I don't have one.

"Just a little nervous," I whisper, and Jai nods sympathetically. He doesn't say anything more as we walk down the hall.

We're getting closer, and I can almost make out the names on the list now.

There is a sudden shove from behind as Lance Tucker cuts between Jai and me.

"Excuse you." He sneers. Jai and I exchange a look that asks, *Why does Lance insist on being such an ass gnome?*

Lance jostles a few more people out of the way and scans the list with his finger until he hits on his name. "Who's Kinky?"

Jai lets out a moan of exasperation. "That's *Kenickie,* not *Kinky.*" His tone has an edge to it, as if he'd like to add, "Can't you read, numbskull?" I admire Jai for keeping this thought to himself.

"Kenickie." Lance sounds the name out, glancing at Jai. "Must be a good part because it's near the top of the list."

"It is," Jai admits, stepping closer to the list. He scans from top to bottom and clutches his chest. Oh no. His name must not be on the list at all. Well, mine probably isn't either, so we can go drown our sorrows in some root-beer floats at A&W now. I'm thinking of the best way to console Jai when he lets out a whoop.

"I'm the Teen Angel! Kick-ass!" Jai does a little hop, not taking his eyes off the list.

"Wow, that's great!" I say. Too bad I won't be receiving such good news.

"Um, Becca," Jai says slowly, "you'd better come here."

Wait, does that mean——? My heart reaches a frenzied cadence. I step forward and look at the top of the cast list.

The Pine Prairie High Players present
Grease
Rehearsals begin Monday, January 12.

<small>Cast List</small>
DANNY: Matt Wooderson
SANDY: Rebecca Farrell
RIZZO: Jamie Whitaker
KENICKIE: Lance Tucker
FRENCHY: Ashli Berg
TEEN ANGEL: James Irving
CHA CHA: Haley Matheson

"Holy—" I reach for the wall for support, wondering if I've read wrong. I'm Sandy? Even after forgetting the words to my audition song, after convincing myself that Jamie had a better audition, after thinking that I didn't even make the chorus, I'm the *star*? My knees go weak.

"Congratulations, you guys!" Katie rushes up and hugs each of us. "I'm so proud to be friends with the stars of the show." Her eyes glow.

Jai clears his throat. "I would hardly call myself a star in comparison with Becca."

I blush, dizzy with excitement. "Oh, stop it, you guys."

"Jai!" a voice shouts. "Hey, Jai!" The three of us turn around. It's Ashli Berg.

"Jai!" Ashli squeals. "Congratulations on your role!" She jumps up and down a few times and claps her hands. I hope that I don't come off as eager as Ashli when I'm around Matt.

Jai smiles at Ashli and eyes the cast list again. "You're Frenchy, Ashli? Wow, I'm so impressed. That's an awesome part!"

Ashli looks like she's ready to swoon over Jai's compliment. "I, um, thanks. Yeah, wow." Then she starts grinning maniacally, her face turning peony pink. She lets out a little squeal. "I was just hoping to get in the chorus. I mean, I've never been in a play in my life. This is going to be so much fun!"

Jai raises his eyebrows like he's not so sure about that. I say nothing, but I'd like to whisper to him, "Hey, look on the bright side. At least someone likes you, even if she isn't an Audrey Hepburn clone. I can't even keep the romantic attention of a freshman who belongs to the Computer Club."

A whiny voice cuts through the silence. "Step aside, losers."

It's Jamie Whitaker, who muscles Jai out of her way toward the cast list.

"Hey!" Ashli shouts. "Don't talk to Jai that way." Jai's eyes widen, like he's thinking that maybe Ashli isn't so bad after all. Because she's really not. Just a little hyper.

Jamie glances at Ashli as if she were an insect on the ground. "I wasn't talking to *just* Jai, you know." She turns back to the cast list.

"Nice," Jai mutters loud enough for Jamie to hear, but she's too busy examining the list to respond.

"Rizzo?" Jamie shrieks. "Just *Rizzo?*" I can't help but feel triumphant.

Before Jamie gets a chance to have a full meltdown over not getting Sandy, Melissa Stromwell and Haley Matheson pounce on the cast list.

"Cha Cha! I'm Cha Cha!" Haley shrieks.

"And I'm in the chorus, but Ms. Miller already said I could be the choreographer," brags Melissa. "I mean, I *am* cocaptain of the dance line."

I'd like to say, "Wow, Melissa, can I touch you?" But I don't.

Haley looks directly at me and then turns to Jamie. "I can't believe you didn't get Sandy. Your audition was the best."

Lance steps forward. "Yeah, Jamie, you were really good. Much better than some people." He glances at me.

Jamie faces me. "Oh, I agree. Ms. Miller made a huge mistake. I was totally *meant* to be Sandy. After all, I'm the blonde. Everyone knows Sandy should be blond!"

Jai examines the top of Jamie's head. "Well, Sandy probably wouldn't have such obvious roots, so I think Ms. Miller made the right choice after all."

Jamie's eyes narrow. "You should talk. Like your highlights are real."

Melissa giggles at this. I'm grateful to Jai for defending me, but I don't like seeing him put himself in harm's way where these girls are concerned. They can be vicious.

Jai frowns, but he doesn't appear rattled by Jamie's dis. "Listen, girls, I'd love to stand here all day and trade beauty tips with you, but—"

"Hey, guys, what's up?" Matt Wooderson in the house.

"Congratulations, dude!" shouts Lance, pointing at the cast list. Matt cranes his neck to get a better look. While he does this I get a better look at his sexy shoulders, which are only about a foot and a half away from my face. Oh, how I'd love to just reach out and—

"Hey, how about that?" Matt says after reading the good news. "Sweet. And good job, Becca. I thought you'd get Sandy. We'll have fun." He smiles right at me, and my legs turn to Jell-O.

"Thanks," I answer. "Um, good job yourself."

"I'm glad I'm not Sandy," Jamie sighs. "Totally boring."

Wow, either Jamie got over her disappointment fast, or she's just trying to get in another dig at me. Her remark about Sandy being boring makes me recall the conversation I had with Katie and Jai about the role the other day. Is it a blah part?

I decide that it's not because Sandy transforms herself by the end of the play. Maybe the role will be therapeutic for me because Sandy goes from being a buttoned-up, play-by-the-rules girl to a freer spirit. I'm in the process of doing the opposite. And if I could do this and also get the guy in the end, like Sandy, that would be even sweeter. But perhaps I'm dreaming just a little too hard.

"*I* don't think Sandy is a boring part," says Ashli. "I think *somebody's* just jealous."

Jamie rolls her eyes at Ashli. "Jealous? I don't *think* so."

Matt smiles at Jamie. "Rizzo's a cool role, Jamie. You'll have fun with it. Especially with my handsome cousin here playing the part of your boyfriend."

Jamie and Lance eye each other.

"What do you mean?" asks Lance.

Matt turns to Lance incredulously. "You don't know, my man? Kenickie and Rizzo are a couple. A very, um, *affectionate* couple."

A huge grin spreads across Lance's face, and he runs his fingers through his overly gelled hair.

Jamie merely raises an eyebrow. It's clearly just occurring to her *now* that she and Lance will be getting busy onstage. And she doesn't look horrified by the idea.

"Ugh," remarks Jai, which sums up my feelings about the Lance/Jamie situation as well. "Becca, Katie, let's go."

"See you later, Jai!" calls Ashli, waving so hard her arm looks like it's going to pop out of its socket.

"Bye, Ashli!" he calls as he walks toward the door with Katie and me.

As soon as Jai, Katie, and I are outside in the gnawing January wind, we really let loose.

"This is going to be so much fun!" Katie shouts, practically skipping to Jai's car.

"Totally," agrees Jai. "And I can give both of you rides home now."

Jai turned sixteen last month and received his father's old car as a birthday present. I relish the prospect of having him as my private chauffeur instead of saddling Dale with driving duties. Although he does his best, Dale often gets sidetracked by simmering pots and bare-bottomed three-year-olds as he tries to get out the door to pick me up.

"The chariot awaits, ladies," says Jai, beckoning toward the ancient Taurus.

"Isn't that a line from *Grease*?" Katie asks.

"Something like that," answers Jai. We break out into another round of excited laughter.

Too Much Information

Upon viewing the cast list for the school musical, Mr. Wonderful picks up Bella and whirls her around.

"I knew you could do it," he whispers, licking her ear lightly.

A tingle runs down Bella's spine, but her joy is short-lived when she discovers that Lord Terrible and Janie Wickeder also have substantial roles in the play and will be onstage lovers.

"That's a bit disappointing, isn't it?" she says to Mr. Wonderful, who nods in that understanding way of his. "But I guess we'll just have to pray that this is an instance in which life will not imitate art."

"Yes, we can pray," Mr. Wonderful says. "But you have to admit that Lord Terrible and Janie Wickeder were cut from the same cloth. They're perfect for each other."

"In a totally gross sort of way, yes," admits Bella.

Suddenly a shrill wail rises from behind her, and Bella jumps.

"Goodness, what *was* that?! Has a kitten just been sucked up a vacuum?"

As it turns out, no. The hideous sounds are being emitted from Janie Wickeder herself. Janie is standing next to the cast list, clad in an electric-yellow baby-doll dress with cap sleeves. The unflattering outfit makes her look like a banana with major PMS bloat.

"Bella didn't deserve to get the leading role!" Janie shouts. "Everyone knows I should be the star! Me, me, me!"

Janie starts jumping up and down and tearing out her highlights, which break off easily because her hair is so fried. After a minute of shrieking and jumping, she collapses on the floor, sobbing into handfuls of hair. Her dress rides up as she writhes, revealing granny panties with clowns on them.

Mr. Wonderful covers Bella's eyes with his hand.

"I'm sorry you had to see that," he says.

A shirtless Lord Terrible leans against the wall, dazed by the spectacle of Janie's tantrum. He strokes his abundant chest hair and lets out a curdling belch.

"Women," he mutters, shaking his head and spitting an oozing stream of chewing tobacco into his palm. "So damn emotional."

Mr. Wonderful frowns at Lord Terrible and squats down next to Janie. "Now calm down. This isn't the end of the world. You still have a good role in the play. And besides, you were meant to play the slutty villainess."

Janie nods meekly and flees the scene. Lord Terrible, who seems to have had a change of heart regarding the intolerable emotional needs of females and is attracted to girls who wear clown panties, chases after her.

"Hey, babe, I got something that'll make you feel

better!" he shouts as he fishes a tin of Skoal out of his back pocket with the hand that doesn't contain his spittle.

Bella and Mr. Wonderful walk into the theater, and E. Jector emerges from the shadows of the lighting booth to congratulate Bella and her boy on their newfound stardom.

"I hope it's not too bold of me to admit that I'm incredibly jealous," E. Jector offers.

"Well, your jealousy is quite understandable, my friend," Mr. Wonderful replies, extending his hand to E. Jector. The two shake, their eyes meeting in some sort of macho understanding, and E. Jector makes his way back to the lighting booth.

He then dims the lights of the theater, pipes "In Your Eyes," the most romantic song ever, into the speakers.

"I think you two could use some time alone," E. Jector says.

Mr. Wonderful leads Bella to the stage, where an enticing nest of blankets and pillows has been laid out. The two lie down and enjoy a tender yet passionate make-out session. Mr. Wonderful tries putting his hand up Bella's shirt, and she totally lets him go for it.

La pièce de résistance!" declares Dale, doing his best Pepé Le Pew. He sets a steaming platter of chicken cacciatore on the table. Dale is a rock-star chef.

"It looks and smells wonderful, Dale," I say.

"Thanks so much for cooking, honey," my mom says. "I'm famished."

I tell them the rest of the cast lineup during dinner, and Mom regales us with the latest scandal at Prairie Perks, which broke out when the head librarian accidentally spilled a decaf mocha on the mayor. Our adult conversation is momentarily interrupted when Nathan has an accident of his own, dropping a glass of milk in his lap.

"Ah!" he shouts. "That's cold! My peanut is frozen." Nathan starts to whimper.

"You know," I remark, "if Nathan were wearing underwear and pants, the shock of the cold milk might not be so devastating."

Once Nathan recovers, we sit in relative silence enjoying the food. I notice that my mother is helping herself to a second chicken breast and piling her plate with huge mounds of pasta and green beans.

"Wow, Mama, you're really hungry tonight!" Nathan remarks, giggling.

"Yeah, Mom," I remark. "You're a bottomless pit. What's that all about?"

My mother clears her throat and smiles into her napkin, eyeing Dale conspiratorially. "Should we tell them, honey?"

Dale's eyes twinkle. "Sure."

Mom puts her napkin back in her lap and faces my brother and me intently. "Becca, Nathan, you're going to have a new little brother or sister this May."

"Where?" Nathan asks, looking around the room.

"Here. In my tummy," my mother answers, patting her abdomen.

Nathan's eyes light up. "There's a baby in your tummy, Mama? Wow! How did it get in there? Did you swallow it?"

I can't wait to hear how my mother explains this to Nathan.

Before she can answer, Nathan lets out a whoop, jumps out of his chair, whips off his shirt, and runs around to my mother's side of the table.

"You can feel it if you want," Mom says, placing Nathan's hand on the little bump that I've failed to notice. Perhaps my brother's near-constant nakedness has prevented me from focusing on the state of my mother's abdomen.

Dale turns to me. "So what do you think, Becca?"

What do I think? *I can't believe they had sex again.* I doubt that's the response Dale is looking for.

It just never occurred to me that my parents wanted another baby. Then again, there are two unoccupied bedrooms in this house. I wonder if my parents are planning to fill both of them. Good grief, I hope not. That's exactly what this family needs: a whole army of little nudists running around the yard as the neighbors stare in horror.

Still, this baby could have been an accident. I mean, it's obvious that I was, but I'm pretty sure Nathan was planned. Somehow, it doesn't seem right to blurt out, "So, was this an 'oops' baby?"

And besides, the new, reformed Becca Farrell doesn't say those kinds of things. But what *does* she say?

"Um," I start, breaking into a nervous giggle. "I'm, ah, surprised."

My mother pries her eyes away from Nathan, who is tenderly massaging her belly and whispering softly to our unborn sibling.

"I can tell you're shocked, honey, but you have almost five months to get used to the idea. And have you forgotten how excited you were when Nathan was born?"

I remembered how, at the hospital, Mom had said, "Becca, this is your brother, Nathan." Then she motioned for me to come sit next to her and the baby on the bed. She pulled back the blanket to reveal Nathan, who was peacefully asleep. I marveled at his gumdrop lips, buttery little nose, and petal-shaped ears. In truth, he looked like just about every other newborn on the planet: a smaller version of E.T. But he was *my* brother. Love flooded through me instantly. Maybe another sibling isn't a bad idea.

On Monday at lunch, I announce the big news to my friends.

"So last night at dinner, um, my mom told me that she's expecting," I say carefully. I intentionally don't use the word *pregnant*. It just sounds more graphic, like it would encourage Jai and Katie to ask me all kinds of questions that I don't think I should be answering.

Jai raises his eyebrows, and Katie stares down at the ends of her hair.

"Yeah," she begins nonchalantly, "I noticed that your mom was carrying a bit of extra poundage the last time I was over. And I assumed that when she poured about two-thirds of that pound bag of M&M's into a bowl and went upstairs, it wasn't because she and Dale had the munchies. I mean, they're not exactly potheads."

"True," I admit, impressed by how observant Katie was. I mean, *I* didn't notice that my mom had gained any weight, and I *live* with her. I suddenly feel pathetic and self-absorbed.

Jai drums the table and looks me in the eye. "So are you weirded out that your parents had sex again?"

I shrug. *Right.* I didn't think of that just like I haven't thought about how amazing Matt would look shirtless and covered in baby oil.

Jai plays with the cuffs of his tuxedo shirt, his lips puckered in thought. "Excuse me, but I think that aliens have abducted my good friend Rebecca Olivia Farrell and replaced her with a prudish clone. Anyone with information concerning her whereabouts can text me at—"

"Don't encourage her," Katie interrupts. "If she doesn't want to talk about it, that's okay." I'm grateful to Katie for shushing Jai, but the way she says it makes me a little paranoid. Maybe Katie is thinking, *Yes! Finally, Becca has stopped mewling about all things gross, sexual, and inappropriate.* I wonder if Katie has resented my many overshare moments all these years and been tempted to tell me off and find some new friends.

I meet Katie's eyes with my own, and she gives me a sweet smile. I'm crazy. No one is more genuine than Katie.

Jai studies his cuticles for a moment. "I guess you're right. Let's talk about something else. How about those Vikings?"

✳✳✳

"All right, future Broadway legends and Oscar winners, let's get going!" shouts Ms. Miller, sitting down behind the piano.

"You gotta love a teacher who believes in her students that much," mutters Jai.

Our first task at rehearsal is to learn the music. The cast crowds around the piano in front of the stage. I notice that Jamie and Lance are standing next to each other and keep exchanging these little looks. Soon they'll probably be exchanging saliva, too. Gross.

After stumbling through "We Go Together," Ms. Miller asks the rest of the cast to start running lines while Matt and I try our solos in "Summer Nights." I get goose bumps just looking at Matt, who is particularly cute in his crisp blue flannel shirt, khaki cords, and steel-toed work boots. His hair is just long enough to tuck behind his ears, and I think I see the beginnings of a soul patch sprouting under his lip. I wish I could kiss it and trace the outline of his lips with my own, brushing them against his perfect cheekbones. And then, he'd—

"Becca!" Ms. Miller barks. My head snaps up. "That's your cue. Try it again."

"Oh, sorry," I say, realizing that my heart is beating more rapidly. Matt's eyes are fixed on his sheet music with such concentration that he probably wouldn't notice if the girls' swim team streaked through the auditorium.

Jamie's obnoxious giggle peals from behind the stage curtain. "You know," she says quietly, but loud enough for me to hear, "it looks like you're in over your head. Maybe you should go see that shrink again, Loony. Seems like you're having trouble coping with the pressure."

Holy crap, I cannot believe Jamie is bringing *that* up right now. When I was eleven, right after my mom and Dale got married, I was having trouble dealing with the changes in our family, especially the fact that I had to answer to two parents instead of just one like I was used to. My mom took me to a psychologist for a few months, and that helped me deal with some of my anger and confusion. Unfortunately, I told some of the kids at school that I was in therapy. Word got around, and I was crowned with the highly sensitive nickname "Loony." Not by everyone, mainly just the people who would have picked on me anyway. Still, I was so upset about it at the time that I actually had a few *more* sessions with the psychologist to talk about the teasing. Funny, but I don't remember Dr. Lund suggesting that I stop telling kids such personal information. Some shrink she was.

I haven't been called Loony since eighth grade, and here

is Jamie, resurrecting that stupid nickname. It catches me off guard, and I feel myself blinking back a few angry tears. I fix my eyes on the sheet music. The notes are blurry.

I need to focus. I've already missed my cue, and if I think too hard about Jamie's little aside, I'll start crying.

"Okay, Matt and Becca," says Ms. Miller, "pick it up from 'We made out under the dock.'"

Ms. Miller's mention of this particular line makes a few people laugh, and I suddenly worry that they're laughing because they know what a fantasy come true this would be for me. Making out under the dock with Matt, I mean.

Then again, that particular activity might not be so great. When I think of docks, I think of the one down at Star Lake, where Dale likes to go fishing in the summer. That dock is covered with weeds and algae in the summer, and right about now it's sitting in several feet of ice and covered with a thick layer of snow. Making out under that dock would be nearly impossible, not to mention freezing. Plus, Matt's tongue could be even bigger than Evan's.

Okay, so I'm *not* fantasizing about Matt and making out and the dock. At all. I hope that people can tell this by the very serious and professional expression I have plastered on my face. It's an expression that says, *Hi, my name is Becca, and I'm the star of this show. I'm* not *Loony. And not at all desperate to be Matt's dock-make-out partner.*

Matt and I continue with the duet, and the chorus backs us up. I get into the music, and by the end of rehearsal, I think we sound pretty good.

After Ms. Miller dismisses us, Jai and I look for Katie so that the three of us can go home together.

"That's okay, guys," Katie says. "I'm going to lay out some set design plans with Ms. M. I'll just call my mom for a ride later."

"'Kay. See ya," I say.

In the parking lot, Jai and I are assaulted by a particularly cruel blast of January wind.

"Damn!" I shout, digging my face into the collar of my coat. I should really be wearing a ski mask. "This is ridiculous."

"Oh my God, yes," agrees Jai, covering his own face with his mittens. We scurry to Jai's car and jump inside. He starts the engine.

"We should probably wait a few minutes and let this thing warm up," Jai says.

"Sure," I respond, shaking my shoulders to try to generate a bit more body heat.

We sit quietly for a minute until Jai says, "So I noticed you looked kind of upset for a while in the middle of rehearsal."

Great. I *so* don't want to explain this. I may have already told Jai a lot, but he doesn't know about the Loony situation. And I'm not going to tell him now.

"Oh, I was just embarrassed because I missed my cue," I say. Which is partially true.

"Yeah, it seemed like you were having trouble focusing," Jai says, shivering a little. "Was something, or more to the point, someone distracting you? Like maybe Matt?"

"No," I say. "I just want to do a good job as Sandy. I was

stressing about it. That's all. Now, don't you think the car has warmed up enough?"

"Okay, what's going on?" Jai says, turning to face me. "What's with the overnight transformation from overshare goddess to tight-lipped mysteriosa? You haven't been yourself since we came back from Christmas break."

I am so busted. What do I do? Vehemently deny everything? Play dumb? Burst into tears and confess? I really need to consult some sort of manual for recovering overshare addicts on how to best handle this sort of thing. I mean, people in rehab develop strategies for dealing with situations in which they might be tempted to fall off the wagon, right? So what's the right strategy for someone who's trying to kick a lifelong TMI habit?

Maybe if I act like nothing's wrong or a big deal, it will calm Jai's suspicions.

"I've just been feeling, I don't know, more mellow lately. Yeah, mellow." I nod at Jai, but I know it's me I have to convince.

"Mellow, my ass. Something's up. And honestly, it's freaking me out a little."

I'd like to tell Jai that it's freaking me out *a lot*. Maybe I should. After all, Jai is my friend. He wants to listen, and I should honor that. I know I'm caving, but I feel relieved as I say, "Okay, I can see that keeping a secret from you is never going to work, Jai."

"No, it's not," Jai agrees. He starts the car, then looks at me attentively. "Spill."

I take a deep breath. "So here's the deal. What I didn't tell you after vacation was that even though I wrote Evan an e-mail and apologized for the whole Wonder Tongue thing, he still dumped me. It made me realize how destructive my lack of boundaries was. I don't want that to happen again. So I made a New Year's resolution to stop oversharing. Plus, I figured that people would benefit from hearing about my life in a little less detail. And I would certainly benefit from not giving out those details. I mean, you see how people like Jamie make fun of me for stuff I've said in the past. They won't let it go. So why should I give them more ammunition?"

Jai nods. "That makes total sense."

His affirmation makes me feel kind of stupid now, like I should have known this all along. I mean, it's obvious, isn't it? Put yourself out there, and someone's bound to take a swing at you. I don't know why I didn't think to protect myself.

"Well"—I sigh—"I thought it would make life easier if I stopped. Oversharing, I mean. I was worried that you and Katie might be disappointed, but I figured you could deal. You can, can't you?"

Jai puts the car in reverse and slowly backs out of his parking space.

"Of course I can deal," he replies soothingly as he exits the parking lot. "Not that I don't enjoy hearing about all of your juiciest thoughts, but that's not the only reason I hang out with you."

I am so relieved, I want hug Jai. I hold back because that would probably cause him to drive off the road.

"Besides," he continues, "I had a feeling that your breakup with Evan might have had something to do with this. I just wanted to hear it straight from you. Now my only question is this: how in the hell are you keeping stuff to yourself? I know you too well. You're going to explode."

"Au contraire," I respond, starting to relax. "I'm keeping a diary."

"How cute!" Jai sings. "Does it have a little lock?"

"Kind of."

"And is it well hidden?"

"Kind of."

✳✳✳

Romance is in the air by the second day of rehearsals. Not between Matt and me, but Jamie is busily flirting with Lance as we all stand around the piano going over "Summer Nights." Jamie keeps turning up the collar on Lance's denim work shirt, and he makes a big show out of putting the collar back down, like he's all annoyed when really, it's clear that he's lapping up the attention. Jamie also bumps her hip against Lance's a couple of times and then innocently stares at her sheet music when Lance looks up. I'd like to tell Jamie that her attention-getting tactics aren't very original. This girl needs to find a new game to play.

Though the mere thought of Jamie and Lance hooking up is repulsive, I'm all for it if it means that they ignore me while they drool all over each other.

Speaking of drooling, Ashli Berg is basking in Jai's awesome presence. After "Summer Nights," Ms. Miller calls Ashli, Jai, and the chorus onstage to do "Beauty School Dropout," which is Jai's big number. It didn't occur to me until now that the Teen Angel sings the entire song to Frenchy, so it's like Jai is serenading Ashli. When they finish the first run-through, Ashli actually wipes tears from her eyes.

"Oh, Jai!" she exclaims. "You were so *good*! Your voice is like silk, and you were totally on pitch. I think this part was made for you. And it's fate that I get to be Frenchy because you're singing to *me*! It's a total honor."

Jai shoves his hands into his pockets and looks at the floor uncomfortably. "Um, thanks."

Although it's embarrassing to watch Ashli fawn all over Jai, I don't see why he can't be a bit more gracious about receiving her compliments. Heck, if Josh Retzlaff jumped out of the lighting booth and told me that one of my solos sounded superspiffy, I'd at least smile. However, I have a feeling that I'm not very well liked in the lighting booth right now.

Toward the end of rehearsal, Matt and I are sitting near the piano running a few lines together. He smells really great today, kind of like the smoke coming from a wood-burning stove on a snowy day. Plus, he's sitting up straight, his shoulders all squared and broad and manly. I just want to bury my face in his chest and have him draw me into his arms. Instead, I read the next line from the script.

"Well, I still think that you and Cha Cha went together."

Instead of reading the next line, Matt looks at me. "I think it's so cool that we got the leads."

"Um, yeah. It is," I say quickly. That was brilliant. I don't understand what my problem is. I say stupid crap when I should keep my mouth shut, and when I need to say something cool, I can't. Sometimes I think I'm destined for a lifetime of verbal lameness.

Matt arches his back and leans against the piano. "Ms. Miller certainly picked the right girl to be Sandy, that's for sure."

"The right boy, too," I blurt out. Matt raises his eyebrows, like he's surprised I said this. "I mean for Danny. You know. You."

Great. That really clarified things. Eloquent is my middle name.

"Thanks," Matt answers, his face betraying none of the thoughts he's probably having about what a doorknob I am. "I'm really psyched to have the role. I was pretty sure Lance would get it."

I manage to keep myself from laughing out loud at this when I remember that Matt and Lance are cousins. I certainly don't want to alienate Matt by bad-mouthing one of his relatives.

"It's good that you got the part," I say. There. That was better and it's totally true. I don't know what I'd do if I had to stage-kiss Lance. Probably hurl. Then again, I may hurl anyway when the time comes to kiss Matt. For different reasons, of course.

"Yeah, it's good?" Matt asks, his eyes twinkling. "Why is that?"

Is it my imagination, or is Matt Wooderson flirting with me a little?

"Um, why is that?" I repeat. "Um, because, well, it just suits you. Not that you're a rebel like Danny is in the beginning, but you seem like a, um, ah—"

"Romantic at heart?" Matt supplies. I must shoot him a pretty confused look because he says, "That's what Danny becomes in the end. A total sap."

"I don't know," I admit. I want to ask Matt if he's a total sap, but it seems like a stupid question. I don't want to embarrass myself any more than I already have.

"I might be," Matt says, patting my upper arm gently. *Oh my God, Matt Wooderson is touching me. I may swoon.* "The sap should practice his lines now."

"Okay. Me, too," I say. We get back to work.

After play practice, I'm dying to go write about Matt and his alleged sappiness on my blog, so I tell Jai that I'll call Dale later for a ride. I flee to the computer lab, which is still open thanks to a Computer Club meeting. I duck into the back row and start madly typing.

"Hey, Becca," whines Josh Retzlaff, "this is a certified geeks-only meeting."

I'd love to snap back, "You're kidding! Geeks? In here? I thought for sure I was staring at the local chapter of Studmuffins Anonymous. Huh, guess I was wrong." Of course I say nothing. Ever since Josh acted as breakup courier, I've resolved to never speak to him again. Except maybe if he came out of the lighting booth and told me I totally rocked one of my solos. As if that would ever happen. Josh complimenting me, I mean. I fully plan on rocking my solos.

Evan whispers something to Josh, and the pair falls silent. And I pay them no mind because my fingers are flying across the keyboard.

Too Much Information

Tuesday, January 13, 5:09 PM

On a sunny summer afternoon, Bella and Mr. Wonderful sit beneath a massive oak tree in the middle of a field, nibbling Brie, baguette, and berries. Mr. Wonderful leans against the tree, and Bella reclines in his arms. He strokes her hair gently, and she reaches up and caresses his silky earlobes.

"I love you, Bella," Mr. Wonderful whispers. "I will never feel this way about anyone else. You're the one—"

"Shh, you big handsome sap," Bella croons gently, turning to Mr. Wonderful. "You don't need to say it. Not just yet." She drapes her arms around his neck, and his lips envelop hers. Classical music swells from somewhere, and pleasure ripples through Bella's foxy body.

Suddenly Bella hears a needle scratch across a record, and the music stops. A shrill cackle erupts from behind the tree. Mr. Wonderful and Bella jump up and are shocked to see that the cackle was actually produced by a male voice. Joshing A. Round, E. Jector's notoriously dippy companion, stands before the happy couple in all of his weenie-fied glory. He's wearing a hooded cloak, tights, wussy fringed suede boots, and a belt with a plastic lightsaber slung through it. Bella and Mr. Wonderful both conceal their laughter when they see the expression of stark rage on Joshing's face.

"I've come to seek revenge on behalf of my best friend, E. Jector," Joshing declares. "It was a grave injustice that you did him, Bella. You had no right to treat him so shoddily and then flee to the arms of another man."

He flicks his head at Mr. Wonderful. "What say you, my man? Are you brave enough to fight me?"

Joshing tries to draw up his saber, but it gets caught in his belt loop, and he ends up having to remove his belt before he can hold it up in the ready position.

"Don't you have anything better to do?" Bella asks. "Seriously, you should just work on becoming a 'World of WarCraft' champion. Focus on your real talents. You'll only embarrass yourself trying to kick my boyfriend's firm, visually pleasing ass."

Mr. Wonderful puts his arm around Bella. "My woman makes excellent points about my physical strength *and* my ass. But if you wish to fight me, I ask that you lay down your sword and use your fists. Let's duke this out like men."

Joshing looks down at his pitiful little sword and bursts into tears.

"But I wanna use my lightsaber!" he shrieks, stomping the ground with his stupid little boots. "It's no fun if I can't use my saber!" He lunges at Mr. Wonderful, who, with the flick of a wrist, blocks the strike of the saber and knocks it out of Joshing's hand. The saber flies through the air, hits the oak tree, and splits in two before it hits the ground.

"My saber!" Joshing A. Round wails. "You ruined it!"
He cries some more and runs to pick up his belt, which
is lying near Bella's feet. The sight of Joshing A. Round
crouched at Bella's feet is too much. She lets out a wisp
of laughter. Mr. Wonderful's shoulders start to shake, and
she looks up to see that he finds the situation equally
hilarious. It's pointless to hold back, and both of them
dissolve into a heap of laughter.

This destroys Joshing. With tears streaming down his
flushed cheeks, he brushes the dust off his cloak and
collects the pieces of his shattered saber. Then he runs
from the oak tree as fast as his stubby legs can carry him,
squealing like a hungry piglet the whole way.

q

Instead of rocking my solo, "Hopelessly Devoted to You," at Wednesday's practice, my voice keeps cracking on the higher notes. It sounds like someone is trying to do the Heimlich maneuver on me as I sing. I thought this was a problem that only guys had. Well, not all guys obviously. Jai and Matt both have silken voices that never crack.

"Cut!" says Ms. Miller before I can finish a particularly bumpy note. "Becca, why don't you take a little break and we'll come back to this later? Go get a drink of water or something."

"Okay, Ms. M," I reply, heading for the door to the hallway, my cheeks burning. Matt catches my eye on the way out, and he gives me a sympathetic half smile.

"Don't sweat it, Becca," he remarks.

Easy for him to say. Then again, I know he's just trying to make me feel better.

"Thanks, Matt," I mutter, trying my best to muster a smile as I head out the door. I feel like such a loser, and I'm sure that plenty of people in the auditorium (Evan, Josh, Lance, Jamie, and her cronies) are thinking exactly that.

After a trip to the drinking fountain, I go to the girls' room. Just as I'm locking the stall door, I hear a peal of laughter as someone enters.

"Yeah, she sucks. Listening to her sing is torture. Not as much torture as listening to her talk, though," I hear someone say. It's Jamie.

"Oh my God, I know," says another voice, which I recognize as Haley's. "Do you remember those stories she used to tell in health class? Like in middle school when we had to do the sex-ed unit, she just wouldn't shut up about how her breasts hurt when they started growing and all that crap?"

Damn, that was forever ago. Don't people around here ever *forget* anything I say? They're like a big herd of elephants.

"I think it was all a lie," says Jamie. "Her breasts have never grown."

Ouch. That's not true, and I don't understand why these girls think they can talk. They're not much bigger than I am. Still, I know that it's my fault that they're talking about my chest like this. Me and my stupid mouth.

"They're like mosquito bites," adds a third voice. Melissa. Great. The gang's all here. "Every time I see her now, I so want to be like, 'Hey, Becca, how are your boobs feeling today? They sure don't *look* any bigger.'"

I'm tempted to waltz out of the stall and say, "I'm a B cup now, thank you very much, girls." But somehow I think that would make the situation even worse. I stay put, not so much as twitching a toenail. I hear three stall doors close.

"What a flat-chested dork. And a pathetic singer. I bet a hyena could do a better job. And I'm sure Ms. M is really regretting her decision right now," I hear Jamie say, her voice rising above the sound of urine streaming. "You know, I was really disappointed at first that I didn't get Sandy, but I'm having fun playing Lance's girlfriend. And with the way things are going, I might get the part in real life, too."

"Yeah," agrees Melissa. "He totally likes you."

"And he's so cute," adds Haley.

"Way cuter than his cousin, anyway," says Jamie. "And cooler, too. I don't understand why everyone thinks Matt's so great."

"Me neither," says Melissa. "He's actually kind of a jerk."

"Oh, I know," says Haley. "Do you remember that one time when we were all over at Darren Nelson's and he—"

Haley's voice is cut off by the flush of a toilet. The girls continue talking as they wash their hands, but I can't make out their words over the noise of running water.

"Well, Matt really needs to learn to keep his hands to himself," Jamie declares, and I hear the girls' room door open and then shut.

I quickly pee and wash my own hands. I step out into the hall gingerly and am relieved to see that it's empty. I can't imagine what would happen if they knew I'd overheard all of that. Then again, knowing those girls, they probably wouldn't care.

When I get back to the auditorium, Jamie is just starting to practice her solo, "There Are Worse Things I Could Do." I sit down with a script in the first row, but I can't focus on it.

I'm reeling from what I just overheard. It sucks that Jamie doesn't think I deserve to play Sandy, but I'm not surprised either. I *did* just make an ass out of myself onstage. I must be overthinking things. Yeah, that's it. I just have to find a way to clear my mind when I'm singing. I have to stop thinking about the fact that Evan, Jamie, and Matt are listening.

And now I'm supercurious about what happened with Matt at Darren Nelson's. Darren is this guy who graduated from Pine Prairie High a couple of years ago, and he is famous for hosting huge parties for high school students, complete with Jell-O shots and kegs.

What was Matt doing at Darren's party? Even though Matt is popular, that doesn't really seem like his kind of scene. And why would Melissa call Matt a jerk? Not that I hold much stock in her opinion, but I'm curious about why she said this. And what did Matt *do* at the party? Did he try to grab someone's ass or something, as Jamie's comment implied? Matt doesn't strike me as an ass-grabber.

"Great job, Jamie," Ms. Miller says after Jamie finishes singing. I wasn't really paying attention to her solo, but Ms. M looks pleased. Jamie must have sounded good. Not like a hyena. "I think this role was tailor-made for you."

"I think you're right," Jamie replies, her voice full of arrogance.

"Okay, thespians, I want everyone onstage for 'We Go Together,'" shouts Ms. Miller.

After we finish, I plop down in the front row to wait while Jai runs to his locker. Evan walks down the main aisle of the auditorium to talk to Ms. Miller. He breezes past me without so much as a glance, but I can tell that he's deliberately not looking at me. His shoulders are all tensed up, which means that he's still mad at me or hurt or both. And with good reason.

My guilt about Evan resurfaces, and it mixes with the shock of overhearing Jamie's dis in the bathroom. I feel so worthless at this moment, I wish I could just sink into the floor. Seriously, I'm ready to lose it.

My face must mirror how crappy I'm feeling because when Jai sees me, he says, "God, what's wrong?"

Tears well up in my eyes.

Oh no. Not here. Not now.

Jai digs his cell phone out of his pocket and hands it to me. "Why don't you call your mom and tell her that you and I are going to A&W?" he says. "I think some onion rings will cure what ails you."

I look around. "Where's Katie?"

"Oh, she told me that she's going to stay a little longer to talk to Ms. Miller about the set. Her dad's picking her up. Now call."

"Thanks, Jai," I say, dialing home. "And I want you to know that next month, when I finally get my license and a cell phone, I'm going to stop being such a mooch."

"Go on. Call your mom, Ms. Thang."

✳✳✳

After Jai and I have settled into a booth at A&W and ordered our food, I start drawing hearts in the steamed window and twist my napkin.

Jai places his hands on the table. He's solemn. "What's going on, Becca?"

I start to get misty-eyed again.

Jai pulls out a sugar packet and starts shaking it. "Come on, tell me. It's killing you not to spill your guts. You've got the same look on your face now as you did the other day in the car, and it's making me nervous. So out with it, if not for yourself, then to give *me* some peace of mind. What's up?"

I take a deep breath. "Well, there's the play, obviously. Evan thinks I'm so evil that he won't even look at me, and Josh gave me the look of death after rehearsal today. Then there's Jamie, who thinks I'm doing a sucky job as Sandy." I'm actually *not* in the mood to give Jai a play-by-play of what I overheard in the girls' room. I mean, it's one thing for me to humiliate myself, as I have many times. It's quite another to have other people say humiliating things about me. Much more painful.

"Let's see, what else?" I continue. "Oh, there was my wonderful performance today. Ms. Miller was pretty nice about it, but I'm sure that she was thinking I sounded horrible. I'm worried that I can't handle being one of the stars of this show." Which makes me think about Matt, another topic that seems dangerous to bring up. No one needs to know how much I like him, especially since liking him is so pointless in the first place.

To avoid talking about the Matt situation, I blabber on for a while about how weirded out I am that my mom is pregnant again. "The new baby will probably be a nudist like Nathan, and they'll gang up on me and make me look like the biggest freak in the family. Like I'm not already a big enough freak."

Jai appears to be taking all of this in when our food arrives. We demolish everything wordlessly. When we're through, he leans forward.

"I appreciate your honesty. I also think that you need to cut yourself some slack. You're an incredible person, both for your talents and your compassion. I admire your motivation to change, but there's no need to go cold turkey on the whole confession thing, particularly since you're trying to get over Evan and deal with all that other stuff."

"Thanks for understanding," I say. "Really, it means a lot to me."

Jai hunches forward and puts his elbows on the table. "And now I want to tell you something that *I've* been keeping inside. Something that I think you should know."

A nervous little smile spreads across Jai's face as his eyes meet mine.

Oh my God, is Jai about to tell me that he has a thing for me or something? That would be too weird for words. Plus, even though I think Jai is adorable and has the best style of any boy at school, I don't have *those* kinds of feelings for him. I need to let him down gently. This is going to be hard.

"So anyway," Jai continues anxiously, staring at the Formica tabletop. "This is really difficult to say because I've never told anyone about this before, but, um, well—"

I smile at him reassuringly. "It's okay, Jai. You don't have to say it. I already know. I just don't want it to change our relationship."

Jai's head jerks up. "What are you talking about? How do you know?"

"Well, from the way that you're acting, it's just really clear," I answer.

"What do you mean 'the way' I'm acting? What way is that?" Jai's neck stiffens.

The pace of my heart quickens. I'm messing this up big-time.

"Um, I guess you're normally not so nervous? And it's perfectly natural for you to be nervous when you're telling someone how you feel about them?"

A smile twitches at the corners of Jai's mouth.

"What, Jai?"

The smile broadens into a grin.

"You think that this is about me having a thing for you, Becca?"

"It's not?"

He laughs loudly, and his eyes twinkle. "No, not at all. Hopefully, your ego can rest easy knowing that we can still be friends."

"Wait. Am I dumb or something?"

"No, you're not. You're wonderful."

"But, I just want to be fr—"

"And I'm gay."

The waitress appears at our table. "You kids want the check, then?"

"Sure," says Jai, his eyes still locked on mine, the same grin still on his face.

I pause and rewind that last ten seconds in my head. "Did you just come out to me?"

Jai is sitting perfectly still, with none of the usual fidgets, smirks, or cartoon eyes. "I did. I wanted you to be the first to know."

I slump back and take a moment to digest this. Jai is gay. Jai is *gay*. Jai is GAY.

This makes total sense. I mean, the kick-ass wardrobe, the

faux hawk, the love of show tunes, and the advanced baking skills all point the boy away from the path of heterosexuality. Man, I'm so dense for having not picked up on this before. *Of course* Jai is gay.

I want Jai to know how much I support him, so I grab his hand across the table and squeeze it. "I'm honored that you came out to me. And I'm honored to be your friend."

"You two make a cute little couple," says the waitress, dropping the check on the table.

Suddenly nothing in the world is funnier. Jai and I laugh until we're crying.

"Come on." Jai manages to say between gasps. "You didn't *really* think that I could be into girls when *Hairspray* is my favorite movie."

I wipe a tear from my cheek. "Yeah, and like any straight boy would have so much Madonna on his iPod."

"Really."

"So I guess all that stuff about saving yourself for Audrey Hepburn was a cover, huh?"

Jai nods. "'Fraid so. She was too skinny, anyway. Plus, that would be an impossible relationship. What with her being dead and all."

"No kidding. Like me and Teddy Roosevelt," I add.

"Right," agrees Jai. "Although he doesn't do it for me, personally."

"It's kind of funny that we're both into guys," I remark. "I just hope we don't fight over any." I wonder how Jai feels about Matt Wooderson.

"I don't see us playing tug-of-war over any boys because, at least for now, I'm staying in the closet. I just don't feel ready to come out to everyone yet. Got it?"

"Of course," I say. "I'll tell everyone you're building an official fan site for Audrey."

"Well, there's probably no need to go that far, but I appreciate the offer."

I pause for a moment. "Does this mean that you're not telling Katie?"

"I *will* tell her, but not just yet. When the time is right, like it was with you here tonight."

"It's funny, though, that you told me and not her. She's the quiet one, after all."

"That's true, and I have no doubt that Katie will be supportive when I do tell her, but after all of the stuff you shared with me tonight and your new goal of not telling secrets, I feel closer to you. And I fully trust you, Becca."

"Thanks, Jai," I say. "That means a lot, especially after what happened with Evan."

"Well, I had a hand in that, and I want you to know that I'm really sorry. I should never have written, you know, what I did on that envelope. It was a mean thing to do." There's real remorse in Jai's voice.

"You're forgiven," I say, patting his hand. I shake my head and start laughing. "And 'The Wonder Tongue' thing was pretty funny, anyway."

Jai chuckles softly, nodding, and stands up. We head out to his car, which, as always, needs a few minutes to warm up before we can depart.

"Have you always known you were gay?" I ask.

Jai fiddles with the defrost button. "I don't know. I mean, I never got crushes on girls during elementary school like some of my friends did, but I played it off like I thought girls were gross. A lot of boys do that."

"I know," I admit, thinking about the painful rejection I faced at the hands of Timmy Wightman in fourth grade, who told me and my icky girl germs to get lost when I invited him to join Katie and me in a game of hopscotch.

"When I lived in Northfield, I became friends with this kid, Shawn Lopez, who moved to Minnesota from Texas in seventh grade."

"You've never mentioned him before," I say.

Jai nods. "I know. I guess talking about him makes me sad. We were instant best friends. He had the best sense of humor. I could be having the worst day, and he could always make me laugh about it. We did everything together: biking all over town, watching movies all night, making these crazy burritos with everything we could find in the fridge at Shawn's house." Jai shakes his head.

"Anyway, he had the most amazing brown eyes and shiny black hair. And don't even get me started on his body."

Hello! I'm a little startled to hear Jai talking about anyone, female *or* male, this way.

"I didn't think about him that way at first," Jai admits. "I didn't know I could feel that way about anyone yet."

"So what happened?" I ask.

Jai blinks a few times, and I realize that he's crying a little. I rub his shoulder.

"Well, one night, it was actually the weekend before school started last September, we fell asleep watching *Weird Science* in the basement at my house, and I woke up and looked over at him. He wasn't wearing a shirt, and I could see his chest moving up and down as he breathed. And I realized, at that moment, that I wanted to kiss his chest."

"Did you?" I ask, my eyes widening.

"No." Jai shakes his head, wiping his eyes. "No, I got so freaked out that I went up to my room and slept there. In the morning, when Shawn and I were eating cereal, I just watched him for a minute. It's funny that he could be doing something totally normal, but I thought he was the most beautiful thing I'd ever seen. And I knew that I was in love with him."

"Did you tell him?"

"No, I was too afraid of how he'd react. Shawn had already had a couple of girlfriends and had kissed them and stuff, so I was pretty sure that he didn't feel the same way about me. He also had this ongoing fantasy about having a three-way with these twin sisters that lived next door to him. He talked about it all the time."

"Huh," I remark. "Kinky."

Jai shrugs. "Whatever, the point is that I valued Shawn so much as a friend that I didn't want to risk scaring him away. And I knew that telling him would freak him out. We never talked about the whole gay issue, but I think he would be cool with it if we were friends now."

"Why aren't you friends now?" I ask. "What happened?"

"As soon as school started, Shawn just got really busy. He

joined the football team, and pretty soon he was eating lunch with the jocks. He also got a new girlfriend and always wanted to spend time with her on the weekends. I was seriously depressed about it because I didn't have any other close friends. I hung out with a few guys from choir, but we never talked about anything important, and they never invited me to do anything outside of school. I was actually kind of relieved when my parents told me we were moving to Pine Prairie."

"Man, that's rough. Do you know what happened to Shawn?"

"The last time I saw him was right before I moved here. I wanted to say good-bye, so I asked him to meet me at a coffee shop. It was way awkward because he couldn't stop talking about his new girlfriend. He told me he was in love with her and that they'd almost had sex. He sounded like a different person."

"Sounds weird," I say.

"Yeah." Jai sighs. "So anyway, when I found out in October that my dad's job was being transferred to Pine Prairie, I thought a lot about what kinds of friends I wanted to make here. I still wasn't over Shawn, but I worried that I could have the same feelings about another guy."

"So when you met Katie and me, you knew you were safe?"

"Exactly." Jai glances over at me and smiles. "You guys like my clothes. And you both just *get* it. But I don't want you to think that I only became friends with the two of you because you're girls and not people I'd want to kiss—"

"I *know*, Jai!" I say.

"Right. You're both so wonderful, so much fun. And the fact that you instantly accepted me into your group was so reassuring. It was the best thing that could have happened to me."

"Oh, Jai," I say, leaning over to hug him. He throws his arms around me and we sit like that for a moment. Then I sit back. "How are you going to break the news to Ashli?"

Jai covers his mouth in mock horror. "Oh no. I hadn't thought about that."

"Well, you could still go to the prom with her," I point out. "Just let her know up front that you won't be making out with her, or any other girls, that evening."

Jai nods thoughtfully and puts the car in drive. "I'll think about it."

"Do you think you'll come out to everyone else while you're still in high school?" I ask.

Jai shakes his head vehemently. "No way in hell."

I nod. "I can see that. I mean, I've heard people say some pretty homophobic things."

We sit in silence for a moment pondering this. It's depressing, so I decide to bring up a more cheerful topic.

"You should move to New York City with me after high school," I suggest. "It's got the Broadway scene, the best thrift stores in the country, and more gay boys than you can shake a Gucci belt at."

Jai smiles. "That would be nice."

As he drives out of the parking lot, I let myself imagine life in New York. "Ooh," I say, "we could get a little apartment together. I could help you decorate it with your impeccable style, maybe with a few Lava lamps—"

"Listen, Becca, before you bury yourself too deeply in this fag-hag fantasy, remember that we still have two and half years of high school left. That's an eternity."

"No, it's not."

"It's not? Think back two and a half years. What were you doing?"

"Um, I was thirteen and it was the summer before eighth grade. I watched *Anne of Green Gables* in my basement like every day, and Katie finally got her per—"

I stop myself, realizing that this is just the kind of thing Jai doesn't want or need to know. I then ponder how much I've changed since that summer, back when I had yet to feel the sensation of someone's tongue in my mouth. Back when I thought winter was this cold everywhere. Back when I was talking about my breast development in health class. "God, you're right. Two and a half years really *is* forever."

"Well, it is when you're sixteen and living in Pine Prairie," says Jai wearily.

We're both silent for a moment, and I stare out the window of the Taurus. We pass Beckman's Furniture Showroom, which occupies a gutted Hardee's. Then we roll by the Church of the Nazarene, which posts a weekly inspiration.

"Oh, look. Nazarene put up a new quote!" I shout. "'If God had a wallet, your picture would be in it.' Wow. That's deep."

Jai doesn't respond. He looks sad, even sadder than I must have looked after rehearsal today. And with good reason. My problems kind of pale in comparison with what Jai is going through. Sure, I have a few enemies, an unrealistic crush, and a sometimes crackly singing voice, but at least I'm not hiding a huge part of who I am the way Jai is.

Wait, that's not true. I *am* hiding something, and it's hard as hell. Still, it's probably not as hard as what Jai's going through.

"What if you did decide to come out?" I ask. "What would be the ideal response you could get from people?"

Jai turns onto Fifth Street and pulls into my driveway, stopping dangerously close to the family minivan. "I would just want everyone to accept me for who I am and not make a big deal out of it. To look at my sexuality like any other part of who I am, like being left-handed or having blue eyes or something. Because really, that's all it is."

I respect Jai's levelheaded attitude about this and wish that his dream could come true, that he could live in a world of acceptance and respect. He shouldn't have to hide. In fact, I think his difference should be celebrated. If I had my way, Jai would come out to Pine Prairie in style.

Too Much Information
Wednesday, January 14, 8:42 PM

Picture a lavish reception hall lined with mile-long tables coated in white linen and loaded with shrimp cocktail, gourmet minipizzas, the chocolatiest brownies ever, gallons of premium ice cream, and a keg of root beer. Picture a crowd of smiling guests outfitted in white-tie attire milling about the hall, helping themselves to refreshments and enjoying live entertainment provided by Madonna. Yes, Madge herself has carved time out of her busy, pelvis-thrusting schedule to perform at this marvelous event: Dr. J's coming-out party. Tonight, he's slamming the closet door shut.

The guest of honor, clad in a white Armani tuxedo, enters through the French doors. The crowd bursts into applause as Dr. J is escorted to the center of the hall by Bella, whose entirely adequate cleavage holds up the strapless white satin evening gown she wears. Mr. Wonderful stands off to the side, looking dapper as usual, and when Bella glances over at him, he blows her a kiss and mouths, "You look gorgeous." Of course Bella already knows this, but it's nice to hear it anyway.

Bella's other friend, K-Style, decked out in equally stunning finery, follows closely behind on the arm of her boyfriend, the brawny captain of the hockey team. K-Style and her boy kiss, and she breaks away from him and takes Dr. J's other arm. The three friends, Bella, Dr. J, and K-Style, stand in the center of the ballroom as deafening cheers of love and support crash against their ears like ocean waves. The girls affectionately kiss Dr. J on the cheek, having considerately blotted their lipstick before the event.

Out of the crowd comes one of the buffest, most

visually pleasing young men Bella has ever laid eyes on. Besides Mr. Wonderful, of course.

The boy walks right up to Dr. J and lays a swoon-inducing kiss square on his mouth.

"Oh, Shawn! I knew you'd come to your senses," Dr. J exclaims after they kiss.

"Yeah," Shawn replies, "I finally listened to my heart and realized that that three-way fantasy with the twin sisters was just a cover-up for my true feelings. I've wanted you all along."

The boys kiss again as the crowd resumes its applause. Bella notices an elegantly dressed young woman sitting by herself in the corner of the ballroom, dabbing her eyes and cursing softly in German. It's Alli Bubbles, who has carried a torch for Dr. J since she first clamped eyes on him. She's clearly heartbroken that Dr. J prefers guys. Bella approaches Alli and urges her to join in the merriment. Reluctantly, Alli rises and follows Bella to the dance floor. She's still crying, but she starts to move with the rest of the crowd.

Then Madonna starts singing "Vogue," and everyone immediately strikes a pose. After that, they all drink root beer and gorge themselves on ice-cream sundaes and dance until their feet bleed.

10

On Saturday afternoon, I'm in the minivan with Dale, and he pulls into the driveway of the Eidsvaags' split-level house, skidding slightly to avoid an enormous patch of ice. There was a minor thaw yesterday, which lasted long enough for a bunch of snow to melt and freeze into a thick coating of ice when the temperature dipped last night. Ah, one of the many perks of living in Minnesota.

"Have fun with Katie," Dale says. "What time do you want me to get you tomorrow?"

"I'll call you," I say, grabbing my backpack and a grocery bag containing the evening's entertainment. "Thanks for the ride."

"No problem."

I exit the van and enter Katie's house without knocking. Katie's parents have gone to St. Cloud to watch her eleven-year-old brother, Blake, compete in a peewee hockey tournament, so we'll have the house to ourselves for a few hours. Jai won't be able to join us because he's up north with his parents at their family cabin.

"Hi, girlfriend," I say, placing the grocery bag on the coffee table.

Katie flashes fake gang signs. "Yo, did you bring the goods, woman?"

"Of course. Behold." I open the bag and pull out brownie mix, M&M's, and the holy trinity of Molly Ringwald movies: *Sixteen Candles, The Breakfast Club,* and *Pretty in Pink.*

"I'm so glad your mom was a child of the eighties," Katie says. "I mean, my parents are too old to know about that stuff. They grew up with crappy seventies movies."

"What about John Travolta?" I ask. "He's our seventies god."

"Oh, right," remembers Katie. "*Grease* and *Saturday Night Fever* are good, but if it weren't for your mom, we'd never know about the glory of the eighties. Most of the teen movies they make today are totally pathetic."

I smile. My friends adore my mother's collection of videos from her youth.

"I'll thank my mom for getting pregnant in high school so that we can enjoy her favorite movies," I say.

"And make fun of the big hair in her yearbooks," Katie adds.

"And scorn her Guns N' Roses cassettes," I say.

Then we rush into the kitchen to get the brownies going.

The evening is a blast. We stay up until 2 A.M. watching all of the movies.

"You know, these flicks actually kind of depress me," Katie says.

"Because Molly always gets the boy, and it makes you want a boyfriend of your own?"

"Bingo." I know she's thinking about Luke like I'm thinking about Matt, but neither of us mentions our respective crushes.

Because really, we both pine for boys we can't have, and getting all "Oh, if only I were making out with my object of lust right now" doesn't change that fact.

I wish Jai were here to lighten the mood. These movies are always better with his wicked commentary on the totally rad eighties hair and clothes in the movies. Then again, I wonder if I would let some random question slip, like "So, Jai, what qualities would *you* want in a boyfriend?" Despite my resolution, I'm paranoid that I'm going to revert to my old ways.

I don't have to worry about that, though, at least not in a slumber party setting. Our parents know that Jai is a platonic friend, but he would never be allowed at a sleepover. I wonder if the parental figures would relax this rule if they knew that Jai has absolutely zero interest in getting busy with Katie or me. Somehow, I doubt it. The fact that Jai owns a pair of functional testicles is enough to send the 'rents into overprotective mode.

After we turn off the TV, Katie and I lie still for a few moments, swimming in a sea of comforters and pillows on the floor.

Katie closes her eyes for a moment, then opens them. "You've been acting differently lately. I've noticed, you know."

I'm too tired to pretend that I don't know what she's talking about. "Yeah, I'm trying to change. I'm on a sort of anti-TMI diet."

"What prompted that? Your breakup with Evan?"

It's funny, I thought I was being so discreet about my quest for self-improvement, but Jai and Katie both know exactly what I'm doing. Am I really so transparent? Or is it just obvious to them that I needed very badly to change? Maybe my friends are secretly glad that I got dumped. It's like Evan taught me a lesson so that they wouldn't have to.

"Well, the breakup was one of the reasons," I admit. "Kind of like the spark that started the fire. I finally realized that I can't just say everything that comes to mind. I need some boundaries."

Katie rolls over. "I could see how you might feel that way, but I've always liked you just the way you are."

"Yeah, but you're much more tolerant than the average person."

Katie sighs. "I'm not sure about that. I think I may just be more boring. I don't exactly generate a lot of gossip around here."

It never occurred to me that generating gossip would be a good thing, but maybe Katie craves a little scandal in her life. Or at least a little more excitement.

"You're not boring," I assure her. "You're artsy and talented and thoughtful. Everyone thinks you're a sweetheart. Nobody ever says that about me."

"Sure, people think I'm nice," Katie says, "but I'd like it if a boy saw me as kissable." I know how she feels, especially given all of my recent brooding about being rejected by Evan and worrying that no boy will ever like me again. It's got to be even worse for Katie, who's never had a boyfriend at all. I wish I could reassure her somehow.

"The boys here are dumb," I declare, quickly realizing how second grade that sounds. "Except for Jai and a few others, of course."

Katie grins sleepily. "Like Matt Wooderson?"

"Maybe." And maybe is the truth. I could tell Katie about

the conversation I overheard in the girls' room, and I'm sure that she would be quite interested, but I hold back. Jamie and her friends could have been talking total crap in the bathroom, and I don't want to go spreading rumors about Matt, not even to Katie.

Fortunately, she doesn't press me for an explanation. Instead, she says, "And what about Evan?"

I sigh. "I feel so bad about what happened, and now he ignores me, which only makes me feel worse. I can't go back and undo my mistakes with Evan, and that's the hardest part."

"That would be hard," Katie agrees. "But at least you got to experience a little romance, even if the tongue grossed you out. I have to admit that I was pretty jealous of all that. I know I should have just been happy for you, and I mostly was, but I've wanted a boyfriend of my own for so long. So even when you were complaining about Evan being a gross kisser, I was always thinking, *I'd love to be grossed out.*"

I know Katie is a romantic, but hearing her say this surprises me. I'd like to tell Katie to be careful what she wishes for, but I don't think she'd appreciate it. I'd just come off as the smug, experienced one. And who's to say that all kissing is gross? It's not like I have anyone to compare Evan to.

"You were jealous?" I ask.

"Yeah, sure. Especially at first, when you were so excited to be going out with Evan, it was hard. I'm trying to be patient, but sometimes I think it'll just never happen for me. My mom tells me that college is a better time to have a boyfriend than high school, but I think she was just saying that because she was kind of a nerd in high school and didn't start dating until college, anyway."

"Well, you certainly have nothing to be ashamed of the way I do. I can't imagine you'd ever treat a boyfriend the way I treated Evan. No one would ever break up with you."

"That's nice, I guess, but it's not much consolation, since no one will actually *date* me in the first place."

"I think it's going to happen for you, Katie," I say, "and I don't think you're going to have to wait until you get to college. The boys around here will come to their senses. I'm sure of it. And when they do, it'll be *my* turn to be jealous. It's not like I'm going to get another boyfriend."

"Why wouldn't you?" Katie asks. She sounds genuinely surprised that I would say this.

"Well, look at who my first boyfriend was. A freshman who plays the bassoon and belongs to the Computer Club. And he dumped me. So who does that leave? I mean, there are few people at school who are less cool than Evan."

I know I'm being mean, but it almost feels good to dis Evan after the way he dumped me. I can't help but still feel angry about it. And humiliated.

"I don't think there are rules to it," Katie says, "like just because your first boyfriend wasn't popular that you can't ever date someone cooler. Not that I'm an expert, but if a boy really likes you, he probably won't care who your last boyfriend was."

"That's a good point," I say. "I hope you're right, and that you get the boyfriend you deserve."

"Yeah, me, too," agrees Katie.

Late Sunday afternoon, I stand at the kitchen sink slicing potatoes and carrots for dinner and staring out the window. It's already dark, and even though I've lived in Minnesota my whole life, I'm always amazed by how little daylight winter offers. It's completely dark when I wake up at six-thirty, and the sun goes down as I arrive home from play practice at five. I may as well be living in Finland.

The lack of sunlight puts me in a foul mood, and I feel brooding coming on. I m making progress with the overshare compulsion, but I wonder if it was wrong of me to write about Jai on my blog. Thoughts from last night's conversation with Katie are still whirling around in my brain. Have I truly learned from my mistakes? Is my life in any way better because I've been biting my tongue? I don't see much of a difference yet, especially since the ghosts of overshares past keep resurfacing, mainly thanks to Jamie and the Rod and Gun Club. Just seeing Evan is a reminder, too.

I'm silent throughout dinner as my mom and Dale discuss the bathroom renovation.

The conversation pauses, and Dale turns to me. "Why are you so quiet tonight?"

Before I can answer, Nathan pitches a chunk of ham at my mother and has to be dealt with swiftly. He is particularly surly tonight, and both of my parents need to participate in disciplining him.

Nathan has been acting out more often recently. My parents finally took my advice and pushed the thermostat down a few degrees in order to keep Nathan's clothes on. And although he's managed to stay fully dressed for several hours at a time, he's found other ways to rebel. In the past week, he's thrown LEGOs down the toilet, overturned a potted plant, and drawn a patchy beard on his own face with a Sharpie. Nathan always emerges from the Seat of Shame with determination to commit a crime naughtier than the previous one. I'm getting worried that he'll abandon his dream of professional nudism and become a small-time criminal.

After dinner, I sit on my bed trying to concentrate on my English homework, but my thoughts swiftly drift elsewhere. I'm worried that my life is again running a parallel too close to Nathan's. Am I merely replacing one bad habit with another? Is confessional blogging just as bad as conversational oversharing? I don't think so. There's a world of difference between writing about secrets and actually saying them out loud. Writing seems safer because it was always talking that got me into trouble in the past.

Suddenly I recall what Josh said to me during the breakup phone conversation: *People don't really change, Becca.*

Is that true? Or is it just that when they do change, everyone else already has a set way of viewing them and refuses to see the change? With the way people keep bringing up my past overshares, it certainly seems that way. But does that mean I'm doomed to wear the Overshare Queen crown even though I've stepped down from my throne?

After twenty minutes of rereading the same three paragraphs,

I give up. I step out of my room and hear Nathan singing softly in his room and stick my head in the door.

"Holy cow, Nathan!"

The room is a sight to behold. Nathan's dresser drawers are all open and empty. He has pushed a few plastic storage bins a few feet away from his bed. Shirts, pants, pajamas, and even underwear are draped over the bed and bins.

"I'm making a fo-ort!" Nathan declares in a singsong falsetto. I am pleased to note that he's wearing pj bottoms. "You can come in too-oo! Welcome to my ho-ome!" He happily places a pile of socks next to his bed.

"What's that?" I ask.

"A bush."

"I see." With any luck, Nathan will abandon his dreams of establishing that nudist colony or committing mayhem all over Pine Prairie and become a landscaper.

"And what's that?" I point to a pair of overalls in the middle of the floor with a balled-up sweater sitting atop the bib.

"My dog, Fluffy." Nathan hops around the room and resumes his falsetto. "Be careful or he'll bi-ite you. He's really, really me-ean."

Dale chuckles as he enters the room. "How's it going there, Captain? Are these the captain's headquarters?"

"Yeah!" answers Nathan.

"Well, it's nice to see that Nathan's clothes serve a purpose after all," Dale remarks, eyeing the fort.

"Yeah, it's great that your money hasn't gone to waste," I add as I leave the room.

I hear a clatter from the bathroom and go to see what my

mom is up to. I know that by doing so, I'm running the risk of being put to work, but I'll take my chances.

I peek into the bathroom to see my mom scraping away at some paint on the windowsill. She's shifting uncomfortably from one foot to another, like she's got ants in her pants.

"What's wrong, Mom?"

"I just feel lousy is all," she says, setting the scraper down. "In fact, can you finish this? I need to go lie down." She hands me the scraper.

"Sure," I say reluctantly. "What's wrong? Pregnancy problems?"

"Yeah. I wish every teenager could see me now. They'd stop having sex and not do it again until they reach their forties." I somehow doubt that, but I'm not about to contradict a pregnant woman holding a paint scraper.

"What's going on?"

"Oh, the usual aches and pains and—" Mom stops herself. "You don't want to know."

"Yeah, I do." I always want to know. That's my specialty.

"Hemorrhoids."

Maybe I really didn't want to know.

Ew.

Too Much Information

Sunday, January 18, 9:17 PM

Like any caring boyfriend would, Mr. Wonderful shows up

at Bella's house with a case of Preparation H for her suffering pregnant mother.

"Here," he says, handing a tube of cream to Bella's startled but grateful mother, "try this. There's no need to live in agony."

"Oh, how thoughtful of you," declares Bella's mother.

"Don't mention it, ma'am," Mr. Wonderful answers. Then he plants a huge kiss on Bella right in front of her mother, who doesn't protest in the slightest at the sight of her own daughter receiving the tongue.

Mr. Wonderful lets out a sigh of satisfaction after the kiss. "Wow, I can't believe how lucky I am. Being with you just keeps getting better."

"I feel the same way about you, Mr. Wonderful," Bella croons sweetly.

Her boyfriend shakes his head contentedly. "Well, I'm sorry that I can't stay, but I have to go volunteer over at the nursing home now." Mr. Wonderful gives Bella another quick kiss and departs.

"Wow," exhales Bella's mom as she emerges from the bathroom after applying the soothing salve. "Your boyfriend is the best. But"—she pauses—"did you *tell* him about my embarrassing problem?"

"Of course not," replies Bella breezily. "Would I do something so indiscreet? Please! Mr. Wonderful just *knows* these things."

"He's certainly a very intuitive young man. And if you

ever want to invite Mr. Wonderful for a sleepover, it's fine by me."

Bella grins. "Thanks for trusting me to be sexually responsible, Mom."

Bella's mom swats the air with her palms. "Heavens, it's not like I expect you to make the same mistakes that I did when I was your age. I know that you've learned from me. And besides, I can see that Mr. Wonderful is a gentleman. He hasn't tried to get in your pants yet, has he?"

Bella purses her oft-kissed lips and shakes her head. "Now, Mother, let's not go asking questions we don't really want to know the answers to."

Then Bella and her mother share a hearty laugh and go shoe shopping.

On Monday morning, I'm at my locker pulling out my algebra book when Katie comes up to me. There are still snowflakes sticking to her peacoat and the black chenille hat I knitted for her as a Christmas gift. It's another moment when I'm startled by how truly beautiful she is, her pale freckled skin hitting a stark contrast against the dark colors of her clothes and nearly burgundy hair. Of course Katie is one of those people who has no idea how breathtaking she is, and telling her so only embarrasses her, so I stopped long ago.

"Hey, Katie," I say. "What's going on?"

"I'm really tired. I was up late working on all that stupid algebra homework Klimstra assigned us. How long did it take you to do it?"

I slap my forehead. "Crap! I totally forgot about that. And I have her first period."

"I know." Katie nods. "I wish I could trade schedules with you, since I don't have her until the afternoon. I'd rather get the suckiness over with first thing in the morning." Katie searches my distraught face. "What happened, Becca? You didn't do the homework?"

Last night, after I scraped paint and blogged about hemorrhoids, I had to help Nathan fold up all of his clothes and put them back in his dresser.

"The evening sort of got away from me," I admit.

"That's not good. The problems took me forever. Maybe you can finish it on the sly during class," she suggests.

"I'll try," I say, but I know it won't be easy. Anyone caught dozing off or passing notes in Ms. Klimstra's class is administered a heavy dose of humiliation. In fact, Rod Knutson was so notorious for sleeping in her class last year that she took away his desk for the entire month of October. He had to stand in the back of the room and take notes on the window ledge. Not that his alert state helped him much, since he's repeating the class this year. He sits behind me and constantly harasses me for answers.

I feel a rush of anxiety as I walk into the classroom. Ms. Klimstra is scary. She's the closest approximation of a grumpy schoolmarm that I've ever seen. She actually wears her graying hair in a tight bun and never deviates from her uniform of a crisp blouse and long khaki or navy skirt. When she gets mad, she starts rubbing her hands together like she's applying lotion. I dread the thought of getting on her bad side, especially since she might categorize me with mouth breathers like Rod.

I take a seat and open my notebook. Rod is immediately on my case.

"Hey, let me copy your homework," he whispers, emitting the vile scent of stale chewing tobacco as he talks.

I'd love to loudly declare, "Rod, for the fiftieth time, I'm *not* going out behind the grain elevator with you. Quit asking." I take a deep breath, reminding myself that comments like that just set Rod and his friends off.

Without taking my eyes off my notebook, I simply say, "No, Rod."

"Man, someone's in a pissy mood today!" declares Rod. "What's wrong, Farrell? You on the rag? That must be it."

I grip my pen more tightly but will myself not to look at Rod. With any luck, he'll soon realize that I'm not playing that game with him today and give up.

"Have they put any super-plus tampons in the girls' room yet? I know you were really mad that they only stocked regulars," hisses Rod. Dustin Schwermer laughs and high-fives Rod.

Ugh. Another overshare ghost rears its ugly head. A few months ago, I was complaining to Katie at lunch about the wimpy feminine protection stocked in the girls' room. The Rod and Gun Club happened to overhear this and went nuts.

This is too much.

"Just leave me alone, okay?" I say loudly. I'd like to add, "Eat a big pile of poo while you're at it." But no, if I start dishing out the insults, Rod will only fling them back at me.

Out of nowhere, Ms. Klimstra swoops down on us. "Is there a problem here, people?"

"Um, no, Ms. Klimstra, everything's fine," I reply. Except that I've just been sexually harassed by this pathetic, tobacco-scented ogre and am about to lose it. But other than that . . .

"Hmm." Ms. Klimstra looks skeptical. "Rodney, I hope you're not bothering Rebecca."

Rod scowls. "I wouldn't talk to *her.*"

"We should all be so lucky," Ms. Klimstra states crisply. She massages her palms together, then turns and walks to the front of the room to take roll. Great, class only started thirty seconds ago, and she's already pissed.

"Ms. Farrell and Mr. Knutson, I may have to separate the two of you if you can't stop talking," Ms. Klimstra announces. The entire class lets out an utterly predictable "ooh" as if I just accepted a tin promise ring from Rod.

Before I know it, I'm blinking back tears, grabbing my books, and running out of the room. Once I get to the hall, I make a beeline for the bathroom, but when I reach the door, I pass it by.

✹✹✹

Principal Bredeson leans back at his desk and folds his hands.

"Sexual harassment, huh? I thought we were over that."

I blow my nose and wipe my eyes. "That's a nice idea, but no."

He flicks a bit of eraser dust off his desk. "Have you tried just ignoring Rod?"

I'm stunned by this stupidity. I wish I could say, "Mr. Bredeson, would you be able to ignore an army tank if it pulled up and parked itself on your lawn?" Somehow I doubt he'd see the analogy.

"Yes, I've tried ignoring him," I say softly. "But he won't stop." Then again, maybe he never would have started if I'd been more careful about when and where I discussed tampons. Once again, the source of my problems can be traced to something lame I said in the past.

"Can't you do something about this?" I ask.

Mr. Bredeson frowns. "Rebecca, I'm surprised at you. You're one of the top students here, a standout in choir, and now have the lead role in the school musical. Why do you want to stir up trouble like this?"

I think Molly Ringwald had a similar conversation with the school principal in *Pretty in Pink*. My wardrobe isn't nearly as fabulous as hers, though, and I don't even have *one* boy in love with me, let alone two.

"I'm not stirring up trouble. Rod and his friends are."

Mr. Bredeson adjusts his tie. "Well, unless a teacher catches one of them acting out, there's not a whole lot that I can do."

A fresh batch of tears springs forth. "Okay then, I'm sorry for wasting your time," I choke out, collecting my books.

"Perhaps you'd like to speak with Mr. Herberger about this."

Ah, yes. Mr. Herberger, Pine Prairie High's esteemed guidance counselor. About as useful as a snowblower in July.

"I'll think about it. Thanks, Mr. Bredeson," I say, walking out of his office.

Yeah, thanks for nothing.

I should have just escaped to the bathroom in the first place, which I do now. A huge knot of anger is lodged in my throat regarding this stupid town and its medieval sexist attitudes. I'm missing algebra, and since my absence is unexcused, I'm going to get a zero on the homework I never did. I don't care. I sit down on the toilet and hug my books as my shoulders shake with silent sobs.

I manage to calm down after about five minutes, but I'm still feeling angrier and more bitter than ever. I need to vent about this. I exit the bathroom and walk toward the computer lab.

Too Much Information
Monday, January 19, 8:56 AM

Bella stands in a pink, princessy dress in the center of the school gymnasium, looking out at the crowd. The bleachers are overflowing with students, all dressed in peasant garb and clutching pieces of rotten fruit. The members of the football team, wearing long robes striped with the school colors, stand on the sides of the gym clutching huge flaming torches. The school principal, Mr. Butthead, who is clad in a hooded executioner's robe, walks to the podium in the center of the gym and raises his hands. The entire gym immediately silences.

Mr. Butthead clears his throat. "It has come to my attention that there are some people at this school who think it's acceptable to act like sexist Neanderthals, torturing the innocent and kindhearted. I've decided that the best way to help them change their behavior is to publicly humiliate them. They need a taste of their own medicine. Boys, step forward."

Four slouching figures shuffle to the middle of the gym. They are shackled together and wearing ripped, filthy rags. A spotlight shines down on them, and their faces come into view. It's the members of the Rod and

Gun Club, which include Lord Terrible, Randy Knob, and the Worm Twins. They walk toward the podium, their gel-saturated heads bent in shame.

"Now, what do you have to say, boys?" Mr. Butthead asks, gesturing toward the podium. "Go on."

Lord Terrible limps forward, his pathetic companions having no choice but to follow, and faces his schoolmates, who immediately begin booing. Bella sees a brown apple sail over her head and hit Randy Knob squarely in the crotch. Randy doubles over in pain, and everyone cheers, whipping soggy tomatoes, drippy bananas, and moldy blue oranges at the boys. Even though Bella is only standing a few feet away from them, she miraculously never gets hit. No one is aiming at her.

Mr. Butthead dodges the fruit as he makes his way back to the podium. "Pipe down, people, and listen to Lord Terrible. He has something he'd like to say."

Lord Terrible looks close to tears as he leans toward the microphone. "Me and the guys are really sorry for being total pricks."

His three friends nod solemnly, and Lord Terrible continues. "We had no right to call so many of you fags and lesbos, and we did it because we have doubts about our own sexuality. In fact, I think the Worm Twins are both pretty hot, so—"

"That's fine," Mr. Butthead cuts in. "Everyone here is aware of your laundry list of offenses, so why don't you get to the most important part?"

The football team lurches forward, banging the floor

with their torches in unison and shouting, "Apologize! Apologize! Apologize!" The crowd joins in and throws more fruit.

Lord Terrible nods and, after ducking a few pieces of flying fruit, straightens. "Yeah, so we extend an extra-special apology to Bella, who has suffered the most at our hands. And we're real sorry for egging your mom's storefront last Halloween. Bella, you are a wonderful and beautiful girl. You are definitely the most talented singer and actress at this school, much better than Janie Wickeder."

Janie Wickeder emerges from the crowd and makes her way toward Bella. "Come on, Bella," she says, extending her hand.

Bella stands up and reluctantly puts her hand in Janie's. Janie leads her to the podium, where the members of the Rod and Gun Club fall to their knees and shout in unison, "Please forgive us!"

Janie picks up the microphone. "Let's hear a round of applause for Bella, who has put up with way more crap than she's ever deserved!"

The crowd roars with approval, and Mr. Wonderful, wearing princely garb, rushes to Bella's side. "Darling, I promise that I'll do a better job of protecting you from creeps in the future. Now let's go practice that stage kiss."

12

I heard you walked out of Klimstra's class today," Jai says as he peels a banana. His face is a web of concern.

"Yeah, me, too," adds Katie. "What happened?"

"Well, between the homework I forgot to do and Rod being his usual prickish self, it was pretty much the worst morning ever," I answer, taking a bite of my pizza. "I even went to talk to Mr. Bredeson about the situation, but he basically told me to piss off."

"He did?" asks Jai. "Why?"

I sigh. "Oh, he doesn't seem to think sexual harassment is a problem anymore."

"Five minutes sitting with the Rod and Gun Club would change his mind really fast," Jai remarks drily and tilts his faux hawk toward the boys, who are currently engaged in napkin races, a cafeteria competition that most kids abandoned back in third grade. They each unfold a paper napkin and clamp their lips down on a corner. Then, using only their lips, the boys see how quickly they can get the whole napkin inside their mouths. I feel sorry for those napkins.

"No kidding," I mutter bitterly. "What a bunch of fugly swine."

"So what did Rod do this time?" Katie asks.

"I don't want to dwell on it right now," I reply. I give Katie and pleading look, and she nods.

"Okay. So who's going to the girls' basketball game tonight?" asks Katie brightly.

I paste a small smile on my face. "I guess I am."

"Me, too," says Jai. "Go Pirates!" He clenches his fist and raises it in the air.

"We need to get you some pom-poms, cowboy," remarks Katie.

We spend the rest of lunch discussing the victorious basketball season that the Pine Prairie High girls' team is having so far this year. Normally, Katie, Jai, and I aren't that interested in sports, but we've heard that the Piratesses (yes, it's stupid, but that's what the female athletes are called) are having an awesome season and want to see it for ourselves. We debate whether or not we should paint our faces red and black to show school spirit. Eventually, we decide against it when Jai points out that face paint is comedogenic.

Katie drops her napkin. "What does *comedogenic* mean, Jai?"

Jai thumbs the lapels of his blazer. "Oh, it's just another way of saying that we'll get zits if we use face paint. Even if we wash it off really well and tone and moisturize afterward." I can't help but think that that was a really gay thing to say, but Katie appears unfazed by Jai's knowledge of skin care.

I manage to get through my afternoon classes without incident, but my respite from trouble ends when I walk into the theater after school. I head up the stairs to the stage so that I can set down my backpack in the dressing room. I flip back the curtain just in time to see Jamie and Lance in a bona fide lip-lock. They're really going at it, their heads rocking back and forth rhythmically. Jamie pulls back slightly, and I see Lance's tongue rotating inside her mouth. I quickly drop the curtain and take a seat on the edge of the stage. I think I'm traumatized for life.

I'm still willing myself not to get physically sick when Matt appears.

"How's it going today, Becca?" he asks, smiling. Matt has the kind of smile that makes his eyes crinkle at the corners, and when I see it, I can't help but feel a little better about the world. Even on a crappy day like today.

"Okay," I say. "How are you?"

"Not bad, but I'm having kind of a tough time learning all of my lines." He smiles again.

I cough. "Um, would you, um, like some help?" With lines, kissing practice, whatever?

Matt pats my shoulder. "That would be fantastic. Would you mind sticking around for a little while after rehearsal?"

"No problem," I answer.

"You're the best," Matt says. He stands up and walks away.

I'm the best? The best what? Actress? Singer? Future girlfriend? What?

After rehearsal, I walk down the steps at the front of the stage. I see Josh talking to Jamie and Lance just outside the lighting booth. It seems strange that Jamie and Lance would even deign to talk to Josh, a lowly freshman and member of the Computer Club, unless they wanted to make fun of him.

I sit down in the first row of seats, and Matt appears after a minute. I'm disappointed when he sits down two seats away, but he probably needs to stretch out his legs.

"Um, why don't we start with the drive-in scene?" Matt says. "That's the one I'm having the most trouble with."

"Sure," I say.

We begin running the lines, and I relax enough to give him a few suggestions about how to make his delivery a little smoother and more dramatic. I blush when we get to the part where Danny and Sandy are supposed to kiss.

"Um, I guess we'll be dealing with that part later," Matt remarks in a businesslike tone.

I nod, unsure of what I could say at this moment that wouldn't sound stupid.

As we run the lines, I start thinking about what Jamie and her friends said about Matt in the girls' room again. What did he do? And why was he at one of Darren Nelson's skanky parties in the first place? Matt hangs out with the serious athletes, and most of them don't drink for fear of getting busted and benched at games. Then again, Matt doesn't do sports, so maybe he does drink and party and I've just never heard about it before. If that's true, then I'm not sure I'd be all that interested in Matt anymore, except maybe as eye candy.

Somehow, I manage to stay focused on the lines while thinking about all of this. After about fifteen minutes, Matt looks up from his script and grins at me, his baby soul patch moving upward with his lips. "I think I'm in pretty good shape now. You're a great drama coach, Becca. Thank you so much for helping me."

"Anytime," I answer. And I want to say, "Now offer me a ride home. Or tell me I'm the girl you think about when you watch the end of *Sixteen Candles* and pine for a romance of your own. Or at least tell me that you were never at one of Darren's parties and Haley Matheson was just talking crap as usual." I suddenly wish I knew Matt better.

Matt stands up, so I do, too. We gather our jackets and bags and walk out of the theater, shutting the door firmly behind us until we hear it latch. I look up at him.

"So how are you getting home?" Matt asks.

"I was going to call my stepdad," I answer. *Tell me that I don't have to.*

"Don't bother," Matt says, zipping up his jacket. "I can give you a ride. You live on Fifth Street, right?"

Yes!

"Yeah. Thanks."

We both walk toward the lobby, and my heart starts to pound. I'm not sure why I should be nervous at the prospect of riding in a car with Matt, but I am. Maybe because it means that I'll have more opportunities to make an ass out of myself.

When Matt and I enter the lobby, there's only one person in it: Evan Johnson. He's sitting on a bench near the front doors, clasping a dog-eared copy of *On the Road* and gazing at the parking lot with a forlorn expression. He looks kind of small and lonely, and I almost wish I could go over and give him a hug, though I don't think that would go over very well.

"Hey, Johnson, what's going on?" Matt asks brightly, walking toward Evan.

I wonder how well acquainted Matt and Evan are. I mean, they've been involved in a couple of the same theater productions, so it's not surprising that they at least know each other's name. Matt is a popular junior and Evan is a geeky freshman, so I can't imagine they've interacted much. I'm not even sure if Matt knows that Evan and I were dating.

Evan turns his head, and his eyes widen when he sees that Matt isn't alone. He slips his book into his coat pocket and coughs.

"Hi, Matt." Evan hesitates and then makes direct eye contact with me. My heart flips around in my chest. This is the first time that Evan's looked me in the eye since breaking up with me. He grimaces slightly, and I can tell that he's deciding what to say next. Finally, still looking at me, he says, "Um, hey."

"Hi, Evan," I say, doing my best to keep my voice even. I don't want Matt to know how weird this is for me. At the same time, I'm relieved that Evan has finally acknowledged my existence, even though his eyes dart away from me toward the floor as I greet him.

"You look like you're waiting for a ride," Matt says to Evan.

"Yeah, I am," Evan answers, fixing his eyes only on Matt. "My mom may have gotten sidetracked at the hospital." Evan's mom is a nurse, and I know that sometimes she has to stay at work longer than she plans to.

Matt reaches into his jeans pocket, fishes out his cell phone, and extends it toward Evan.

"Here. Call her and tell her that you've found a ride home," Matt says.

Oh, no.

Evan takes the phone from Matt cautiously. "You sure?"

"Yeah. You live in town, right?" Matt asks.

"Darwin and Tenth."

"No problem," Matt answers cheerfully. "That's totally on the way, and there's no point in your waiting here. Give your mom a ring and we'll get going."

Evan takes Matt's cell phone and makes a quick call.

"I guess we're set, then," Matt says. "Let's head out."

As Matt strides toward the door, I glance over at Evan, who is peering at the floor. I almost want to shout, "Wait! I'll just call Dale and have him come pick me up." I know that it doesn't make any sense to do this, and there's no way to explain to Matt that this is going to be one of the most awkward car rides of my life, so I follow the boys out to Matt's car, a really beat-up Buick LeSabre.

"My Ferrari is at the shop," Matt jokes as he unlocks the car and throws a couple of empty pop cans into the backseat. "So my grandpa was kind enough to loan me his old car."

Evan and I don't say anything and just stand there by the side of the car as Matt leans across the bench seat and unlocks the passenger-side door, which Evan opens.

"You'll both have to ride shotgun because my backseat is so full of junk. Sorry about that," Matt says. I peer at the backseat and see an Igloo cooler, a sleeping bag, several plastic gallon jugs half full of ice, hockey skates, assorted fast-food wrappers, and a bunch of books strewn all over the place.

"I should really clean this thing out," Matt admits. "I still have stuff in here from the camping trip Lance and I took this fall."

Evan and I are still standing awkwardly next to the car.

"Get in, you guys," Matt urges us.

"You first," I say to Evan, gesturing toward the bench seat. I don't think I could handle sitting between the two of them.

"No, you can go," says Evan. "I live closer, so I'll have to get out first." His tone isn't hostile, but I can tell that he's in as much agony as I am.

I quickly realize that Evan's right, so I slide into the car next to Matt, accidentally bumping into his shoulder.

"Sorry," I say.

"No problem," answers Matt, adjusting the defroster. His posture is relaxed, and he's got his legs spread out, like he deserves to take up as much room as he wants. His right thigh is touching my left one.

Evan gets into the car and shuts the door. I consider moving to the right a little so that I'm not touching Matt, but if I do that, I'll certainly bump thighs with Evan. No thanks.

Evan and I both fish around for our seat belts, and Matt puts the LeSabre in drive.

And we're off. I cannot believe I'm sitting here sandwiched between my current crush and my ex-boyfriend, who is keeping as close to the passenger door as possible, probably to avoid any contact with me.

"So how are things in the lighting booth?" Matt asks Evan.

Oh, good. The boys can do all of the talking and I'll keep my lips zipped.

"They're okay," Evan answers.

Silence fills the car. I wish Evan would say something else, but he looks about as mortified as I feel.

"Well, that's good to hear," Matt says. "I'm sure you can see how well things are shaping up onstage. I think we have an awesome cast. Becca here has really helped me learn my lines. Don't you think Becca's doing a great job?"

Hearing Matt compliment me in front of Evan feels like a triumph. I look over at Evan, and it's clear that he's in no mood to listen to someone sing my praises.

"I don't know," he answers quietly.

I am so tempted to say, "Evan, it's fine. You don't have to say anything nice about me because what could you say, really? That I told my friends about your sloppy kissing technique? Or that you were so disgusted with me that you couldn't even break up with me yourself?"

I'm suddenly furious with Evan for not having had the decency to tell me to my face that he wanted to break up. Not that that conversation would have been fun, but it would have been the mature thing to do. Then again, how much maturity could I have expected from a freshman?

I have so many questions for Evan, and here he is, right next to me, and I can't even ask them. I want out of this car. I feel like I'm suffocating.

"Hmm," begins Matt. "I suppose you and Josh have a lot to

concentrate on when you're doing the lights and sound, so maybe you haven't noticed. But you should pay attention the next time Becca sings 'Hopelessly Devoted to You.' She's really good."

Is Matt joking? The last time I sang that song, I sounded like a sea lion with laryngitis.

"Okay," Evan answers. "Um, that's my house right there." He points toward his driveway.

"All right. See you tomorrow," says Matt, pulling up next to the back door.

"Thanks a lot. See you." I notice that Evan only looks at Matt when he says this, and he darts out of the car and slams the door.

"Next stop, your place," Matt remarks. I don't think he has any idea that the amount of angst in his car has just been reduced by half. More than half, actually, because I feel so much better now that Evan is gone. I'm also proud of myself for not blurting out all of the questions twirling in my head, all of the things I never got to say to Evan.

Still, I look at the empty space that Evan has left and realize that I'm buckled up right next to Matt. Should I unbuckle and move over, or will Matt think that's weird? My shoulders tense up, and I'm not sure what to do.

Matt leans over me and fiddles with the defroster again, so I quickly unbuckle and slide over. I really hope that he doesn't say anything about this.

"You warm enough?" Matt asks.

I wonder why he's asking. Is it because I'm no longer sitting right next to him? Or is he just concerned about my well-being?

"I'm fine," I answer.

The LeSabre rolls down the darkened street, and we ride in silence. A couple of blocks later, Matt is pulling into my driveway. I didn't even need to point it out to him.

"Thanks so much for the ride, Matt," I say, finally relaxing a little.

"My pleasure, Becca," Matt answers, giving me one of his gorgeous grins. My heart does its second flip-flip of the evening, but this time it's for a good reason.

"Well," I begin as I grasp my backpack and open the car door, "see you tomorrow."

"Yeah, see you."

I get out of the car and shut the door, then head down our icy driveway, taking care not to fall on my ass, as Matt hasn't backed up yet. I look back at him when I reach the back door and he waves and then gestures for me to go inside. I wave back and open the door. A cloud of warm air hits my face, and I race for the computer.

Too Much Information

Monday, January 19, 7:02 PM

Questions Bella wishes she could ask E. Jector:

1. Are you over her?
2. Do you ever wish you'd broken up with her yourself instead of making Bella suffer through a phone conversation with your cheesy best friend?

3. Do you ever wish you hadn't broken up with her at all?

4. Do you still think she's cute?

5. Do you realize that you have an abnormally large tongue?

6. Have you considered seeking medical care for this condition?

7. Can you please tell your mother to pick you up on time in the future so that Bella can get a ride home from Mr. Wonderful without worrying about touching thighs with you and you silently hating her guts?

8. Is it possible for you to stop being so damn dramatic and just look Bella in the eye and say hi to her when the two of you cross paths?

The responses she'd like to receive from E. Jector:

1. No.
2. Yes.
3. Yes.
4. Yes.
5. No, but thank you for telling me.
6. I will now.
7. Yes.
8. Yes. I appreciate your constructive criticism.

Questions Bella would like to ask Mr. Wonderful:

1. Do you think she's cute?
2. Have you ever partied at a certain skank's house with Janie Wickeder and crew?

3. Does Bella stand any chance in hell of ever winning your affections?

The responses she'd like to receive from Mr. Wonderful:

1. Of course.
2. No, never.
3. She stands more than a chance. I can hardly keep my lips off her when she's around.

13

The next evening, I'm sitting next to Jai and Katie at the girls' varsity basketball game. The Pine Prairie Piratesses are playing their biggest rivals, the Litchfield Dragons. The bleachers are nearly full, which means that practically the whole town has shown up for the game.

"Hey." Katie nudges Jai. "There's your girlfriend." She cocks her head to the right, and my eyes follow to see Ashli Berg coming toward us with a bag of popcorn. She's carrying a backpack and wearing a gold, red, and black sweatshirt that says OKTOBERFEST 2007 on it. Her hair is back in a high, bouncy ponytail, and she has a huge smile on her face. For once, I don't find myself wondering if I'm as dorky as she is and if Matt thinks so. Instead, her happy energy comes as a huge relief. And after dealing with a few contempt-filled glances from Jamie and company at rehearsal, it's nice to see someone who's so genuinely pleasant.

Ashli plops down next to Jai. "Hi, you! Enjoying the game?" she asks perkily.

"Sure, Ashli." Jai looks like someone just stomped on his big toe. I'd like to nudge him and say, "Dude, you could be a *little* friendlier," but I know he's afraid that Ashli could interpret it as romantic interest. Still, I totally envy Jai for having someone so obviously infatuated with him, even she isn't the right sex. Considering my own grim prospects in the love department, I think I'd be thrilled if some girl professed a lesbian crush on me. At least I'd know that one person on this planet wanted to make out with me.

"Want some popcorn? I have pop, too," Ashli says, opening her backpack. "I didn't know what you liked, so I got Pepsi, Mountain Dew, and 7UP."

Jai gives me a microglance and smiles slightly. "Wow, Ashli, that was really thoughtful of you, but I'd feel a little rude partaking in front of my friends here."

"Oh, that's all right." Ashli shrugs and looks over at Katie and me. "Help yourselves to whatever you want. I already have a beverage." She holds up a can of Diet Pepsi.

"Thanks, Ashli," Katie replies, reaching for the 7UP.

"I wanted that one," Jai says.

Ashli shoots up like an arrow. "You did? I'll go get another one. Be right back!" She leaves her backpack sitting next to us and takes off down the bleacher stairs.

I turn to face Katie and Jai. "Wow. Our own personal concession stand."

Jai rolls his eyes. "Too embarrassing for words."

Katie purses her lips. "You know, I think it's really sweet of her. And you should consider yourself lucky. At least *somebody* likes you, even if it isn't the girl of your dreams."

I'm glad to hear Katie voice the thoughts I was just having, even if she isn't aware that Jai dreams about boys, not girls.

"Yeah, she's more like a nightmare," admits Jai. "She's constantly cornering me backstage at play practice and I still pull the old 'gotta pee' routine, but I have to think of a new avoidance tactic because yesterday, Ashli was like, 'Um, Jai, do you have a bladder infection?'"

"Poor, poor little Jai," I whimper. "It must be hell to have someone so crazy about you." I know I'm making fun of him a little unfairly, but my own bitterness about this issue has grown so rapidly that I'm having trouble sympathizing about the Ashli problem.

"Yeah, please spare us," Katie echoes.

"Fine, we can talk about something else," says Jai, straightening and looking full of importance. "It just so happens that I have an announcement."

An announcement? My heart races. I'm stunned that Jai would tell Katie something so private in such a public place. And especially when Ashli Berg could come waltzing back at any moment. Then again, she's the person who would benefit most from this information; she could stop wasting her time pursuing a guy who thinks she curves in all the wrong places. Maybe I should try to change the subject.

No, Jai needs to do this in his own way. I bite my lip to keep from talking.

Katie's eyes widen. "What is it, Jai?"

I realize that I'm holding my breath.

"I might be leaving Pine Prairie."

"What, like for spring break?" guesses Katie.

"No, next year, I'm thinking about moving to Minneapolis

and living with my aunt and uncle. I want to go to the Minnesota Performing Arts High School," Jai states.

This is news to me.

"Really? Isn't that expensive?" I ask.

Jai shakes his head. "Not necessarily. They offer scholarships. I applied for one."

Katie's mouth drops open. "You did? You're serious about this?"

"Very." Jai's jaw is set. "Why are you guys so shocked? I moved from one part of the sticks to another. Pine Prairie is even more conservative than Northfield, and I'm practically suffocating here."

Hearing Jai say this pisses me off a little. Suffocating? That seems a tad dramatic. I want to say to Jai, "Listen, I know that you think you have to stay in the closet here, but it's not that bad, is it? I mean, you're friends with Katie and me, and you're in the school musical. Plus, someone, even if she *is* a girl, wants to make out with you." But then I'd be outing Jai *and* belittling how hard it must be to be a gay teenager, particularly in a town like this.

I stay quiet and let Katie respond to this.

"Look," she says, "I know that Pine Prairie sucks, but I don't think you should go. What would we do without you?"

"You'd come visit." Jai smirks. "What do you say, Becca?"

Well, usually I say the first thing that pops into my head, and right now I'm thinking about my own selfish interests. If he leaves, the level of suckage in my life will definitely increase, and I totally don't need that. Especially not right now. I need his friendship. I don't think this is what Jai wants to hear right now, so I take a deep breath and put on an act.

"I'd definitely miss you, but if it made you happy, I'd be happy for you," I say softly.

Just then, Ashli reappears with a can of 7UP. "Here you go, Jai!"

Jai accepts the pop. "Thanks, Ashli. That's very sweet of you."

Ashli beams. "Anything for you, Jai. Absolutely anything."

Jai's lips part, but he obviously can't think of a response. Not that Ashli is anticipating one; she turns her attention to the game and starts cheering, "Go Pirates!" so loudly that even the other fans start to stare at her.

I lean toward Jai and whisper, "Do you really want to miss moments like these?"

"I'll take my chances," is all he whispers back.

❋❋❋

After play practice on Thursday, Josh approaches me.

"What's new in your zoo, Becca?" he asks, raising a can of Mountain Dew to his lips.

"Um, I'm okay," I say cautiously. With the exception of his announcement that I was intruding on the Computer Club meeting, Josh has done nothing but shoot me dirty looks since the play began. Why the hell would he start talking to me now? Hmm, maybe he wants to turn over a new leaf. I mean, we weren't exactly friends when I was dating Evan, but we did hang out a little. We even talked about how much we both love New York City blogs one time. Maybe I should give Josh a chance. Besides, if I'm rude to him, he'll certainly tell Evan about it, and I can't bear the thought of Evan having more reasons to think I'm scum.

"How are you?" I ask.

"Everything's dandy in Joshland!" Yep, that's Josh for you. I do my best not to wince.

"Great. Um, see you later, Josh." I smile at him and then turn toward the door. I think I've been sufficiently cordial.

"Wait, Becca!" he shouts.

I whirl around. What *is* it with this boy? What could he possibly want?

He drains the last of his pop, sets the can on the floor, stomps on it, and kicks it under a row of theater seats.

"Not into recycling?" I ask.

"Whatever," Josh grunts. "So how's your mom doing? I heard she's pregnant."

I eye Josh suspiciously. "She's fine?"

Except for the hemorrhoids, of course. Not that Josh needs to know any of this. I'm not sure I would have told him about this back in my overshare days, anyway.

"Oh, excellent. I have to go to a Computer Club meeting now. Later, skater!" And just like that, Josh is gone.

Before I have time to process that little exchange and fish the Dew can from under the seats so I can put it in the recycling bin, Jamie and Lance walk up to me. Lance's hand is grasping the back of Jamie's neck, like she's a horse he's leading to the barn.

"So your mom is preggers, huh?" Lance grins lasciviously. The word *preggers* rolls off his tongue in the most vile way. Lance snickers and readjusts his enormous belt buckle, which features a large fish and the inscription DON'T LET THIS ONE GET AWAY.

"Yeah, she's having a baby," I reply.

Why in the world would Lance even care?

"Is she feeling okay?" Jamie asks.

What *is* this?

"Um, she's all right," I reply, again remaining intentionally vague. I'm sure Lance and Jamie would have a field day with any embarrassing information I gave them about my mother. They'd probably post a sign on the door of Prairie Perks reading OWNED BY PREGGERS HEMORRHOID LADY. Then I'd be in real trouble because I'm sure my mother wouldn't be too pleased to have her physical discomforts advertised like that.

"She's feeling fine? Oh, well, that's good then," says Jamie, and she collapses into a fit of laughter.

"Later," says Lance, barely concealing his own laugh attack. I hear him let loose as soon as he and Jamie are out in the hallway.

"Congratulations," says a voice behind me. Matt. I turn around. "So you're going to be a big sister again, huh?" he asks.

I nod. "How did you know about the again part?"

"Oh, I go into Prairie Perks all the time, and your mom was talking to another customer about when she's due. I also noticed those pictures your mom has of you and your brother behind the counter. He's a cute little guy." I wonder if Matt would think Nathan was so adorable if he knew that the boy ran around in his birthday suit half the time.

Matt smiles and stuffs his hands into his pockets. He's looking particularly delicious today in a black turtleneck sweater. Very Seattle coffeehouse. Or so I'm guessing, since I've never been to Seattle.

"Yeah, it's a good thing that Nathan's cute because it keeps my parents and me from strangling him when he's naughty," I remark. Naughty or nude. Or both.

"He can't be as bad as my sister," Matt says.

"Your sister?" I ask. I now realize that I know nothing about Matt's family. In fact, I know very little about Matt at all.

"Yeah, Emma is six years old and thinks she's the bomb because she's a big, bad first grader now. A couple of years ago, one of her favorite hobbies was coming into my bedroom and scribbling all over my Jon Krakauer books. I had a signed, hardcover copy of *Into Thin Air*, and Emma totally mutilated it. Her dimples were the only thing that saved her."

"That sucks," I commiserate. "I know how you feel. Nathan got into my yarn stash one afternoon and unwound all of the balls around my bedposts." I turn red, realizing that I've just said the word *balls* in front of a boy I like. "Anyway," I continue, "it took me hours to get everything straightened out again."

"So you like to knit?" asks Matt.

"Yeah, I do that quite a lot. Especially on like a Saturday night sacked out in front of a good eighties movie." Oh God, did that make me sound pathetic or what? Matt's got to be thinking, *How lame is it that this girl has nothing better to do on a weekend evening than make scarves and rewatch* The Breakfast Club*?*

But Matt's face doesn't betray any kind of judgment. Instead, he says, "You're into eighties movies? Me, too. What's your favorite?"

"Man, that's a tough question," I admit. And if Matt is a true aficionado of these films, he might be asking me about my favorite to scope out my personality. "*Heathers*, maybe?"

"Ooh," says Matt, rounding his lips. "Good one. A bit violent, though."

"And what about you?" I ask.

"*Risky Business*. Hands down."

"I haven't seen that one. What's it about?"

"Oh, it was one of Tom Cruise's first big movies. It's the best. I'll lend you the DVD."

I wish Matt were inviting me to watch the movie with him, but that would be wishing for a little too much. Still, we're actually having a real conversation that's not about the play, and I'm not all tongue-tied like I usually am. It's cool to know that Matt and I actually have some stuff in common, too. Maybe there's potential for a friendship here. And if Jai really is leaving Pine Prairie, I could use another friend.

Too Much Information
Thursday, January 22, 5:48 PM

Bella wonders if there's something seriously wrong with her. Her whole life, she's felt like this big freak who can't seem to control whatever comes out of her mouth, and she's paid a huge price for it.

For one thing, until very recently, she had only one

friend. Bella has always assumed that K-Style is an unusually tolerant person. Even though she's stuck by Bella for many years, Bella continues to worry that K-Style will someday come to her senses and ditch her. Not because K-Style is that kind of person but because Bella doesn't trust herself not to screw up.

Bella feels like she screws up a lot. She certainly screwed up with E. Jector, who still can barely stand to look at her. Bella wants so much to talk to him, to tell him how sorry she is. If E. Jector were willing, Bella would love to be friends with him, even if it meant that his annoying pal, Joshing A. Round, would tag along like he always does.

Perhaps it's just wishful thinking, but Bella sees another friendship on the horizon, and it's with Mr. Wonderful. He's been very friendly toward Bella lately, and she senses that he's sincere. And while she's dreamed about the two of them being more than friends, Bella knows that that's not realistic. Plus, given a few things she's heard about him lately regarding the company he keeps and places he may or may not be putting his hands, she's not sure Mr. Wonderful is really the unicorn of high school boys anymore.

14

After lunch on Friday, I go to my locker only to find that someone has defaced it. Written in pencil, in block letters about half an inch high, the words are clear:

I WANNA HAVE MATT W'S BABYS.

I look around suspiciously. People are going about their usual business of begging one another for gum and sifting through stacks of crumpled papers for work sheets they're never going to find. I quickly erase the sentence and rush off to American history.

I have trouble focusing on Mr. Huhn's lively lecture about Reconstruction after the Civil War. He's my favorite teacher, and normally I'd be hanging on his every word, taking copious notes, but I can't stop obsessing over my locker.

I'm not exactly the most popular girl in school, but I'd like to think that I don't have a lot of enemies. There are definitely people who dislike me, like Evan, who wasn't exactly friendly during our car ride with Matt the other day. I'm not sure where I stand with Josh after our last interaction, but he doesn't appear to hate my guts anymore. That's progress. Then there's the issue of Jamie. She seems to be over the fact that I got the lead in *Grease,* but hearing her talk about me behind my back confirmed what I've always suspected: she thinks I'm a loser. Still, Jamie seems way too self-absorbed to go to the trouble of vandalizing a locker.

Maybe one of the Rod and Gun Club boys did it. That makes more sense, given the way Rod was hassling me the other day in Ms. Klimstra's class. Or it could have been Lance, who loves to deface clean surfaces and blow stuff up. Neither of them can spell worth a damn either. Yes, these two are definite culprits.

But then, why would they write about Matt? It's not like I drape myself all over him at rehearsals. He got a little flirty with me that one time, but I don't think anyone noticed that. I make an effort not to openly drool or stare when he's around. And I definitely don't want to have his, or anyone else's, babies.

"Ms. Farrell, what is your answer?" Mr. Huhn is standing right in front of my desk.

"Um, can you repeat the question?" I hear a few snickers from the back of the room.

"What did I just ask her, Ms. Stromwell?" I glance over at Melissa, who is sitting up straight with her pen poised above her notebook.

"You asked her what a carpetbagger was," replies Melissa. She smiles, revealing an obscene abuse of Crest White Strips. Crap, did her front tooth just twinkle and make a little dinging noise? Obnoxious.

"It's, um, a person who bags carpets? Like a grocery bagger but at a carpet store?" I say lamely. "Although the bags would need to be really big to hold rolls of carpet?"

The entire class erupts with laughter.

"Nice," I hear Justin Schwermer say. "Paper or plastic?" I suppose he thinks he's clever.

Mr. Huhn bites his bottom lip and eyes me critically, like I just told him that he would make a really sexy prison guard. I never would have said anything like that even in my weakest overshare moments. I'm not the kind of girl who talks back to teachers. I have been known, however, to make a few squirm with my questions about breast development and comments about Teddy Roosevelt's sex appeal.

"Ms. Farrell," says Mr. Huhn sternly, "I don't know what planet you're currently inhabiting, but I suggest you take the next shuttle back to Earth."

"Sorry," I say weakly. My face grows hot, and I hunch over my notebook. In the past week and a half, I've received more negative attention from school authority figures than I previously had during my entire life. I need to focus now. I can't be obsessing about who thinks I want to have Matt's babies.

✳ ✳ ✳

Jamie and Lance arrive at play practice with matching hickeys on their necks. I've never understood the appeal of hickeys. It's like, "Hey, I'm into you, so let me give you a bruise. I'll just latch on to your neck like a leech and suck on your skin until I break enough blood vessels to leave a mark. That way everyone will know just how much I care about you."

Evan never tried to kiss my neck, but if he had, I would have told him to keep his lips moving. I look up at the lighting booth and catch Evan staring back at me through the little projector window, but he quickly ducks out of sight. Maybe I should just go back to the lighting booth and tell him that he doesn't need to hide from me, that he should just act normally. I know that Josh is back there, too, and he doesn't need to be present for any more pivotal moments between Evan and me.

Rehearsal itself is fairly exhausting. We start learning the moves for the big school dance scene. As choreographer, Melissa Stromwell seems to be deriving a lot of pleasure from bossing everyone around, but I relax and start to enjoy myself when Matt and I partner up, his left hand clasping my right. He lightly pushes on the small of my back to twirl me, and the motions feel smooth and easy. I lock back into his grasp, and we maintain eye contact and grin at each other. I wonder if Matt's smile belongs to him or Danny. Mine is one hundred percent Becca.

After the dance sequence, Ms. Miller summons Matt and me to try the drive-in scene.

"Becca and I spent some extra time practicing the lines for this one, Ms. M," Matt says. "Hopefully, I can still remember them. Becca never seems to have a problem. She's the professional here." I wonder if Matt means that, or if he's just saying it in a show of false modesty.

"Let's see what you guys can do. I just want to run the lines and do rough blocking today," Ms. Miller says. "We'll work on the stage kiss later." I'm shocked by how casually she mentions this. My heart is racing.

Matt and I sit side by side in two folding chairs. The chairs will soon be replaced by a cardboard convertible, which Katie and the rest of the stage crew are already designing.

"Matt, put your arm around Becca and start," orders Ms. Miller from the front row.

Matt swings his arm over my shoulder and I nearly faint. Matt Wooderson is touching me. Or, more precisely, my sweater. I envy my sweater.

I take a deep breath and try to adopt an expression that communicates that I most definitely do not want to have any of Matt's babies. Not even one small one. Just in case the person who wrote that is watching.

Matt and I manage to block the scene minus the kiss, and then Ms. Miller has the whole cast go through "Summer Nights." I lose myself in the singing and dancing and actually enjoy myself. I don't worry about Evan and Josh watching me in the lighting booth, and I don't freak out when Jamie bumps against me as Matt and I harmonize at the end of the song. For once, I feel like one of the stars of the show, and I'm pretty sure I deserve it.

After rehearsal, I'm backstage looking through my backpack to see if I have all of my homework. I feel a tap on the shoulder and turn to see Matt standing behind me.

"Hey," he says, handing me a DVD case. "This is for you."

I look at the cover. "*Risky Business.* Cool." Matt remembered to bring me the movie. Which means that he thought about me outside of school. Which makes my toes tingle.

"Enjoy. And there's no rush to give it back. I've seen it a million times."

"Thanks, Matt. I'll watch it this weekend," I say, smiling.

It's a relaxed, happy smile. I'm definitely feeling more at ease around Matt these days.

"Let me know what you think," Matt adds as he walks away. So not only did Matt think about me outside of school, he wants to have a conversation with me. Now my ears are tingling.

"I will," I answer. "Have a good weekend."

"You, too." And Matt turns and gives me a little wave with the tips of his fingers before he walks out the stage door.

Sigh.

Too Much Information
Friday, January 23, 6:46 PM

After rehearsal, Mr. Wonderful approaches Bella.

"My goodness, you look gorgeous today," he says. "And the way you sang at rehearsal—well, guys don't usually admit things like this, but I had a lump in my throat by the time you were done. And goose bumps."

"Oh, Mr. Wonderful," begins Bella, modestly tilting her head toward him, "that's so sweet of you to say."

"Well, it's the simple truth."

"You were amazing, too."

The two lovebirds stand before each other for a moment, drinking in each other's visual appeal and animal magnetism. Bella can tell that Mr. Wonderful is absolutely dying to kiss her, but, being a gentleman, he would never put the moves on her with so many other people around.

"How would you like to come over to my place tonight and watch *Risky Business* with me?" he asks.

"Why, I'd love to," Bella replies, batting her naturally long, lush eyelashes. "Will anyone else be joining us?"

"Heavens, no. I've asked my parents to stay at a hotel for the night so that you and I might enjoy some private quality time together. They were incredibly understanding. In fact, my mother volunteered to cook a sumptuous gourmet meal for us and leave it warming in the oven."

"My, that's so thoughtful," Bella responds. "I can see why you're such a caring, loving person. You've been raised right."

"I'm very lucky," Mr. Wonderful admits, gazing into Bella's eyes with an inextinguishable passion.

It suddenly occurs to Bella that Mr. Wonderful might expect, well, certain *things* from her if she stays the night with him. Things that could lead to a Baby Bella or Mr. Wonderful Jr. if the young couple were careless.

Mr. Wonderful must read Bella's thoughts because he gently takes her hand in his, lightly caressing her palm.

"I know what you're thinking, Bella, and you don't need to worry. We'll let Tom Cruise handle the truly risky business, and we'll just see where the evening takes us."

15

The next afternoon, I invite Jai and Katie over to my house for one of our typical weekend get-togethers. It seems like all we ever do is make cookies and watch films in which a large portion of the actresses sport permed, ratted bangs and blazers with huge shoulder pads. Then again, Pine Prairie doesn't leave us with a lot of other options.

A few minutes before Katie and Jai are due to arrive, I walk into the living room and see Nathan sitting on Dale's lap, looking somber.

"You promise?" Dale says.

"Yeah," Nathan replies glumly.

"Then repeat what I just said," Dale instructs.

Nathan heaves a sigh. "I will wear clothes while Becca's friends are here, um, um—"

"Or I can't hang out with them. I have to stay in my room."

Nathan repeats this, his little hands folded piously in his lap like he's reciting a prayer. It's so cute, I have to suppress a giggle.

"Good," Dale says, smiling. "Now let's go get you dressed."

"Thanks, Dale," I say as he leads my brother upstairs. Dale flashes me a thumbs-up, and the doorbell rings. I let Katie and Jai in, and we go to the kitchen to make chocolate-chip cookies.

Within a couple of minutes, Nathan bounds into the kitchen, resplendent in a turtleneck, overalls, and even socks.

"Hi, guys!" he shouts, pulling a chair from the dining room into the kitchen. He wedges the chair between Katie and me and climbs up onto it. "I want to help!"

"Here, buddy, I've got a job for you," says Jai, who motions for me to move over. Jai picks up the electric mixer and holds it over the mixing bowl, which is already full of sugar and butter. "Let's do this together. It's much better if two people hold the mixer." Jai places Nathan's tiny hand on top of his and turns on the mixer. Nathan scrunches up his face in concentration as he "helps" Jai.

After they've creamed the butter and sugar, Nathan gazes up admiringly at his new idol. "That was fun! And I helped!" He jumps up and down on the top of the chair, clapping.

"You were a big help," Jai says. "I couldn't have done it without you."

Katie looks over at me, the corners of her mouth twitching. "Oh my God, that's so sweet, I think I'm going to cry. Jai, I had no idea you were so good with kids."

Nathan still has his eyes fixed on Jai, like he worships him. "Jai," he asks, "do you have hair on your peanut?"

"Nathan!" I shout sharply. Jai starts laughing and coughing at the same time, and Katie's "aw, ain't that cute" expression morphs into one of shock.

Nathan remains unfazed by our reactions. "Well, *do* you?"

I'm ready to haul Nathan upstairs for Dale to deal with, but Jai pats Nathan on the shoulder. "Actually, I'm allergic to peanuts. Now let's get these cookies in the oven so that we can go watch *Risky Business*."

"Jai," I say, "you have just become my personal hero."

I watch Jai and Nathan scoop the dough onto cookie sheets, thinking about how cute they are together and remembering my worries about Nathan's personality paralleling my own. Nathan prefers nudity to clothing, but he's willing to put aside that preference to get something he wants. Have I done the same thing by clamping down my oversharing ways? Am I getting what I want? Do I even *know* what I want?

My brain isn't coming up with any answers to these questions, so I shove them aside and join my friends and brother in a sugary eighties fest.

Fifteen minutes later, I'm carrying a wailing Nathan up the basement stairs.

"Why can't I watch the movie with you guys?" he shouts. I know the shouts are going to dissolve into tears any minute now.

"Because this isn't a movie for little kids. It's a movie for big kids and grown-ups," I answer. Which I would have known if I'd even bothered to read the description of the movie on the back of the DVD case, not to mention the R rating.

"But I'm a big boy! You and Mommy and Daddy tell me that all the time," Nathan protests, sniffling. He makes an excellent point.

"I know we do, but you won't like this movie. It's boring," I say lamely.

I hand a whimpering Nathan off to Dale, quickly explaining that the movie we're watching isn't exactly a Disney classic. Dale nods understandingly and manages to calm Nathan down quickly by asking him if he'd like to take off his pants. Works like a charm.

I rejoin my friends in the basement and we get back to *Risky Business*.

When the movie finishes, I sit back on the couch and face Jai and Katie. "Well, what did you think?" I ask.

"That was such a *guy* movie," says Katie with disdain. She glances at Jai. "No offense, but that was kind of sick, actually. I mean, do teenage boys really want to do it with hookers?"

Jai adjusts his sweater-vest as he thinks of the best way to handle this question. Should I just jump in and say something so that he doesn't have to? Not that I would tell Katie that Jai is gay; that's his news to tell when he feels the time is right, but I feel like I need to spare him from answering Katie's question. I'm just afraid that I'll screw it up and out Jai and then he'll be all pissed, even if it is just Katie who's finding out.

Jai is still quiet, and I can't stand it anymore, so I say, "You don't have to answer that."

Jai's eyes meet mine, and I can't quite decide what he's trying to tell me with his expression. Does he want me to shut up?

Katie is oblivious to this because she says, "Well, I know Jai doesn't have to answer my question, but I really want to know. I feel like I'm clueless about how guys think, and Jai can help me."

"Maybe Jai doesn't feel comfortable helping you with that," I blurt out. "Why don't you just leave him alone?"

Oh, no. That was probably the wrong thing to say. Katie sits back on the couch looking a bit stunned.

"Becca, can I talk to you in private upstairs for a minute?" Jai asks flatly.

So that *was* the wrong thing to say. Crap.

"Sure," I answer.

"What's going on?" asks Katie, her voice streaked with confusion.

"We'll be right back," replies Jai, heading toward the stairs. "Come on, Becca."

I give Katie my best "I have no idea what this is about" look and follow Jai. We head into the living room, and he sits down on the couch, gesturing for me to join him. I do.

"What are you doing?" Jai asks. He doesn't sound angry, exactly, but his tone is clipped.

I fiddle with a throw pillow. "I, uh, I just thought you might not want to talk about, you know, what Katie wanted you to talk about because—"

"Because I'm gay."

"Well, yeah," I admit. "I was just trying to help."

Jai sighs and stares at the floor. "The best way for you to help me is just to be my friend. I already know that you support me, and I trusted you with my biggest secret. But, you don't need to answer questions for me. I'll handle it. In fact, based on what just happened, I feel like I owe Katie an explanation."

I agree with Jai on this point. I feel terrible that she's just sitting down in the basement wondering what the hell we're talking about up here. "You should tell her if you want, but don't do

it just because you feel like if you don't, I will. Because I won't."
I really hope that Jai believes me when I say this.

"I know you won't," Jai says, and just hearing this fills me with relief. He still trusts me.

Jai stands up. "Tell you what. I'm going to drive Katie home, and I'll have a talk with her. I mean, I'll tell her. And I'll explain that you already know and that I told you and not her because there was a good moment for it, not because I don't trust her."

"That sounds like the right thing to do," I say.

Jai walks out of the living room, and I hear him shout, "Hey, Katie! Get your coat. We're leaving."

❋ ❋ ❋

Katie calls me an hour later in tears.

"I feel so left out!" she wails.

"Why?" I ask, even though I'm pretty sure I know the answer.

"Because Jai came out to you first!"

I sigh, but it's not an annoyed sigh. I'm so glad that Jai told Katie because now I can stop pretending like I don't know he's gay. We don't have to have any more awkward conversations like the one we had today in the basement.

"He only told me like a week ago," I say, hoping that this calms her down a little. I'm not going to admit to Katie that it's been a long week and that there have been several moments, especially at the basketball game, when I was holding my breath and wondering if Katie would guess that Jai was gay or that I would open my big old mouth and give it away. I'm quite proud of myself for not doing that.

"Fine, so it was only a week ago, but the point is that he only told *you*. Why not me?" Katie sniffles. I didn't expect her to be so hurt by this. I guess I thought that she'd just be happy to be let in on the secret and that she'd feel even closer to Jai the way I did when he told me. How wrong I was.

So what should I say to Katie now? Should I just tell her about how Jai came out to me at A&W after I spilled my guts to him? That might make her feel even worse, since she wasn't present for that either. It's not like we intentionally excluded her; it just happened that way.

Finally, I say very simply, "I don't know, Katie."

I hear her heaving on the other end of the phone. I haven't known Katie to get emotional like this very often. In fact, the only time I can remember hearing her cry like this was when her dog Rollie died in sixth grade.

I don't say anything for a moment because I want to give her a chance to calm down. I can hear her breath deepening, and after a moment she says, "I guess I've felt insecure ever since we met Jai and became friends with him."

"You have?" I ask incredulously. "Why would you feel that way?"

"Well, when we first met him, he seemed so fascinated by you and all of your oversharing, and I kind of felt like the boring tagalong."

"Whoa," I say. "This is news to me. It's strange, too, because I remember feeling jealous of Jai's compliments to you, like when he called you a doll. I assumed that he liked *you* more. I mean, you're so much sweeter and more laid-back and beautiful and—"

"Becca!" Katie protests. I forgot that it weirds her out to hear that, especially the part about her being beautiful, but I'm not going to apologize.

"Well, you *are* all of those things, and Jai knows it, too. I think he likes us both equally."

I hope this is true, but I have no way of knowing for sure. It's not like I'd call up Jai and say, "So tell me, if you could only be friends with just one of us, would you choose me or Katie?"

"Do you really think so?" Katie asks.

"Of course. And I'm sorry that you felt left out. Believe me, I was surprised when Jai told me what he did and I definitely remember thinking, *Why isn't he telling Katie, too?* However, I think that what we need to do is just support him and not judge him for coming out to us at different times. He's already dealing with enough. I mean, imagine that you were in Jai's shoes. It would be hard to know what to do, right?"

"For sure," Katie agrees. "I didn't think about it like that." She sounds much calmer. I feel proud of myself for talking her through this. Maybe I'm better with words than I thought.

"Now, the next thing we have to do is think of how we're going to convince Jai to stay in Pine Prairie. I don't want to lose him so soon."

"Neither do I," Katie agrees.

Too Much Information

Saturday, January 24, 7:04 PM

Ways to Keep a Teenage Gay Boy in Hicksville, U.S.A.

1.   Convince Cher to go on tour again and make a special stop in Hicksville.

2.   Get local salons to stock more faux-hawk-building products.

3.   Eliminate the high school wrestling squad (nobody goes to their matches, anyway) and pour the funds into the drama program.

4.   Import several gorgeous, love-hungry gay foreign-exchange students.

5.   Really have the coming-out party Bella described in her January 14 entry.

6.   Remind area homophobes of the old adage "If you can't say anything nice, don't say anything at all."

7.   Better yet, send all Hicksville homophobes to rehab for sensitivity training.

8.   Gently steer Alli Bubbles toward a nice straight boy who might actually return her affection.

9.   Open a thrift store that sells everything one might need to dress like a Scottish rock star.

10. Organize a local unit of the Fashion Police and make gay boy the chief.

11. Promise to share secret blond brownie recipe with boy if, and only if, he stays.

16

I don't sleep very well Tuesday night because I know that to-morrow, Matt and I are going to do the stage kiss for the first time. My stomach is in knots all day on Wednesday, and I have to make seven trips to the bathroom. By the time I actually get to play practice, my insides feel raw and empty.

Jai senses my nervousness as we stand backstage. The boys of the T-Birds are practicing "Greased Lightnin'," and the rest of the cast is waiting to go out into the hall and get measured for costumes by the ancient home-ec teacher, Mrs. Rick.

"You ready to kiss the boy of your dreams?" he whispers, nudging me playfully.

I look around tensely. "Shh, Jai! And if by *ready* you mean that I'm currently sucking on my fifth Altoid of the afternoon, then yes. Totally ready to rock-and-roll with Matt's lips—"

"And/or tongue," Jai cuts in.

"There will be no more talk of tongues!" I hiss. In my limited experience, the tongue, both as an instrument for kissing and for speaking, can cause a lot of trouble. Especially in my case. One might say I have tongue issues.

Jai pats my shoulder. "You'll be smashing, darling. And I'd like to point out that it would be far more nerve-racking to kiss Matt if you two were dating. Can you imagine making out with your boyfriend onstage in front of everyone?"

"No," I say curtly. This comment sets off a whirlwind of thoughts in my brain. Jai has just reminded me, as if I don't already remind myself enough, that I blew my one chance at a boyfriend. Couldn't I have just shut up and dealt with Evan's tongue? Why did I have to go blabbing about it to my friends?

"I didn't mean to bring up a sore subject," Jai says softly. "I'm sorry."

"It's okay. I know," I reply.

Jai and I both gaze at the boys singing and dancing onstage. Matt is looking particularly sexy today. I notice the stark contrast between him and Lance. Although they're blood relatives, Matt stands tall and slim, his gorgeous muscle tone creating juicy contours under his T-shirt and jeans. Lance is considerably shorter and sports the beginnings of a grimy little mustache, which Jamie probably loves. To me, it screams pimp. Not that I've ever seen a pimp, unless Tom Cruise in *Risky Business* counts.

After the boys finish their number, Ms. Miller calls Matt and me to rehearse our drive-in scene. Now I'm really shaking, like I just skipped two meals in a row.

"So we're going to block this scene today, you guys," announces Ms. Miller.

Matt nods but doesn't look at me.

"So take a seat in the convertible." Ms. Miller puts air quotes around the last word. The convertible, a product of Katie's creativity and elbow grease, is more than the sum of its parts, which are a cardboard front with folding chairs behind it. It's totally adorable, with a mint-green-and-white-exterior and the bumper done up in shiny silver paint. And even though it's two-dimensional, it almost looks like a real car.

"Now, Matt," Ms. Miller begins, "you'll want to have your arm around Becca throughout the scene, but make it more casual at first and pull her closer as the scene progresses."

"'Kay," Matt answers. He sounds like I do when my mom asks me to stack all of the towels in the same direction after I fold them.

"And, Becca, you need to look really nervous."

I nod. No need for acting there.

"Remember, Sandy's uptight," Ms. Miller states.

Jamie giggles from offstage. "Method acting!"

"Um, actually, Jamie, it's not. You should really look that term up before you use it," Ms. Miller responds, her voice edged with irritation. It never occurred to me before that Ms. Miller might have noticed what a petty little stain Jamie can be, but now that I think about it, teachers would have to be blind not to see it.

I turn to look at Matt, and he gives me a warm smile.

"Ready?" he asks.

No. Yes. Maybe. I don't know.

"Ready or not, here we go," I reply, wondering if this cliché sounds dumb. Matt just smiles again and nods.

Ms. Miller asks Matt and me to do the beginning of the scene several times. Matt doesn't make his usual little jokes between tries. I start to wonder if he's nervous, too, but it's hard to tell by looking at him. He *seems* calm. I, on the other hand, can hardly take a full breath.

Matt isn't oblivious to my condition. "We'll be fine, Becca," he whispers as Ms. Miller examines her notes. "Just take it easy."

His arm is still around me. He pulled away after we did this scene every other time. Why isn't he moving his arm?

Ms. Miller's head snaps up from her clipboard. "For the kiss, I want you to cup Becca's face in your hands at first, Matt. Be sweet at first, but then get greedy. You'll start pushing Becca down in the seat like you're getting serious about things."

"Yeah, let's get serious for once!" shouts Lance from behind the curtain.

"That's enough, Mr. Tucker," yells Ms. Miller. "Now calm down back there."

I look over and see Jai standing next to Jamie and Lance. Jai glances at them and shakes his head as if to say, *Pay no attention to these chuckleheads behind the curtain!*

"Go ahead, Matt and Becca." Ms. Miller hugs her clipboard to her chest.

Matt gives my shoulder a little squeeze. I'm too nervous to look at him, so I just stare straight ahead even though the stage lights are blinding. My eyes adjust to the light, and I can make out the first few rows of seats. My gaze travels up the rows and rests on the lighting booth, where I see Evan peering through the window. I can't make out any particular expression on his face, but he's going to watch me kiss Matt.

Oh God, I don't know if I can do this. I take a deep breath, and Ms. Miller says, "Let's take this scene from the top."

Miraculously, my voice comes out clear and strong, and the dialogue creeps toward the moment of truth. Matt and I both look straight ahead as our characters pretend to watch the drive-in movie. I will myself not to let my eyes wander toward the lighting booth. I need to stay focused here. I will die if I screw this up.

Suddenly Matt scoops me into his arms, softly holding my chin, and presses his lips against mine.

I'm hot and cold at the same time. This feels nothing like it did with Evan. Matt's lips are completely dry, and his tongue is safely tucked away behind his teeth. His whole jaw is tense, like a hinge that needs oil. The motion feels mechanical. I move with him, and Matt lowers me onto the chair with his weight.

"Start to resist him, Becca!" Ms. Miller calls.

Instinctively, I place my hands on Matt's shoulders and lightly shove him away. His lips break from mine, and he quickly sits up. I immediately turn five shades of red. I feel like I just did a striptease in front of the entire cast.

"We need to try that again, guys," says Ms. Miller. "Becca, you need to resist more, and Matt, you can't break away from the kiss so easily. Remember, Danny's an aggressive boy."

Matt nods. "Got it, Ms. M."

I wonder if he's even the least bit weirded out by what we're doing. Then again, it's not like he has any ex-girlfriends watching him do this. At least, I don't think he does, unless he hooked up with one of Jamie's friends at Darren Nelson's party.

Ew.

We try the scene several more times. The kisses start to get a little wet, and the force of Matt's body on mine is a bit suffocating.

After about ten incredibly long minutes, during which Ms. Miller yells, "More resistance, Becca!" at least three times, she's satisfied.

Ms. Miller then calls the chorus to practice the final number, and I do the run-through in a daze, just going through the motions. I can't stop thinking about the fact that I just kissed Matt Wooderson. In front of Evan and God and everyone. I would definitely rank it as one of the weirdest experiences of my young life.

After rehearsal, Jai, Katie, and I are heading for the door when Jamie sidles up to me. Great. Just the girl I want to talk to.

"Have fun today?" she asks, a mocking amusement in her voice.

Ugh. I don't need this. Besides, I don't know if I'd call stage-kissing Matt fun, exactly. I continue walking toward the exit as if Jamie doesn't exist.

"Well, *did* you?" she persists.

I still say nothing, and neither do my friends. They're both probably hoping that she'll just go away if we all ignore her, too.

"You looked pretty freaked out onstage," Jamie remarks. "Terrified, in fact."

Nobody says anything, and I start walking a little faster. Jai, Katie, and Jamie match my stride.

"You looked like someone who couldn't handle the situation she was in," Jamie states.

I can also tell that Jamie is not going to let this go, so I turn to her. "Um, in case you weren't aware, I was doing a little something called acting. Sandy is freaked out that Danny is putting the moves on her. That's why I looked terrified and like I couldn't handle the situation."

Jamie grins, and her eyes narrow. "Oh, I don't think you

were acting. I think you were scared out of your mind because you're like psycho-obsessed with Matt. Today was your big fantasy come true. Although from what I hear, Matt isn't a very good kisser, so maybe you were disappointed."

What does she know about Matt's kissing abilities? What did she hear? I immediately start wondering if Matt did this allegedly bad kissing at one of Darren Nelson's keggers, but I have a feeling that Jamie wouldn't be a willing font of information about this.

I'm just standing there in front of Jamie with my mouth hanging open like a moron. I don't know how to respond to what she's just said. I run through my mental Rolodex of comebacks, but I don't come up with anything that won't feed her fire. Fortunately, I don't have to say anything because Jai stops, turns, and glares at Jamie.

"Leave her alone," he demands.

"Let's go," Katie whispers to Jai and me.

"Touchy, touchy, aren't we?" Jamie remarks as she examines her nails. "But I guess you *would* be touchy after watching Becca and Matt kiss. It must have filled you with jealousy."

My cheeks are on fire, and my heart is beating like a thousand times a minute. It's everything I can do to keep myself from strangling Jamie. It's one thing for Jamie to make fun of me, but hearing her dig into Jai is too much. She just stands there with an incredibly smug expression on her face.

Jai looks over at Katie. "You're right. We should go. This is such a waste of time."

Katie nods, and the three of us complete the short march to the auditorium exit.

"Hey Jai, the *J* in your name stands for *jealous!*" Jamie shouts as we walk out the door. I'm sure she thinks that was really clever.

Once we're out in the parking lot, Jai looks over at me.

"What the hell was that all about?"

"Um, ah," I fumble, "I'm not really sure."

Because I'm not. But I *am* freaked out. Does Jamie know Jai is gay? And how does she know? Did she just guess? I suppose it's possible. I mean, after Jai came out to me, I felt a bit dense for not having picked up on the clues before. However, Jai is the first openly gay person I've ever met, so it's not like I have finely tuned gaydar.

"Well," begins Jai, unlocking his car, "her comment to me was certainly ambiguous."

"Ambiguous how?" I ask.

"She said that I must have been jealous watching you and Matt kiss. But who did she think I was jealous of, exactly?"

"That's a good point," remarks Katie. "She could have meant you were jealous of Becca for kissing Matt *or* Matt for kissing Becca."

I hadn't thought of that. I'd automatically assumed that she was suggesting Jai wanted to be kissing *Matt*, that she'd guessed Jai was gay. I don't say this, though, because the very thought of Jamie figuring out that Jai is gay fills me with dread.

"Whatever," Jai says, sliding into the driver's seat and unlocking the doors. I get into the car and shiver. "I don't care if Jamie thinks I want to kiss you *or* Matt. Because, and I mean no offense here, neither you nor Matt is really my type. I'm holding out for the right boy."

"Me, too." Katie sighs.

"And I hope your first kisses are everything you want them to be and more," I reply, feeling a little world-weary.

Too Much Information

Wednesday, January 28, 6:59 PM

Bella wonders if her readers can relate to the feeling people get when they finally experience something they've always wanted, like going to Disney World or bungee jumping. Once they're actually in the moment, they realize that what's happening is nothing like they expected, and they're not sure if they should be disappointed or pissed off or just roll with it.

Well, for Bella, kissing boys falls into that category of life experiences. When she was twelve, she used to practice making out with her pillow even though she knew that no boy's lips would feel like cotton or smell like Tide. Still, she imagined that it would be soft, dry, and nice. And when she watched people kiss in movies and on TV, the act always looked kind of organized as the actors tilted their heads this way and that.

Now that Bella has kissed two boys (one for real and one for pretend), she knows that it's nothing like this. And she's feeling a little worried that it's not going to get better. Kissing is just a whole lot weirder and messier than Bella's twelve-year-old mind imagined it would be.

What's more, Bella's especially anxious that she's
not going to have many chances to find out if it gets
better. Sure, she's still young, but people can remain
dorks their whole lives and continue to be rejected until
they finally just give up. Bella learned that when she saw
The 40-Year-Old Virgin last summer.

Of course, if the kissing she's experienced is as good
as it gets, then Bella isn't sure that she even cares if she
never does it again.

Wait. That's a lie. It has to be better, otherwise why
would people make out so much and have sex and things?
If people couldn't stand to get past kissing, then the
human race would eventually die off, wouldn't it?

Now Bella's starting to confuse herself. But one thing
she knows is that if Mr. Wonderful ever wanted to
practice those pretend kisses somewhere quiet and
private, she'd be willing to go along with it. For the sake
of the survival of the human race, of course.

I walk into the auditorium on Thursday and am immediately accosted by Josh Retzlaff.

"Hey Becca, how's it hangin'?"

I eye Josh skeptically, and I notice that Evan is watching from the little window in the lighting booth. He immediately ducks away. It makes me feel like I'm this little witch that haunts the theater and only Evan can see me.

"Um, I'm fine," I say. "How are you?"

Josh shrugs. "Same old same old. You must be pretty tired, though."

I give Josh a look that says, "And why would that be?"

"From practicing," Josh replies.

"What? My lines? No, I got off book pretty quickly," I reply. I realize that I'm bragging, but Josh is being so weird that I don't even care.

"Oh, just things. I hope your pillows are holding up okay," Josh says, smirking. Then he scampers into the lighting booth.

My pillows? Was Josh referring to my breasts? Because despite how microscopic Jamie and her friends claimed they were, they're not exactly pillowlike either. And even if they were—

Oh, no.

I wrote about pillows in my last blog entry.

I'm positively robotic when rehearsal begins, but I have no

choice but to throw myself into the singing and acting. The minute I walk offstage, I practically have a panic attack. If Josh has read my blog, then he's probably told Evan about it. Oh, no. I so cannot handle this. I sink to the floor and put my head between my knees, taking in some deep breaths. I start to feel calmer after a few moments.

Maybe Josh doesn't know anything about my blog. Maybe he was just talking crap as usual. He says a lot of meaningless things. Still, the pillow reference was pretty specific.

I want to march to the lighting booth right now and confront Josh about this, but I know I can't. If he doesn't know about the blog, he'll surely go looking for it. And though my name isn't on my blog, I know that Josh has mad geek skills and could probably find some way to track it down.

I suddenly feel a hand on my shoulder. I would have jumped about a foot if I hadn't already been sitting down. It's Jai.

"Are you okay?" he asks. "You look sort of sick."

"Um, I'll be all right. I'm experiencing, um, female trouble," I lie. I know it's terrible of me to overshare like this, especially when it's not even true, but I absolutely, positively cannot tell Jai about this.

"Oh," Jai says uncomfortably.

Jai sits down next to me, and we watch Matt and the T-Birds do "Greased Lightnin'" again.

"Say," Jai says, "I have to cut out of rehearsal a little bit early tonight. My aunt and uncle are in town, and we're having a family dinner at the supper club. I'm sorry I forgot to tell you before. Can you find a ride home?"

"Um, yeah. Sure," I say, still staring at Matt as he leaps

around the stage. He looks so yummy. Maybe I can get a ride from him.

Unfortunately, after rehearsal, Matt is nowhere to be found. He must have just dashed out the minute Ms. Miller finished reading the stage notes. I trudge to the lobby and give Dale a call.

✳✳✳

I think Dale senses something's wrong when I get into the minivan.

"You hungry?" he asks.

"Starving," I reply.

Instead of going straight home, Dale drives us to the Parkside Café, where we get a table for two.

"Maybe we should call Mom and Nathan to join us," I suggest, but Dale shakes his head.

"Your mom is still at the coffee shop working on some accounting stuff, and Nathan is over at Aunt Susan's. Besides, we've never had a father-daughter date before."

I smile sourly. "You may be the only male I can get a date with anymore."

Dale clears his throat and picks up his menu. I hate it when he doesn't answer me like this, but I decide to cut him some slack. He's taking me out to dinner after all.

As Dale studies the menu (I don't need to because I always order the same thing when I come here), I realize how rarely I look directly at him. It reminds me of *Our Town*, because one of the main characters makes the observation that family members usually look *through*, instead of *at*, one another. Dale's forehead is creased with concentration, and I see the beginnings of crow's-feet forking out from the corners of his eyes. Dale is thirty-five years old and has been a part of my life for six years. I start to wonder what he was like as a teenager. How did he get those crow's-feet? Was he out on the beach in Oregon squinting at the sun? He says that he misses hiking in the mountains of the Northwest. I can envision Dale as a college student in sturdy boots, treading through the hills and chomping on granola bars.

"Oh, it's Becca and Dale! How're you two doing?" Vi, the waitress, exclaims.

"Hi, Vi. We're great," answers Dale.

I'd like to tell Dale that he should speak for himself. After all, he's not the one whose innermost thoughts and feelings have most likely been discovered by an ex's best friend. It would be far too complicated to explain this to them both, so I keep my mouth shut.

"And how are you?" he asks.

"Can't complain. So what'll it be?" she asks, pen poised.

"I'll have a patty melt and a turtle shake," I say. The cook here is a master at welding onions, cheese, and beef together and slapping it all between two slices of pumpernickel.

"And for you?" Vi turns to Dale.

"The pork-chop dinner. French dressing on the salad, and a baked potato."

Vi takes our menus and leaves.

Dale folds his hands and tucks them under his chin, looking at me seriously. "So how have you been holding up?"

"Okay?" I eye him quizzically. I wonder why he uses the term *holding up*. Has he noticed that I'm looking more stressed than usual? Or is he just referring to the daily trials any fifteen-year-old faces? I don't want to ask him to explain because it might give away how I really feel. Which, right now, is fairly craptastic.

Dale starts stroking his goatee. "I mean, what with the stress of school, the play, your mom's pregnancy, and being a teenager, I figure that life hasn't been too easy for you lately."

I decide to lie again. "I'm fine."

I figure it's better just to pretend that everything is fine because if I start talking about my worries, I know I'm going to burst into tears right here in the middle of the restaurant. I start twisting the corner of my paper napkin.

"Mmm." Dale takes a sip of water. "I only ask because I've noticed some changes in you lately."

"Oh?" I feign ignorance. "Like what?"

"Well, you just seem quieter and less open than you used to be. Are you having any problems you'd like to talk about?"

"I just told you I'm fine, Dale," I insist, but my eyes start filling up with tears.

Vi arrives with my shake and Dale's salad.

Dale smiles up at her. "Thanks, Vi."

"Not a problem." She tosses me a sympathetic look and rushes away.

I dab my eyes with my twisted napkin.

"Life can't be too bad if I have a milk shake in front of me," I say, trying to make light of the situation. Dale smiles slightly but doesn't say anything. I can understand why my mother married him. Dale is nice, and a really good guy.

I spend a few moments enjoying my shake as Dale watches me. He hasn't touched his salad. I finally realize that he's waiting for me to speak again. Should I tell him anything real? I mean, I expect Dale would probably listen sympathetically, and I don't think he'd judge me.

I take a deep breath. "My New Year's resolution was to be a bit more selective in the personal information I share with people."

Dale simply nods and starts in on his salad, so I continue. "I guess I used to think that I couldn't control my confessions, that it was just something about me that I was born with, like my hair color. I always wished that people wouldn't be so uptight when I talked about bodily functions or who I had a crush on, but I had this revelation lately that maybe *I* was the one who needed to change. You know, that maybe it wasn't other people that had a problem." I play with my straw. "Maybe it was, um, me. My problem."

Dale calmly ponders this. He eats some salad. "Becca, I think it's a wise decision to have boundaries, especially as a way to protect yourself from ridicule and disapproval. And to make other people more comfortable. I know how sensitive and thoughtful you are, so I always assumed that it was never your intention to make anyone uneasy."

"Even though I did. Many times."

"Has it been difficult holding in all of the things that you used to talk about?" Dale asks.

"I've actually been writing things down in a journal."

On the Internet. For all the world to see. Including Josh Retzlaff. I wonder how good Josh is at keeping secrets. The thought of him telling anyone about my blog is enough to make me stop drinking my shake.

"Has writing been helpful?" Dale asks.

"I guess it's been beneficial in some ways. Like when I have a bad day—which seems to be every day lately—I write about how I wish my day had gone. I've created kind of a fantasy world for myself. Which is a nice escape, but I can't stay in that fantasy world. I always have to leave it and deal with things for real."

"Yeah, that's a problem, isn't it?" Dale remarks.

"Uh-huh, but it's also life. And right now, life sucks." I expect Dale to try to tell me to look on the bright side, but he doesn't.

Vi sets our entrées down in front of us, and we silently dig in.

When we've finished our food, I feel much calmer, although still unhappy. "Does life get easier, Dale? Like once I'm out of high school, will I be happier? And will people be nicer?"

Dale strokes his goatee as he contemplates this. "Not easier, exactly, but you'll deal with different kinds of stress, like the stress of college, then finding a job and supporting yourself. None of those things are easy. And as far as people being nicer, well, yes, I think most people mellow in their twenties, but there's still plenty of unpleasantness. The big thing I've learned is that people will never behave exactly how you want them to, so you have to focus on improving yourself. And if you're happy with who you are, then that's the best you can do."

I sit there, taking all of this in while Dale settles the tab with Vi. I *have* been trying to better myself, but I'm messing it up.

As we leave the restaurant, Dale does something unexpected. He puts his arm around me. "I'm sorry you're having such a hard time right now, Becca. Just remember that I love you, and I'm always here for you. So is your mom. Nathan, too." He grins.

"Thanks, Dale," I say. "I'm lucky to have such a caring stepdad."

"I'm lucky, too," says Dale, and we leave the restaurant.

Talking with Dale has given me strength, and I now know what I need to do.

Too Much Information

Thursday, January 29, 8:03 PM

Note: If readers are looking for previous posts or archives, they won't find them. Bella has erased them, and she's about to explain why.

Bella had an interaction today that has left her quite anxious. She's afraid that someone she knows has discovered this blog. Bella wonders if this person would use his/her knowledge of her secrets for good or for evil. She hopes that the reader wouldn't *use* the information for anything. But she can't be sure one way or the other.

Bella knows that the Internet is simultaneously public and anonymous, which is what makes it so exciting and interesting. However, Bella fears that her identity is not as well hidden as she initially thought.

This blog was meant to be a tool to help Bella share her secrets in a healthy way. She wanted to better herself for the benefit of her friends and family and prevent some of her past problems from repeating themselves, but Bella doesn't feel she's been successful in achieving her original goal. Instead, she has traded one kind of problem for another.

So what is to be done? If anyone out there reading this actually knows Bella, she urges them to show her a little compassion. Most of her stories are harmless, a product of her imagination and burning need to confess her innermost longings and frustrations. Bella firmly believes that everyone needs such an outlet, no matter how repressed they may be or how hollow they feel inside. Maybe Bella should have written down her musings in a diary and stuck it under her mattress, but she hoped that her words would be a source of comfort to others. Apparently, she was wrong. Again.

Bella is tired of screwing up and being skewered for her failings. She's already been dumped by a boy she really liked. She gets crapped on at school. Plus, she lives with a three-year-old nudist, guards her friend's biggest secret, and still tries to make the honor roll. It's all a bit much, so if people could cut her just a smidgen of slack, she'd be most grateful.

18

I wake up on Friday, my throat and forehead burning. My mom and Dale agree that I should stay home from school. They leave for the day with Nathan, and I fall right back to sleep in the quiet of the empty house.

Around eleven, I reawaken and realize that I'm feeling a little bit better, so I have some toast and juice. I pick up *Forever . . .* by Judy Blume, one of Katie's favorite books. I know a bunch of people read it in like seventh grade, but I refused to be one of them because I was going through my nonconformist phase. But now curiosity has finally gotten the better of me since Katie mentioned that the main characters totally have sex and the girl orgasms and everything.

For the next two hours, I'm lost in the love saga of Katherine and Michael, whose common denominator seems to be their fondness for getting naked and playing with Michael's thing. At one point, Katherine asks Michael if she can put aftershave on his balls. Hmm. I guess my relationship with Evan was far more chaste than I realized. We never got to the aftershave-on-the-balls stage of things.

After I finish *Forever . . .* I flip the book facedown on the table and bring my toast plate into the kitchen. As I rinse it off and look at the snow-frosted trees in the backyard, I start thinking about things.

Evan. It's only been a month and change since he dumped me, but it seems like eons ago. I miss him, especially our phone conversations and even hanging out in the basement with him while trying to dodge the Tongue. The experience was kind of nerve-racking, but it was also exciting. I didn't think about much else except for him while we were dating. When I think about Evan these days, I still feel bad about the way I treated him. I can't believe I was so inconsiderate of his feelings that I would just tell my friends everything about our relationship.

And Jai. Sweet, dear, still-mainly-in-the-closet Jai. How could I have been so careless with his secret? I'm scared as hell that I've done irreparable damage with my blog. I can just imagine Jamie, Lance, and Josh doing something terrible. Jamie in particular has never been known for her open-mindedness. Combine that with Lance's penchant for infantile pranks and Josh's increasingly strange confrontations, and the future does not look good for Jai.

I don't want to deal with these thoughts right now, so I go back up to my room and drift off into a nap. I awaken at about three-thirty to the sound of the doorbell. I peer down at the front stoop through my curtains to see who it is.

Evan Johnson is standing at the front door. Evan Frickin' Johnson. Holy crap.

I smooth down my hair and pull an old sweatshirt over my tank top so that Evan won't see me nipping out when I open the door and let in the freezing air.

As I hobble down the stairs, I wonder why he's here. Is he going to apologize for dumping me via Josh? I wish. Does he want to get back together? Whatever brought Evan to my door must be something serious. I mean, he still hardly even *looks* at me at school. What could he possibly want?

I shakily reach for the door and open it.

"Evan!" I exclaim breathlessly. "Hi!"

Evan looks alarmed to see me, which is weird. I live here, and he would have noticed that I was absent from play practice. Still, maybe he was hoping that I wouldn't be home. Or maybe he's embarrassed to see me in my pajamas. Come to think of it, I'm pretty embarrassed to be standing here in pajamas. Why didn't I change into a normal outfit before answering the door?

I stand there for a second while Evan collects himself. I can tell that he's conflicted about something. He probably can't believe that he's actually here, standing at my front door. Maybe he lost a dare or something.

"Um, hi," Evan mutters, his shoulders tightening. He looks like he's ready to sprint across my lawn, all the while thinking, *Get me as far away from this crazy girl as possible!* That's what I'd be thinking if I were in his shoes.

I realize that it's up to me to act normal, since Evan is obviously paralyzed by fear.

"What are you doing here?" I ask. "Why aren't you at play practice?"

Evan lets his shoulders drop and sighs.

"Apparently, there's a huge flu bug going around, and so many people missed school today that Ms. Miller decided to cancel practice."

"Oh," is all I can say. I'm glad that Evan didn't sneak out of rehearsal or anything, and I'm really glad to know that someone awful like Melissa Stromwell isn't standing onstage right now playing Sandy.

Evan and I face each other uncomfortably for a few moments.

"Um, can I come in for a second?" Evan stomps his feet and claps his mittens together. His cheeks are really pink, so he must have walked over here from school. It's not that far, but the temperature can't be above zero degrees today, which would make those ten blocks feel like a trek across Antarctica.

"Of course," I say, stepping aside. I feel a little dumb for not inviting him in sooner, but I guess I just got flustered. "Come on in."

I'll have to shoo Evan out the door again in a few minutes. My mom will be coming home soon, and she won't be happy if Evan's here. She'll probably think we did it. With no birth control. In her and Dale's bed.

It's like Evan can read my mind. "I know your mom would probably get all pissed at you if she knew I was here, even though we're broken up, so I'll be quick."

He doesn't even take off his hat or mittens, just stands there on the front hallway rug with snow dripping off his steel-toed work boots. He doesn't seem nervous anymore, which makes *me* nervous. It's like he's about to tell me something awful, like he's a doctor and I'm a patient about to hear that my tumor is malignant. Still, I have to try to act normal.

"Um, do you want to sit down?" I motion toward the dining room.

"Nah, that's okay." For some reason, this stings. I guess I'm just hypersensitive to any type of rejection from E. Jector.

"So what's up?" I try to keep my voice neutral, but I'd really like to shout, "Why the hell are you here? Now? After weeks of avoiding me and not talking to me and basically making me feel like an evil troll?" Somehow, though, I don't think that's the right way to play this.

Evan takes a deep breath. "I have a confession, Becca."

"Yes?" I reply anxiously. "What is it?"

"I've read your blog," Evan states. "'Too Much Information.'"

Oh, no. That means he knows how I feel about tongues and making out. He's seen my fantasy that he'll still be pining for me on his deathbed. And my lustful feelings for Matt. And all that unflattering crap I wrote about Josh. So my suspicions about Josh's pillow comment at rehearsal the other day were correct.

Then there's Jai. Oh, no. I've done something terrible. Evan needs to leave so I can go die now.

"So how did you find my blog?" I ask.

"I didn't. Josh did. When he saw you walk into the lab during a Computer Club meeting a couple of weeks ago, he was curious about what you were doing. So after you left, he checked the Internet history, and he found the link to 'TMI.'"

I want to bang my head against the door frame. How could I have been so stupid? I'm not a computer geek by any stretch, but I should have known better than to leave a trail. Now that I think about it, blogging from a school computer was about as public as reading aloud over the speakers after Mr. Bredeson's daily announcements. And I'm sure Evan is thinking about how foolish I am and how glad he is that he dumped me.

I must look positively nauseated because Evan says, "Hey, it's going to be okay. I haven't told anyone else about your blog, and I don't think Josh has either."

"I'd like to believe that's true, but I know that I'm not exactly Josh's favorite person," I say, recalling the dirty looks he was giving me when the play started. After a while, he replaced the looks with his questions about my mother, which seemed weird at the time but now make sense. Still, each time he talked to me, he risked revealing that he knew about my blog. Why would he do that? It occurs to me that Josh and I are alike in that we both have trouble stopping ourselves from saying the wrong thing. I don't think he could help it.

"Well," begins Evan, "it's true that Josh has been pissed at you ever since the, uh, incident with the poem."

Oh, so I'm not the only one who told her friends about the details of our short-lived romance. Interesting. I stand there nodding, doing my best to hide my anger. I don't think I'm doing a very good job.

Evan gives his eyes a semi-roll. "I'm not going to defend Josh's behavior. I told him that it was wrong to go snooping around the computers like that, but he wouldn't listen to me."

"Well, I appreciate you sticking up for me," I say. I'd like to add, "Especially considering what a pseudo-intellectual, loud-mouthed, unalluring girlfriend you thought I was." But I don't. There's no need to add any more tension to the situation. Besides, I wonder if Evan even remembers that he told Josh to say those things to me.

Evan purses his lips and glances at the floor. "No problem. Anyway, Josh and I haven't been hanging out much lately. We weren't getting along, for reasons that had nothing to do with you. He started acting kind of strange when we were dating."

We. The word hangs in the air like our breath does outside, reminding me that Evan used to be my boyfriend. It's too depressing for words, but even in the midst of my despair, curiosity gets the better of me.

"So you came by just to tell me that? That you and Josh have seen my blog?" I ask. It seems like enough of a reason, but definitely not the sort of thing that I would expect Evan to go out of his way to do.

Evan shuffles his feet on the rug. I used to think it was so cute when he did that, but now it just makes him look like a skittish little kid.

Evan stops shuffling and straightens, looking at me directly. "I just want to thank you, Becca, for what you wrote about me on your blog. And for the e-mails you sent me over Christmas break. I should have responded to them, but I was too angry at the time. I could see that you were truly sorry for the way you treated me, and I wanted to tell you that I'm sorry for the way that I, ah, ended things. It was kind of middle-schoolish of me."

Evan Johnson is apologizing to *me?* And he even admitted that the way he broke up with me was lame. I'd like to ask Evan to repeat his apology just once more, maybe after I go find Dale's digital video camera. I want to record this for posterity.

"I hope you didn't feel too bad about it," he continues. "It was nothing personal."

Yeah, right. Like dumping someone isn't about the most personal thing you can do.

"Oh, well, you know," I bumble. "I *did* feel bad about it. I liked you."

Evan swallows and starts massaging his Adam's apple, which is looking much more prominent than it did a couple of months ago. I also see a few thin whiskers sprouting from his chin. This observation makes me supremely embarrassed, because I remember reading in one of my puberty books that boys don't typically start growing facial hair and chest carpeting and stuff until their genitals are fully developed.

I'm suddenly anxious because I'm standing in front of this boy who probably has an adult-size penis, and I'm wearing monkey pajamas. Dumb ones. Still, I know this is my chance to clear things up with Evan, even if it means hearing unpleasant things.

"Um, since we're speaking so frankly, I was wondering if you really made Josh say all of those things on the phone about me being a pseudo-intellect and not all that, um, alluring."

Evan's face twists into horrified amusement. "I should really get going."

At this moment, Evan looks a bit like a weenie standing in my dining room with his mittens drooping off his hands. Like some nosebleed who still keeps *Choose Your Own Adventure* books tucked under his mattress and only recently discovered that it's a bad idea to attempt chin-ups on the shower-curtain rod.

Oh, how I'd love to say something like "So did you tell Josh to say that stuff or not? Be the man that your whiskers reveal you to be, you freshman weenie!" Instead, I just stand silently in my monkey pajamas.

Evan hoists his backpack onto his shoulders. "I know you're trying to change your ways and not tell everyone so much. But you might want to consider another resolution: don't try to force people to give out information they aren't willing to share. Just something to think about."

"Um, okay," I reply, dumbfounded.

"I'll see you around, Becca." Evan backs toward the front door.

"Oh, well, thanks for stopping by."

"Later," Evan says. He opens the door, blasting both of us with snot-freezing air, and heads out into the snowy abyss. I go to the living-room window and watch him walk down the icy street until he's out of view.

19

I still feel like crap on Saturday, so I spend the day in bed alternately reading and napping. Nathan brings me toast and makes sure I'm "all tucked in right," which is sweet and cheers me up a little. On Sunday morning, I wake up feeling much better, so I give Katie a call and we make plans to hang out. Jai won't be joining us because he went with his parents to their family cabin up north.

I'm actually relieved that I don't have to face Jai this weekend. I feel incredibly guilty knowing that I've outed him to Josh and Evan, even though I don't think either of those guys will do anything heinous with the information. At least, I know Evan wouldn't. And I'd like to think that Josh wouldn't either, but I don't know for sure. Josh can't have anything against Jai except for his association with me, but that doesn't seem like enough of a reason to spill someone's biggest secret.

Katie shows up at my house in the afternoon. Instead of our usual bakefest and movie marathon, we settle into the living room with our latest knitting projects. My mom is at Prairie Perks, so I can work on her birthday sweater, which I've decided to give her even though it won't fit over her pregnant belly by mid-March. Katie's making herself a very cool shoulder bag.

"You should make one of those for Jai," I say. "I bet he'd love it."

"Hmm, maybe," says Katie, finishing off a row. "I'd probably want to use different colors, though. This one looks sort of feminine."

Then Katie puts down her needles and looks up at me. "Do you think because Jai is gay, he would even think about that?"

"I don't know," I answer.

"I wonder if he has a crush on anyone. I've been too shy to ask him," says Katie.

"I don't think he does," I reply, unraveling a row a bit to pick up a dropped stitch, "but he probably wouldn't mind you asking. I mean, if he can't tell *you*, who can he tell?"

"He could tell you, I guess," says Katie, an edge of sadness in her voice. "I mean, he told you he was gay, didn't he? Before me, I mean."

Man, are we going to go through this again? I thought my phone conversation with Katie about this last week cleared the matter up, but it's obvious that she still feels bad about it. I guess if the tables had been turned, I might have been a bit hurt, too. I'm not sure if there's anything I can say to Katie to make her feel better about this, so I just knit in silence for a few minutes.

"Do you think anyone at school suspects he's gay?" Katie asks.

I jerk my head up from the sweater and stare at her.

"What? Why do you look so horrified, Becca?"

What can I say that won't incriminate me as the person who

let the cat out of the bag? I'm going to have to think of a lie. A good one. And fast.

"Um, ah"—I waffle—"I guess the thought of some people at school knowing about Jai's sexuality does horrify me. Like the Rod and Gun Club. Can you imagine what they'd do if they knew for sure that Jai was into guys?"

I picture Jai's car, spray-painted with some grammatically challenged epithet like WIMPFAG! or GET OUTA HERE, GAY BOY! I see Jai walking down the hall, and one of the guys trips him and everyone around them starts laughing hysterically. I imagine Jai entering a classroom, and everyone just stares at him with their slack jaws and judgment.

Katie frowns at her knitting. "You sound pretty paranoid. I mean, I know those guys are jerks and hicks and everything, but I'd like to think that these days, people are more open-minded."

"That's a nice thought, but I wonder if it's really true," I remark, recalling the first day that I saw Jai in the cafeteria. Rod Knutson made a crack about Jai dropping the soap on purpose, which was definitely a gay joke. And Rod didn't even know Jai yet. I bet he could tell that Jai wasn't straight, though.

I also think about the way I've been treated recently, especially by the Rod and Gun Club and Jamie. They keep bringing up all of the stupid stuff I said in the past, not even noticing that I've changed. It's like everyone gets put into a little box early on, and they stay there because it's easier to hang on to the past than move forward.

Then again, maybe I'm a hypocrite for thinking that people

like Lance and Rod wouldn't be sensitive to Jai if they really knew he was gay. Maybe they were just teasing him that first day because they *didn't* think it was really possible that he could like boys. I mean, kids talk so much crap, and I don't think they mean what they say a lot of the time.

"Well, it doesn't matter if people here are open-minded or not," Katie remarks, shaking me from my thoughts, "because Jai has made it clear that he's not coming out until after high school."

"If he stays here," I point out. "I bet you anything that if he goes to the performing arts school, he'll openly flirt with guys the first day he gets there. Otherwise, why would he want to go there so badly? To keep hiding?"

"I really don't want him to go," Katie admits, picking up a ball of baby-pink yarn and swapping out the black yarn she was using on the last row.

"Me neither. But if that's what he wants to do, I don't think you or I can do much to stop him."

"It's sad. Like Jai won't really even give Pine Prairie a chance. I mean, he practically just got here. It's only been like two months."

"I know, and he made friends with us and he's in the musical and everything—"

"And don't forget about Ashli Berg." Katie giggles.

"Oh, of course. Just in case he changes his mind about being gay."

Katie sighs. "Maybe he just needs a bus ticket out of this boring town."

"Yeah, maybe. I mean, I want that, and I'm not harboring a big secret like he is."

The moment I say this, I realize that I really *am* a hypocrite. And a liar. I've been keeping a blog for the last month, and I haven't told anyone except Dale about it. And then Josh and Evan found out about it, too, although I didn't mean for that to happen. So I do have a big secret, and my secret also involves revealing Jai's secret. I suck.

I don't sleep very well on Sunday night. My conversation with Katie makes me wonder if I should just come clean to her *and* Jai about the blog and admit that there are a couple of people who know some very personal information about him. Not the worst people, but perhaps that doesn't matter. The fact that anyone outside of Katie and me knows about this is bad enough, because it's not what Jai wanted.

On the other hand, telling Jai might create a lot of unnecessary drama and strife. I've already cleaned the slate, so to speak, by removing all of the posts except the last one. And as long as Evan and Josh don't say anything, no one else will ever know that I wrote embarrassing things about Jai, Matt, Josh, Evan, and my mom. Oh, and I guess I had Katie dating the captain of the hockey team in one entry, which was a rather thinly veiled hint about her crush on Luke Kleinschmidt.

Still, I wish I had some kind of assurance that Josh Retzlaff isn't going to spill. He made a reference to my blog the other day to my face when he talked about the pillows, and that makes me uneasy. Who's to say he won't just mention something offhand to one of his Computer Club buddies—or worse, to Matt?

Maybe I should talk to Josh about this. Then again, it could be humiliating, groveling to this dork not to tell anyone what he read.

As I drift off to sleep, I decide that the best course of action is to keep things as they are. There's no need to go looking for trouble. If there's trouble to be had, it will show up in the end, anyway.

20

We're doing a full run-through today! Everyone in their places for the opening number!" Ms. M shouts.

Katie pulls the curtain shut, and Matt and I stand in the center of the stage. I look over at him slouching slightly in the soft glow of the dimmed stage lights. He must be getting himself into the Danny mind-set, because Matt normally stands with his delicious shoulders squared. He looks so sexy in his leather jacket and tight jeans. His hair is still wavy and loose today, but he'll have to slick it back for the performances. There's a stray curl that's hanging near his eye, and my hand twitches with the temptation to brush it back.

Matt glances back at me, but he doesn't smile like he usually does. In fact, the way he's looking at me makes me feel a little weird, like I've done something wrong.

"Are you okay?" I whisper.

Matt gives me a half smile and faces front again. Before I can think of anything else to say, the opening music starts. And we're off.

Rehearsal goes along fine, but I'm incredibly nervous as the drive-in scene approaches. I expected that it might become as routine to me as brushing my teeth or clipping my nails, but no—it's always bizarre, and after it's over, I always feel like I just pranced around the stage naked.

As Matt and I settle into our chairs for the drive-in scene, again he doesn't look at me. In fact, he looks downright uncomfortable. Wait, isn't that supposed to be my part? Matt's been so cool about the kiss all along, and *I've* been the one freaking out about it. But today, Matt looks more freaked out than I've ever seen him.

The scene doesn't go smoothly. Matt's movements are all stiff and artificial, and he's way less aggressive. Ms. Miller stops the scene just before I'm supposed to throw Danny's class ring at him and hop out of the car.

"Let's take this again from the top. A little more passion from you, Matt," she says.

"Sorry," Matt says flatly.

"You were fine, though, Becca."

It's nice to hear that, but I'm a little too confused by what's going on to really feel good about Ms. Miller's compliment. When we get to the kiss again, Matt's face flies into mine, and we bump teeth. Hard. A bolt of pain radiates into the roof of my mouth.

"Ouch!" I call out, jerking my face away from his.

Matt lets out a loud groan.

We both sit back with our hands over our mouths. There is major snickering going on backstage. And judging by the high pitch, I'd say that it's mostly Jamie, Haley, and Melissa.

Ms. Miller stands up. "All right, why don't we just forget about this scene and start fresh tomorrow. Matt, you can start your solo now."

"Right," Matt mutters, rubbing his lips over his teeth and wincing.

I walk offstage, my cheeks burning in humiliation. I can hear

Matt start in on his solo, "Sandy," in which love-stricken Danny implies that he'd like to marry his girl someday if she'll have him. I wonder if Danny would feel that way if he and Sandy had ever had major tooth clash. Doubtful.

The first person I see when I push aside the curtain backstage is Jamie.

"Have a little trouble making out with Mr. Wonderful?" she asks, barely stifling a giggle and then scampering into the darkness backstage before I have a chance to say anything.

Oh, no.

No, no, no, no, no!

So Josh didn't keep my blog to himself. He had to have told Jamie. There's no other way she could have known about the whole Mr. Wonderful thing.

What should I do? Sprint to the lighting booth, whip off my poodle skirt, and choke Josh to death with it? Tempting. I wouldn't even care that Evan would be standing right there, watching me murder his best friend in my underwear.

No, I have to try to stay calm. If Jamie wants to pick on me about my blog, I'll deal with it, though I can't imagine that she can limit her snide comments to just me.

In fact, she probably said something to Matt or showed him my blog, and that's why he's been so weird today. He must know. He must have read the things I wrote about him. And why wouldn't it weird him out? After all, some of my fantasies were fairly, um, heated. And strange. After all, I'm the girl who imagined him buying hemorrhoid cream for her pregnant mother.

I think I'm going to throw up. As I stand behind the curtain trying to keep what's left of my lunch down, Jai walks up to me.

"Are you okay?" Jai asks.

"No," I admit.

"Hey, don't worry about the tooth-bumping thing back there," he says soothingly.

I'd already forgotten about that. I wish that were my biggest problem right now.

"Thanks, Jai," I say. "I think I just need to sit down for a minute."

"Yeah, just take it easy," he replies. His tone is so caring that it makes me feel guilty. I wonder how nice he'd be to me if he knew that I'd handed his most private information to one of the bitchiest girls in school.

I so need a shovel right now. That way I can just dig a hole and crawl in it.

"When rehearsal is over, let's get out of here right away," I whisper to Jai.

"Sure," he says. "I'm starving, anyway. Maybe we should go to A&W?"

"Good idea," I reply.

Jai sits with me for a few minutes, and we listen to Jamie sing her solo, "There Are Worse Things I Could Do." The title of the song carries more meaning than it should in real life. If she wants to make fun of me, that's one thing. But the worst thing she could do is pick on Jai.

After Jamie finishes singing, I have to be onstage again for the final scenes. Somehow, I manage to get through them even though I feel shaky all over.

Once we finish the run-through, Ms. M gathers everyone together and goes over a few notes. The minute she says, "Good work. See you all tomorrow," I leap up and run down to the dressing room. I yank off my costume, throw on my jeans, sweater, and boots, and dash up the stairs as the rest of the cast walks down them. I pass Jamie, Melissa, and Haley, who all smirk at me and burst out laughing. My heart sinks.

I walk onstage, praying that Jai is already waiting for me.

I don't see him. Ms. Miller and Evan are sitting in the front row discussing something, and Katie is sitting to the left of the stage, sanding the edge of a two-by-four. I sit for a few minutes on the edge of the stage and then walk over to Katie.

"Did you see where Jai went after Ms. M dismissed us?"

She shakes her head. "I assumed he'd be up here by now. I'm ready to go anytime."

"Yeah, me, too," I admit. "Jai said he wanted to go to A&W. Are you up for that?"

"Yeah, totally. But I should probably call my mom."

"Me, too." I gesture toward the lobby, and Katie puts down her sandpaper, brushes some dust off her jeans, and we head out of the theater to the pay phones. I'm counting down the three weeks to my sixteenth birthday, when I'll finally have my own cell phone.

There's still no sign of Jai after we've both called home, so Katie and I decide to go back into the theater to look for him. Just as we walk through the doors, Jamie and Lance pass us.

"Looks like you just lost a friend," Jamie remarks.

"But he's just a fag, so who cares, right?" Lance adds. The two of them laugh as they head to the lobby.

Oh, no. No, no, no, no, no.

This can't be happening.

"Becca, um, what's going on?" Katie asks, her voice filled with fear and confusion.

"I, ah, oh—"

My throat starts closing, and I actually feel like I'm choking. My eyes scan the theater for Jai, and I finally see him sitting on the edge of the stage. He's holding a piece of paper, and his face is paler than I've ever seen it.

My legs are telling me to run out of the theater, but I move slowly toward Jai. I have to see if my worst fears are confirmed.

Jai looks up, and his face turns from ashen to bright pink in about three seconds.

"Jai, I—"

"Don't," he whispers. His hands are shaking, and he thrusts the paper at me. "Here's a little gift I just got from Jamie and Lance. So thoughtful of them." Jai's voice isn't angry, just hollow, like he isn't fully present.

I stand there clutching the paper, too afraid to look at it.

"Come on, Katie," Jai says. "Let's get out of here."

"But wait, what's—"

"I'll explain everything in the car. Let's just go," Jai insists, so softly that I almost can't hear him.

"But you're coming, too, right, Becca?" Katie asks.

"Well, I don't think, um—"

I stare down at the paper Jai just gave me. It's a printout of the January 14 entry of my blog, the one in which I write about Jai's coming-out party. On the other side is my list from January 24, about how to keep a gay boy in Hicksville, U.S.A. He knows that I wrote it because I mention things that no one else would have known, like how Shawn abandons his fantasy of having a three-way with the twins next door when he realizes his true feelings for Jai. I didn't bother changing Shawn's name because, at the time, it didn't seem important.

I've so blown it. And now Jai's going to tell Katie, and I'm going to lose two friends. Because who would want to be friends with someone who could do something so heinous?

"He's right," I reply, my voice trembling. Tears are forming at the corners of my eyes. "You should go. I'll see you later."

"Are you sure?" Katie asks. "Can't you guys just tell me what's going on?"

"Jai will," I answer. "Just please go."

"If you really want me to," replies Katie, looking doubtful.

"I do. See you," I say mournfully. The tears are running down my cheeks now. I rush toward the theater door, passing Evan on my way. He flashes me a look of sympathy as I duck into the hallway and race toward the girls' room.

As soon as I've locked myself in a stall, I sink to the floor. My breathing is shallow and rapid as I choke back sobs. I try to get a full breath, but it feels like Nathan is sitting on my chest.

I'm the most hideous person on the planet. The winner of the Worst Friend Ever Award. How could things have spiraled so far out of control? I should have known better.

Jai will leave for the performing arts high school for sure now. He wanted to get out of Pine Prairie *before* all of this happened, when no one knew he was gay.

Maybe Jai has the right idea. About leaving. I stare up at the bathroom ceiling, thinking of possible ways that I could escape Pine Prairie. I could go postsecondary, but that wouldn't start until next fall. I could call up my uncle Gary in Portland and see if I could move in with him and my cousin Tricia, who live in an apartment downtown. No, that wouldn't work. Too crowded. And I certainly wouldn't want to stress out my parents by running away from home.

I'm not going to solve anything sitting here on the cold tile floor, so I hoist myself up, dry my eyes, blow my nose, and head to my locker to retrieve my coat and backpack. The school is utterly abandoned, with not so much as a junior-varsity wrestling meet scheduled this evening. I don't especially feel like calling Dale and explaining why I'm not at A&W right now enjoying onion rings with my former best friends.

I put on my coat, hat, and mittens and open the front door of the school, ready to brace myself against the February chill. My house is almost a mile away, but I don't care. If I get frostbite, it's probably deserved.

The next morning, I sit up in bed and look out the window. White flakes whirl in the air with such fury that I wonder if they'll ever find their way to the ground. I can barely make out the trees in our yard, and I can't see our neighbors' houses at all because it's snowing so hard. I doubt the streets have been plowed yet, which means that school will be delayed today, or maybe even canceled. I hope.

I lumber downstairs and find Dale reading the paper and drinking coffee at the foot of the dining-room table. I'm exhausted. I finally fell asleep around 3 A.M. as I tossed and turned over what happened with Jai. I still can't believe I didn't see any of this coming, and now I have no idea how to fix it.

The thought of going to school today makes me want to throw up, but I'm not sure that I have much choice, especially since I missed school last week. I don't know how I'm going to face Jai, not to mention Jamie, Lance, Josh, Evan, Matt, and God knows who else has found out about my blog and the stuff I wrote.

Despite my nausea, I fix myself a bowl of cereal and then take a seat at the head of the dining-room table. Dale looks up briefly from the editorials, winks, then resumes reading.

"Where are Mom and Nathan?" I ask, crunching on Grape-

Nuts. I know that Dale gets annoyed when anyone interrupts his reading, but I'm now noticing how quiet the house is. Usually, Nathan is tearing through the dining room wearing one of his capes and nothing else, shouting about the forces of evil. I always wonder exactly how he's going to defeat these forces. With the blinding light that his pale, bare bottom radiates?

Dale continues reading, totally ignoring my question. I hate it when he does this.

"So where are they?" I repeat.

Dale finally looks up and sighs. "Your mom went back to sleep. She's not feeling very good today, and since the roads haven't been plowed yet, she didn't see the point in opening up the shop until later. Your brother's watching *Sesame Street*."

"Oh," I answer. "So do I have school today?"

"Nope," Dale answers. "It was announced on the radio this morning. The Pine Prairie School District has canceled classes for today."

I push my bowl of cereal aside and start to sniffle. I can't help it. Even though I don't have to go to school today, I'll have to go tomorrow and deal with this whole mess. It's so overwhelming and depressing, I don't even know what to do with myself.

"Is something wrong, Becca?" His voice is neutral, devoid of any traces of sympathy. He probably thinks I'm wasting his time, which I am.

I'm a waste of everyone's time. And now I'm crying for real.

Dale sets down his coffee cup and folds his arms. He says nothing and walks around the dining-room table, grabbing the box of Kleenex off the sideboard en route, and sits in the chair next to mine, patting my back as I alternately cry into my hands and blow my nose.

We sit this way for a few minutes until I've calmed down. I blow my nose a few more times, and Dale continues to circle his hand on my upper back.

"So what's going on, Becca?" he finally asks.

I wonder if it's worthwhile to try to stick to my resolution and not tell Dale about everything. I'm tempted, though, because I've already screwed things up so royally I doubt they can get any worse. Plus, Dale might have some advice for me. I'll take anything I can get at this point.

"You know how I told you I was trying to overshare less by keeping a diary?" I ask. Dale nods. "Well, that diary was actually a blog. On the Internet. When I started writing it, I didn't think anyone I knew would ever see it, so I just wrote about everything. And a few weeks ago, Jai and I had this big talk at A&W, and he ended up coming out to me. He's gay."

I search Dale's face for traces of shock, but he sits calmly, his eyes fixed on me.

"I also wrote about having a huge crush on Matt, one of the guys who's in the play with me. In fact, I made up some pretty elaborate fantasies about the two of us getting together. I didn't think there would be anything wrong with writing about such private things on my blog. I mean, I changed everyone's names. I never mentioned where I live. I thought I was safe.

"Then last week, I found out that my blog wasn't a secret at all. See, I sometimes wrote in the school computer lab and Josh Retzlaff found the address to my blog. He hinted that he'd read it, and I took the blog down off the Internet really soon after that, but it was too late. It didn't stop bad things from happening."

"What bad things?" Dale asks.

"Well, Josh let the word leak about my blog, and Jai found out about it. I've basically outed him to the whole school, and now I don't know what's going to happen."

Describing all of this gets me so worked up that I lay my head down on the dining-room table and start sobbing again. Dale rubs my back, and we stay like that for a long time.

Finally, I sit up, and Dale inhales sharply. He rubs the top of his smooth head and slouches back in his chair, taking his hand off my back.

"Becca, I'm going to be very honest with you. Are you ready to listen?"

Dale's tone suggests that whatever is coming next can't be good, and I'm probably not ready to hear it in the state I'm in. I mean, I'm a mess. Then again, what could he say that would be worse than the things that have already happened?

"I'm listening," I say quietly.

Dale pulls at his goatee uneasily. He sits back up and fixes his eyes on mine.

"I've read your blog."

Crap. Crap, crap, crap, crap, crap.

"All of it?" I squeak out.

"Yes, all of it."

I cannot believe this. How much humiliation can a girl endure before it kills her? I try to ask Dale if my mom knows about "TMI," too, but only a cough comes out.

"In case you're wondering, I didn't tell your mother."

"Thanks," I mutter between hiccups. I feel so out of control right now. My entire body shakes.

"Take some deep breaths. You're going to be fine." Dale lowers his face to meet mine. "Do you hear me? You have to believe me. You're going to be okay." I stare at him through my sore, red eyes.

Dale straightens. "I want you to repeat after me. Everything's going to be okay."

I hiccup loudly. "Everyth—hic—ing is going—hic—to be okay. Hic."

"I'm here for you, and so is your mother. There's no problem that's too big for us to solve. Trust me, we're going to help you get through this," he says.

I hiccup again. "So you read my blog. How—"

"I was tinkering with the computer one evening a few weeks ago, and I looked at the Internet history. I noticed a new URL and clicked on it."

So Dale found my blog the same way Josh did. And he read all of it, so he knows about my horny feelings for Matt, outing Jai, my thoughts about kissing, everything. I can't even imagine what he must have thought as he read all of that stuff. He was probably really disappointed. Some of my entries were pretty mean. Others were just pathetic and desperate. Dale has got to be thinking that I'm horrible. I mean, what sort of person *writes* stuff like that?

I feel a lurch in the pit of my stomach, but I manage to swallow it back.

"Oh my God, Dale, I am so embarrassed. Like let-me-die-now embarrassed," I say.

"You don't need to be embarrassed. I really respected your decision to try to change. I figured that your blog was a positive outlet for you. You wrote some funny stuff."

"Funny?" I repeat. "You thought it was funny?"

"Some of it, sure," says Dale, grinning. "Like that fantasy about Josh and the plastic lightsaber."

"I guess so," I admit. I'd forgotten about that entry, which is one of the few I'm still not sorry that I wrote. In fact, I should have portrayed Josh as a bigger loser than I did.

I look at Dale, who is still smiling, and I feel a little betrayed all of a sudden.

"But weren't you, like, invading my privacy by reading it?" I ask.

"Becca, it's not like I went into your room and rooted around until I found your diary and then picked the lock with a paper clip. You were broadcasting your thoughts on the Internet. I had as much right to read it as anyone else. Maybe more. I actually care about you and want the best for you."

Even though I believe Dale, anger wells up inside of me.

"Well, if that's true, then why didn't you ever talk to me directly about my blog? Like when I wrote about Jai being gay. You must have known I was making a mistake. You could have helped me prevent this whole mess. Why didn't you *say* anything?" I know that my voice has a combative edge to it, which makes me feel a little guilty because Dale is being so understanding. But still, how could he just stand by while I made such a huge mistake?

"I—" Dale stops midsentence, clearly struggling for a way to explain himself. "I didn't want you to feel like I was invading your privacy. I figured that your blog was anonymous enough. Obviously, I was wrong about that."

"We were *both* wrong about that," I say bitterly.

Dale ignores this comment and continues. "And if I'd known that you were writing at school, I definitely would have said something. Blogging on a public computer is risky."

"I know that *now*," I say. "But at least I took it down. Now no one else can see it."

"Well, that's another thing," says Dale, uneasiness in his voice.

"What?"

"You can shut down blogs and Web pages, but they don't totally go away. Once something is on the Internet, it can float around for a while."

What? Oh, no. He can't be saying this. The situation was already bad enough with Jai seeing what I wrote. What if everyone else sees it, too? For the first time in my life, I actually care about everyone knowing my business. I may still be the Overshare Queen, thanks to my blog, but I would never go up to a boy that I like and *tell* him that I want to lick his neck. I'm beginning to see that I do have some boundaries. There are certain things that I would never want people to know about. But now they're going to know everything.

Of course the blog isn't just about my business, which is embarrassing enough. No, I dragged Jai and other innocent bystanders into my sick little world of confessions. And now it turns out that that sick little world can't be erased.

"How does that work?" I ask, kind of afraid to hear the answer.

"Well, Google, for example, saves copies of Web pages in what's called a cache for a few weeks, even after they've been deleted."

Google sucks.

This also clears up a little mystery I'd been contemplating last night. I wondered why Jamie would have waited a few days after printing out those entries about Jai to actually give them to him. This makes more sense now. She could have found out about the blog just yesterday, tracked it down on the Internet, and then printed it out.

"So is my blog out there forever?"

Dale shakes his head. "No, because Google regularly updates its cache, and if a Web site is broken or has disappeared, then Google won't be able to store it in the cache."

"So how long before my blog is out of the cache?"

Dale scratches his head. "It's hard to say. Not very long. A few weeks, max."

I don't take much comfort in this information. After all, a few weeks is plenty of time for the word to spread. In fact, I expect that most of the school will have read it by the time it disappears. I can already picture how it's going to go. I won't be able to walk down the halls without people pointing and laughing, asking me if I've sucked on any tongues lately or how my gay ex-friend is doing or if I've done it with Mr. Wonderful yet. No one is ever going to forget this, and there will probably be a special caption under my senior yearbook picture that says, *Biggest Overshare Loser Ever.*

I rest my face in my hands. "Man, I've really screwed things up."

"Becca, everyone makes mistakes. Yours just happens to be a very public one, which is why you're so upset. It's understandable." He gets up and retrieves his coffee cup from the foot of the table and takes a sip as he stands by the window, gazing out at the bright winter sun through the pine trees. "Your blog has now impacted Jai's life considerably, and of course that worries me."

"Yeah, me, too."

To put it mildly. I mean, it's bad enough that Jai isn't ever going to speak to me again. But word is going to get out. I know it will. And he's going to have to live with the consequences of that. I feel so guilty, I want to tear my toenails out.

22

The snowplow drives by our house around eleven, pushing enormous mounds of snow to the side of the street. I'm sure Nathan will go out later and try to ride a sled off the piles, as they're the closest thing we get to hills out here in flat Minnesota.

My mom eventually gets up and goes to Prairie Perks, and Dale decides to work at home for the day. He shuts himself in the computer room, and I know he won't want to be disturbed. Nathan goes to Aunt Susan's as usual, and I'm relieved to be left on my own. I think I'd go ballistic if I had to spend the day cooped up with Nathan jiggling his privates all over the house and my mom horsewhipping me into helping her sand the baseboards in the bathroom.

I spend most of the day in the basement knitting and watching some of my old favorites: *Heathers, Some Kind of Wonderful,* and *Ferris Bueller's Day Off.* The movies provide enough of a distraction that, for short moments, I sometimes forget about Jai and the whole blog mess. I'm so glad I get at least one day of peace before all hell breaks loose, as I expect it will when I get back to school.

I consider calling Katie, but I'm afraid to. For all I know, she and Jai sat in A&W for hours last night talking about how much I suck and how they're never speaking to me again. After that, they probably went to Jai's place and threw darts at a picture of me, then wrote some haikus about what an awful person I am. I compose a few in my head as I help myself to an afternoon snack of cinnamon toast:

> *Rebecca Farrell*
> *Very unkissable dork*
> *The worst "friend" ever*

> *Overshare Queen has*
> *Lost her crown, hopefully for*
> *Good. We hate her so.*

> *We're glad she's out of*
> *Our lives because we can have*
> *More fun without her.*

Why would Katie and Jai stop at just a few harmless haikus? I bet they've already started a blog of their own, full of stories about all of the crap I used to talk about. They've made lists of my top ten most disgusting anecdotes. They've e-mailed a link to their blog to every student at Pine Prairie High and are encouraging other victims of my overshares to post comments and share horror stories of their own encounters with me. I'm sure Ms. Schwenke, my eighth-grade health teacher, has a few things she'd like to get off her chest about me. She's probably a regular columnist, as is Jamie Whitaker. The blog will provide a lot of healing for all of the people I've tortured over the years.

As I'm reading entries from Katie and Jai's mythical blog in my mind, the phone rings. It's Katie. Oh, no. I'm totally not ready to deal.

"I'm coming over to talk to you," she says, her tone crisp and businesslike.

"Is it about Jai?" I ask shakily.

"No, the beautiful weather we've been having," Katie replies with razors in her voice.

Crap. This isn't going to be pretty. And since when did Katie get so assertive?

I cough. "Okay, okay, I get it."

"I'll be there in five minutes." The line goes dead. I don't really know else what to do while I wait for her, so I head to the kitchen and start preparing a peace offering in the form of Katie's favorite snack: ants on a log with cream cheese and Craisins.

A few minutes later, I see Katie's dad pull into our driveway, and Katie hops out of the passenger's side. She runs across the backyard and lets herself in.

"Hey, Katie," I exclaim cheerfully as she kicks her shoes off in the back hallway. "I made you some food!"

I hold up the plate, but Katie just shakes her head. Wow, this is bad.

"Let's go upstairs to your room," she demands.

I follow Katie meekly up the stairs, still clutching the food like I'm her servant. We both enter my room, and she shuts the door and sits uncomfortably close to me on the bed.

"How *could* you?" she asks. Her voice is even, and her eyes are full of rage. "How could you do something like that to Jai? He showed me that thing you wrote last night, and then we went online and looked at the rest of your blog."

So Dale was right; my blog is still out there and very easy to find. This whole situation just keeps getting worse.

"I can't believe some of the stuff you wrote, Becca," Katie declares. "It's really . . . what's the phrase I'm looking for here? Too much information."

Oh, no. I cannot handle this. For the first time in our five-year friendship, I'm actually afraid of Katie. I'm not afraid that she's going to hurt me. I'm not even all that scared of what else she could say to me. Hell, I don't even care if she's written hai-kus about me or thrown darts at a picture of my face or even started a blog at www.ifrickinhatebecca.com. Mostly, I'm afraid that I've already lost her.

"So tell me, how could you do that?" Katie repeats. She looks like she's ready to grab my shoulders and start shaking me.

"I don't know," I whisper. My forehead sinks into my palm, and I start crying. Not just a few tears, but a full-blown howl. I sound like a sea lion. Katie remains close by my side on the mattress, but it's not a supportive closeness. It's more of an up-in-my-grill closeness.

We just sit there for a few minutes while I alternately sob and blow my nose, and Katie doesn't say anything. I somehow manage to calm down, and I look at Katie through my puffy, tearstained eyes.

"I never meant any harm. If you read all of my blog, then I hope you can see that. I was trying to do something good."

Katie presses her thumb to her lips as she contemplates this. I can tell that she's trying to think of a reasonable way to react.

"Yeah," she says finally, "I guess I can see that, but it doesn't sound like you were very smart about it. I mean, how in the world did Jamie find out? Did you blab about it?"

By the look on Katie's face, I'm sure she thinks that's exactly what I did.

"No, honestly, I didn't tell anyone. Not exactly."

"Not exactly?" Katie repeats. "Get to the point, Becca."

"Well, I made the mistake of writing a couple of blog entries on a school computer, and Josh Retzlaff was able to track them down. He was the one who told Jamie about my blog, I'm certain of it. He told Evan, too."

"How do you know that?" Katie asks.

"Evan actually came over here on Friday when I was home sick and told me. It was like he wanted to warn me or something."

I decide to leave out the part about Evan apologizing for the way he dumped me because I don't feel like talking about it. Plus, it's not that important, anyway.

"Evan *talked* to you?" asks Katie, her eyebrows rising.

"Yeah, I could hardly believe it either," I admit. "He said that he would never tell anyone about Jai or any of the other stuff I wrote on the blog."

"Wow," remarks Katie. "Good guy."

"Yeah, he is," I agree. "And I totally wrecked my relationship with him. I was so focused on the whole making-out thing and how it didn't seem to be working. I should have been more focused on Evan as a person and thought more about his feelings. I'll never be able to win him back."

Katie and I are silent for a moment.

I snap to my senses. "I can't even believe what I'm saying. Sure, I lost Evan, but we only went out for a month. Jai is my friend, which is way more important, and he's never going to forgive me for this. I've lost him forever. This is so much worse than a breakup." A few more tears roll down my face.

Katie says nothing. She just stares at the floor, her face a palette of sadness. She's not going to volunteer any information about Jai, so I decide to ask her the million-dollar question.

"Does he hate me?"

"I don't know, Becca."

"Well, he obviously talked to you about me last night, so I want to know what he said," I say. I don't want to be too demanding, but how else am I supposed to know how Jai feels? I have a feeling that if I call him up, I'll hear a dial tone before the words *I'm sorry* make it out of my mouth.

"I'm not sure how much I should say," Katie admits, her shoulders tensing. "I mean, I feel really in the middle here. I'm sure it won't surprise you to know that he's incredibly upset. He also said that he doesn't want to talk to you right now."

Even though I had already assumed these things, it hurts to hear that they're true.

"Do *you* hate me?" I ask. I don't think I can take it if the answer is yes, but I need to know.

Katie looks me directly in the eye for a few moments, like she's seriously debating her answer to my question. "No, I don't hate you," she says finally, and I exhale, not realizing that I have been holding my breath. "I mean, I think what you did was terrible, but I didn't come over here to make you feel worse about everything. It's clear that you already feel bad enough."

"Then why did you come over?" I ask.

If Katie tells me that she doesn't want to be friends with me anymore, I will totally deserve it. And then I'll self-destruct.

"I came over because I'm really concerned about what's going on, and I wanted to hear your side of the story."

"I appreciate that," I answer. "And now that you've heard it, what do you think?"

"I'm mostly really disappointed that you outed Jai," Katie says, "and I can't say that I'm exactly happy that you wrote about my crush on Luke Kleinschmidt."

Oh, I forgot about that. It was only in the coming-out-party entry, and I barely even mentioned Luke. But for anyone reading my blog in Pine Prairie, I gave away more than enough information. Again, how could I have been so dumb?

"Katie, I'm really sorry," I say. "I should never have mentioned Luke on my blog. That must have been pretty embarrassing for you to read."

"It was," Katie agrees, pausing to pull her hair off her face. "But in the grand scheme of things, it's not that big a deal. I mean, sure, anyone who reads the blog and knows you wrote it is going to figure out who my fantasy boyfriend is. But lots of girls have crushes on Luke, so it's not exactly newsworthy. Plus, even if Luke finds out, he'll be like, 'Katie who?'"

"Maybe I should have called you Kelly in my blog," I joke, and even Katie smiles at this.

"Maybe," Katie concedes, starting to look a little sad.

"Luke's just eye candy when it comes down to it. I mean, in art class, he *still* calls me Kelly even though I've been correcting him lately."

"That's lame," I remark. "But I'm glad you've been speaking up. It's about time."

We're still sitting on the edge of my bed, but I feel my shoulders relax a little.

Katie eyes me intently. "I guess I'm still confused about why you wrote your blog at school. Didn't it occur to you that Evan and Josh would spy on you in the computer lab?"

"Honestly, it didn't," I answer. "And there were days when I felt like I couldn't wait until I got home, like I was going to explode if I didn't get it all out immediately. But you know, I'm starting to wonder if, subconsciously, I wanted to be discovered."

"Hmm, that's a weird idea," remarks Katie. She leans forward and cups her chin in her hand thoughtfully. "I'm really bummed about what you did, and I didn't enjoy picking Jai up off the floor last night."

"Yeah, I bet that was less than fun," I say. It occurs to me that Jai and Katie probably didn't write haikus and talk about how terrible I am. Their conversation was likely much more focused on Jai. Sometimes I forget that not everything is about me.

"Still," Katie continues, "I believe that you never meant to hurt anybody. And you certainly aren't responsible for what Jamie did to Jai. That was her choice."

"Thank you," I say.

We sit facing each other for a few moments.

"So," I begin timidly. "Do you still want to be my friend? I mean, I could understand if you didn't. What I did was pretty unforgivable."

"You've been my best friend for a long time, and I'm not about to drop you because you screwed up. If I were in your position, I'd want to be forgiven."

"Oh my God, Katie, I totally don't deserve you!" I exclaim, jumping up to hug her. She puts her arms around me and pats my back.

"Sure you do. After all, you've been the one with all of the entertaining stories. I've just been the audience."

"Which is exactly what I've always needed," I say.

23

I'm relieved that Katie is able to forgive me and will still be my friend, but I also feel guilty about the awkward position it puts her in. I know she wants to be friends with both Jai and me, but that's going to be difficult as long as Jai refuses to have anything to do with me.

I manage to get a few hours of fitful sleep and wake up with my stomach knotted in anxiety. The roads were plowed yesterday, and it stopped snowing in the late afternoon. That means school is definitely in session today. I'm perfectly healthy, and I know that there's no way I can convince my parents to let me stay home. I have to face the consequences, whatever they might be.

I manage to get a bit of breakfast down, but just before I head out the door, I dash to the bathroom, and it comes back up again. I know that I need something in my stomach if I'm going to even stand a chance of handling the stress at school, so I grab a yogurt and a granola bar and rush out to the minivan, where Dale is waiting in the driver's seat.

"You okay?" Dale asks as I get into the van.

"Um, sort of," I answer. "My stomach's a bit disagreeable today."

"Well, that's not surprising," Dale says, and we spend the ride to school in silence.

Just as Dale pulls up in front of the school, he looks at me.

"You're going to be fine, Becca. Remember that, will you?"

I still don't really believe him, but I nod and grab my backpack.

"Bye, Dale," I say, getting out of the car.

At least he didn't tell me to have a nice day. Like that would even be possible.

I take a deep breath and walk through the doors into the school lobby. I'm half expecting a crowd to be waiting for me, ready to lob rotten tomatoes at my face or chant, "Traitor! Traitor!" but everyone and everything looks like it always does. Kids are milling about by the pop machines, purchasing Mountain Dew for their A.M. caffeine fixes. Derrick and Brookie are fondling each other by the trophy case as usual. No one has taken any notice of my arrival, so I start heading for my locker, certain that it's going to be plastered with printouts of my blog or some more graffiti about my wish to give birth to a tiny Matt Wooderson.

But when I get to my locker, I see that it's unharmed. No one is standing by it waiting to harass me. People are still just going about their business, so I guess I just have to go about mine and hope that nothing terrible happens. I mean, I've only been at school for like thirty seconds, but so far, so good. I open my locker, put away my coat, and pull out my books. Then I glance over to my right and see Katie at her locker, scooping up textbooks. I walk over to her.

"Hey," I say, praying that I don't sound as defeated as I feel.

Katie looks up. "Oh, hey." She stands up with an armload of textbooks and folders, hugging them to her chest.

"I haven't seen him yet. Have you?" she asks.

"Nope."

I don't need to tell Katie that I'm a seething stress ball. She lowers herself to the floor and scoots up against her locker, motioning for me to join her.

Katie flips open her history notebook and her eyes scan the pages. I don't think she can concentrate on what she's looking at, but she's making a pretense of being normal. I follow suit by spreading my algebra book open in my lap and gazing at a page of equations we haven't studied yet. They may as well be written in Greek for the amount of sense they make to me.

After a few minutes, Katie gasps. My head shoots up, and we both see Jai walking down the hall, completely collected, his jaw set. He's resplendent in one of his signature rockabilly wannabe outfits, which includes black jeans, a bowling shirt, his favorite belt (which displays a portrait of Bettie Page on the buckle), and an enormous chain jangling between his wallet and belt loop. I notice that Jai is wearing his wingtips, which is the only flaw in his ensemble, but I know that he is still saving money for a pair of red cowboy boots. Still, despite the footwear problem, he looks awesome.

Jai walks to his locker, which is right next to Katie's.

"Hey, Katie," Jai mutters. "How are you? Did you study for Huhn's history test?"

"Sure," replies Katie. "Did you?"

"Yep."

Despite the hurt I feel for being publicly dismissed by Jai, I breathe a sigh of relief. I'm just thankful that no one threatens to beat Jai up or ask him if he has a poster of an oil-drenched male underwear model in his bedroom.

I collect my books and head down the hall to Ms. Klimstra's room. On my way, I pass Jamie and Lance, who are intertwined in front of Lance's locker. I pretend to ignore them. I know they see me, but they don't say anything either.

I brace myself for Ms. Klimstra's class this morning, fully expecting Rod Knutson and Dustin Schwermer to say something to me about Jai. After all, they're Lance's best friends, and I can't imagine that Lance would keep something from them as newsworthy as the presence of a gay boy at Pine Prairie High. When I walk into the classroom, I see that Rod and Dustin have their heads bent over the latest issue of *Guns & Ammo*. They don't seem to notice me at all. I'm relieved by this, but also a little disturbed by their choice of reading material.

Second-period biology is just as uneventful as algebra, and I almost forget about my problems by the time I get to study hall the next hour. I start doing my algebra homework. Two rows behind me, Haley Matheson starts whispering to Kennadie Meier, the kind of girl who laughs hysterically when people trip and bang their knees on sharp corners. My ears perk up.

"Yeah, he walked into Huhn's class this morning, and the room went, like, silent," mutters Haley. "Everyone just stared. The only person who talked to him was Katie Eidsvaag."

My heart sinks. I know they're talking about Jai because he and Katie have history with Mr. Huhn first period. With Jamie. I remember this because I've heard Jamie complaining about how it's not fair that she has to take a class first thing in the morning that actually requires her to concentrate and take notes.

This is just great. If people stopped talking when Jai walked into class, the word must be out. Which means that *Jai* is officially out, whether he wants to be or not. I wonder how Jai feels about it.

"Oh, Katie likes everyone," says Kennadie with disdain, as if liking people is somehow uncool. My hand tightens around my pen as I will myself not to say anything. I should just stay out of this. I'm sure that these girls are trying to get a rise out of me. It's not like they forgot that I'm sitting right in front of them.

"Yeah, I know," agrees Haley. "And she's so shy that she doesn't really have that many friends. Well, any worth mentioning. So I guess that's why she has to hang out with a gay boy. But hey, at least they can talk about their guy crushes. And speaking of which, I heard she has a thing for Luke Kleinschmidt. Right, like that'll ever happen."

I turn around.

"What?" asks Haley, as if she has no idea what the problem is.

I just glare at her, my lips clamped under my teeth. I hope I can say everything I need to without opening my mouth. Haley stares back, and I think she's getting the message.

"Oh, that's right," she says, letting out a chirpy little laugh. "I forgot. Sorry."

My heart starts to pound, and before I can stop myself, the words come out.

"You didn't forget anything," I retort. "And if you're planning to talk any more crap about my friends, you could at least do it in a place where I don't have to listen to you."

Kennadie's eyes widen, and she nervously picks at the fraying cuff of her jeans. "Jeez."

Haley opens her mouth to speak, but before she can think of anything really nasty to say, Mrs. Knochenmus advises us to "Pipe down back there, people." Haley pulls out a pot of lip gloss and applies it with her middle finger while keeping her eyes on me.

✳✳✳

At lunch, Jai eats with Ashli. I'm glad that he has another friend, but it still hurts that he's avoiding me. This drama goes unnoticed by the rest of the kids in the cafeteria, some of whom are openly gawking and pointing at Jai. I guess the kids who didn't know about him when they got to school found out during their morning classes. I bet some of them didn't even know who Jai was before today, since he's still one of the newest kids in school. It's clear that everyone knows who he is now, given the number of slack-jawed stares in the cafeteria. I'd like to break out the fire hose and drench them all for being so rude. I want to shout at them, "Ass hats, it's not like there's a llama in the cafeteria. It's just Jai, a perfectly normal and wonderful gay boy. Get over it!"

"So," I say to Katie as I open my carton of milk, "was the reaction to Jai in Huhn's class as dramatic as Haley Matheson claimed?"

"What did she say?"

"Oh, she was talking to Kennadie Meier in study hall about how you were the only person who talked to him and everyone else was just staring like a bunch of dumb asses."

Katie stirs her tapioca pudding. "Yeah, pretty much. Mr. Huhn didn't even ask what was going on. I think he knows."

"Oh God, did Jamie tell frickin' *everyone?*" I say, burying my face in my hands. I wonder how many people now know about my blog, too. I can just imagine students rushing to the computer lab to see my blog for themselves. I'm sure many of them are already discussing how pathetic I am.

I pick up my sloppy joe and wrinkle my nose. It smells gross, but I'm starving. I take a bite. Actually, it's not that bad, just a little greasy. I wipe my mouth and set it down on my tray.

Rod Knutson walks by Katie and me holding his lunch tray, grinning like he just visited one of the hookers in *Risky Business.*

"Looks like Jai found somewhere else to sit today. You two must be lonely without your little gay friend hanging around," Rod says, looking pretty pleased with himself. "But I guess if you're bored, you can just reread the stuff you wrote about him on that stupid blog."

The rest of the Rod and Gun Club overhears this, and Lance and the Schwermer twins let out a few guffaws. I wish they would all stop wasting the oxygen in this cafeteria.

"Shut up, Rod," Katie says, leaning back and crossing her arms. She glares at him. The grin immediately fades from Rod's face, and he retreats to his table with the rest of the Rod and Gun Club. I stare at Katie in awe. I think she's just become my personal hero. I don't think there would have been anything *I* could have said to make Rod leave us alone. But since everyone thinks Katie is so sweet, a little hostility must shock them into submission.

"Man, that was so rude," Katie remarks, still obviously disgusted.

"But you let Rod have it. That was awesome."

"Yeah," agrees Katie, but not in an egotistical, "look at how much ass I kick" sort of way. It's more like she's realizing her own power. Then she shrugs. "Well, it's not like I'm just going to sit here and let Rod pick on Jai *and* you."

"I don't care that much if people want to pick on me about my blog," I say. "After all, it's my fault, so I should have to deal with it. But I can't stand the thought of Jai getting crap from people about this."

"I can see why you'd feel protective of Jai, but maybe you're being a little too hard on yourself," Katie suggests. "I mean, I wouldn't be surprised if people picked on you a little bit about this, but you don't have to take it. And you certainly don't deserve it."

"I don't know about that," I answer.

These days, I'm beginning to think I deserve exactly what I get.

24

Within a matter of hours, it seems to that everyone in school has found out about my blog, and now they're curious. As I walk down the hall after lunch, several people snicker at me, staring.

A tiny little freshman steps up to me right before I get to my locker. "Hey, did Evan really dump you?" he asks, barely concealing his laughter. Based on how big his glasses are, I'd guess that this kid is a member of the Computer Club.

I remember what Katie said about me not having to take crap from people, and I think about how she handled Rod in the cafeteria. So I just tell him, "Get lost, will you?"

The boy's eyes widen, and he scampers off down the hall. I can't help but laugh to myself. I don't need to be scared of these people. They don't really know me, not even after reading my blog. And I've already lost Jai's friendship, so what does it matter if they want to poke a little fun at me? It certainly wouldn't be the worst thing that happened to me this week.

I walk into Mr. Huhn's class feeling empowered, so much so that I don't even care when Melissa Stromwell laughs and asks me, "So, how are things working out with Mr. Wonderful?"

"Ha ha," I reply, taking my seat.

I get a few more comments throughout the afternoon about my blog. It's surprising, but most people seem more interested in my love interests than they do in Jai's life. In fact, no one even asks me if Jai is really gay or makes any homophobic remarks or anything. Maybe they already suspected that he was gay. I mean, he dresses differently from all of the other guys at school, and everyone could see that when Ashli was falling all over him, he was having none of it. Maybe other people aren't as naive as I was. Maybe things won't be so bad for Jai *or* me after all.

Then again, maybe they will. Jai won't even look at me at rehearsal, not even when I say hi to him. He and Ashli hang out backstage between scenes, and anytime I come near them, Jai stares at the floor, like he's holding his breath until I go.

Jamie makes things almost as unpleasant. She doesn't actually say anything to me, but her smug expression says it all. I'd like to shout at her, "You think you really got me, don't you, Jamie? Well, I hope you can live with yourself, knowing what a sneaky, petty bitch you are."

Of course it would be hypocritical of me to tell Jamie off, since it's my fault that this happened at all.

If I confront Jamie, I know it will just blow up in my face, and that's the last thing I need right now. Still, I feel like I need to stand up for myself more.

❋❋❋

I've gotten myself pretty worked up by the time rehearsal finishes. I see Katie give me a guilty look as she joins Jai and Ashli for a ride home, but I flash her my best "don't worry about it" expression. I'd already asked Dale to pick me up today.

I peer out the lobby doors and don't see any sign of the minivan, so I sit down at one of the tables next to the pop machines. I see Josh walk out of the theater and toward me. Even though my hands are stuffed in my pockets, I can feel my knuckles whiten as he approaches me.

"Hey, Bella, how's it going?" he asks, walking over to the pop machine. He inserts some change and retrieves a can of Mountain Dew from the bottom of the machine.

"Fine," I answer, my mouth tight and hard.

"What's the matter?" asks Josh jovially, opening his drink. He takes a long swig. "Can't handle a little friendliness from your old pal Joshing A. Round? By the way, I was wondering if maybe you could ask your friend Jai where I can get my hands on some stupid fringed boots."

Josh cracks up at this, like he can't believe how clever he is. "Don't worry, though. I still have a plastic lightsaber," he says, his eyes twinkling. "That was almost funny, by the way. But not as funny as the coming-out-party thingie you wrote about Jai. That was priceless."

I've just about had it with Josh. This whole situation is clearly amusing to him.

"I'm glad you enjoyed it," I say drily. "I just wish you would have kept it to yourself."

I know I'm running the risk of getting into it with Josh, but I don't care. He's the reason the whole school knows about my blog, and I feel like I need to take him to task for this.

"Well, Becca, you're such a brilliant writer and you have so many deep thoughts that I felt they needed to be shared with a wider audience."

"Gee, thanks," I say sarcastically. "You're too kind."

"Well, you put all of that stuff on the Internet, so you wanted people to read it, right?"

"Yes and no. And I know you're not an idiot, Josh, so I'm sure you could see that I didn't mean for just anybody to read it."

Josh is quiet for a moment. He drains the rest of the pop from the can and tosses it in the trash, which is right next to the recycling bin. I guess that's a step up from throwing it under the auditorium seats.

"Yeah, I know you didn't think anyone you knew would ever read it."

"So then why did you tell people about it?" I ask, trying to keep the volume of my voice even. I don't want to show Josh how angry I am with him, not if this conversation is going to go anywhere. "I mean, I can understand why you told Evan. He's your best friend, and maybe you both had a laugh over some of the stuff I wrote. But why did you go to Jamie? There was nothing in that for you, and you knew that she'd spread the word."

"I was really pissed at you for the way you treated Evan," he answers. "Do you know how hurt Evan was that you told your friends about all of the kissing stuff and then showed them the poem?"

"I can imagine," I reply, my voice soft.

"I don't think you can! Evan was absolutely crushed. He was so excited to be going out with you. I mean, he really liked you, Becca."

I feel awful all over again about Evan. "I know. I liked him a lot, too."

"Then why did you mess with his head like that?" Josh looks quite angry now, and it makes me nervous. Then again, what could he possibly do that would be worse than what he's already done?

"I didn't mean to," I say. "I just wasn't thinking."

"You sure weren't," Josh responds in disgust.

"And what about you?" I ask, rage growing inside of me. "How much thought did you give to telling Jamie about my blog? Didn't it even occur to you that it would affect anyone besides me?"

"I guess I didn't care."

"Well, you should have cared. It's fine if you don't like me, but what could you possibly have against Jai?"

"Nothing. He seems like a really cool guy."

"He is," I agree. "And now he won't speak to me because I outed him to the whole school. Thanks to your help, of course."

"Listen, I get it, okay? I see your point. I just didn't think about that."

"And you still haven't explained why you went to Jamie."

"I was still pissed about what happened with Evan, and I was mad about the things you wrote about me."

"But you knew Jamie would tell everyone and then they'd all get to read about you."

"Whatever. I just knew it would make you look bad. Plus, I thought Jamie would think I was cool for telling her about the blog."

I may throw up. Of all the reasons that Josh spread the word about my blog, this has to be the most pathetic. I will never understand why anyone would want to impress Jamie. She's mean and shallow and lives to put other people down. Plus, I doubt she'd *ever* think that Josh was cool, no matter what he did or said.

"Could you just do me a favor in the future? If you have a problem with me, take it up with *me*. You could tell from the blog that I felt terrible about what happened with Evan. I still feel terrible. Why did you think I needed more punishment?"

Josh frowns, and for the first time in our conversation, I feel like I may have gotten through to him.

"I'm sorry," he says finally.

Hearing those words isn't exactly a relief, but the apology is a small concession.

"I forgive you," I say.

Outside, I hear a horn honk. I stand up and look out the window to see Dale in the minivan.

"See you around," I say as I head toward the door. I rush out to the van and get in. Dale looks over at me warily.

"How was school today?" asks Dale, pulling out of the parking lot.

"Not as bad as I expected, but worse in other ways. Jai won't talk to me."

"That's too bad," Dale answers. "Have people found out about your blog?"

"Yes, and I'm sure they're all at home reading it right now."

"Hard to say," Dale admits. We ride along in silence for a while, and then something awful occurs to me.

"Um, have you told Mom about my blog?" I ask.

Dale inhales sharply. "Yes."

"Why did you do that?" I wail.

"I want her to be prepared in case anyone walks into Prairie Perks and hands her a tube of Preparation H."

"Oh my God!" I practically shout. "I'm going to die. I just know it."

"I don't think so," counters Dale, his voice tranquil. "If you survived school today, I think we can safely assume that you're past the worst of it."

"I really hope you're right," I respond. "Still, do you think I should apologize to Mom for what I wrote about her?"

"It certainly couldn't hurt. Why don't I drop you off at the shop? She's just closing up now, and I'm sure she could use your help."

✳✳✳

My mom unlocks the door to Prairie Perks, and I step inside. I rarely come here, since when I do, Mom is always asking me to run errands and wipe down the tables, but I would love it here if someone else owned it. It's a very inviting space. The wooden tables are all different, since Mom scoured antique stores for bargains before she opened the shop. On each table is a small vase filled with water, cranberries, and a few twigs. A bookshelf in the corner of the café holds a collection of games, everything from CLUE to Parcheesi to UNO. The cold case, which is normally filled with sandwiches, salads, and pastries, stands empty. The menu of drinks and snacks is on the wall behind the counter. Hand-painted flowers swirl in colorful patterns around the border of the menu. Potted spider plants hang in the front windows.

"What are you doing here?" my mom asks.

"I thought you could use some help closing up," I reply, even though it wasn't my idea. I'm sure my mom already knows that.

"Well, the cold case could really use a good scrubbing."

I peer inside the case. It looks pretty clean to me.

"All right," I say. I have no energy to argue with my mom about this.

"I'm going to change out the table centerpieces," my mom says. "Those twigs and cranberries are starting to get slimy. Time to break out the tea lights and marbles again."

My mom walks back into the kitchen, and I follow her. While I'm filling up a bucket with soapy water, she pulls the materials for the centerpieces out of a cupboard.

"So Dale told me about your Internet diary thingy last night."

"My blog," I say, grabbing a rag and tossing it in the bucket.

We both walk back into the front of the café and start our respective tasks.

"A blog. Right."

"Um, did you read it?"

"No, I haven't had time," my mom says.

"Well, you really don't need to. I'm sure that Dale told you everything."

We both work for a while in silence. I worry that my mother isn't talking because she's pissed about what I wrote. I have to find out how much she knows.

"Um, what did Dale tell you about my blog?" I ask.

My mother looks up from the vase she's filling with marbles and puts her hand on her belly, which seems to have grown overnight. "Well, he said that you wrote about Jai being gay."

"Did that surprise you?"

"What? That Jai's gay or that you wrote about it?"

"Um, both?"

My mom puts her hand on her hip and thinks about this. "Neither, I guess."

Her words sting a little. I'm mostly disappointed in myself, though.

"What else did Dale tell you?" I ask.

My mom shrugs and puts a votive candle in the vase. "Not that much. He mentioned that you were upset about Evan breaking up with you and that you wrote quite a bit about that. Oh, and that you have a crush on Matt Wooderson."

"That's all true," I admit.

I'm not sure if I should press my luck and ask my mom if she got a lot of detail about Matt. Anyway, if she wants to find out for herself, she still can, and there's not much I can do to stop her, outside of begging her not to read my blog. I'm not going to do that. It would make me look like I've got something to hide. And at this point, whether I like it or not, I have almost nothing that I *can* hide.

Once I've finished cleaning the cold case and my mom has put out the new centerpieces, she asks, "Should I make us some tea?"

"Sure."

She goes behind the counter and fills two mugs with hot water from the espresso machine. I pick out a lemon verbena tea bag and get my mom chamomile, which is the only kind of tea she drinks when she's pregnant.

We sit down at one of the tables.

"I'm so ashamed," I admit, taking a sip of my tea, which burns my lips a little. A few tears roll down my cheeks.

My mother places her hands on her belly and looks at me tenderly.

"You know, I hate to see you suffering this way. My main wish as a parent is to never see you in pain. But sometimes I think that the only way to truly learn something is to go through painful experiences. It's part of growing up."

I dab my eyes. "Man, this sucks so much."

"Sure, it does," my mom agrees. "I'm not thrilled that the world can read about my hemorrhoids—"

"I'm *really* sorry about that," I cut in. "And I know that you would never let a boy sleep over in my bed. It was just a fun little fantasy."

"I know," my mom replies, patting my shoulder. "I've already dealt with being a pregnant teenager in this town. People have talked so much trash about me over the years, both to my face and behind my back. If they want to discuss my butt, let 'em. I've heard worse. And people had better be nice to me, anyway, because if they piss me off, I might just shut this place down and leave town, and then people will have to drive twenty miles to get a cappuccino."

I laugh, and my mother smiles. I wonder if I will ever be able to be as strong as she is.

Her face grows serious again. "Rebecca, I want you to really think about what I just said. Not the part about cappuccinos, but about what you wrote on your blog. Aside from Jai being gay, is there anything else on there that would be damaging for everyone to know about?"

"No," I reply slowly. "Just embarrassing. And really personal."

"But you used to talk about those things with everyone anyway. So if you think about it, it's like you never made your resolution."

I contemplate this for a moment. What if I hadn't resolved to stop oversharing? Would I have told everyone that Jai was gay? Would I have cornered Evan and forced him to explain why he had Josh dump me? Would I have confessed my feelings to Matt? Actually, I don't think I would have done any of those things, but I don't want to contradict my mother when she's being so understanding.

"Sure," I agree. "But resolution or not, I never would have *told* people about Jai. Not out loud. And I didn't think I was doing that on my blog, but I was wrong."

"Yeah, gossip has a way of spreading. Like a fungus," my mom says, scanning the café, which, now that I think about it, is probably one of the biggest gossip hubs in town.

"So what now?" I ask.

"I have an idea," my mother replies.

25

Jai won't talk to me, but there are some things I need to say to him. On Thursday, during the weekly free write in Ms. Sommerfeld's English class, I start composing a letter of apology to give to him during play practice.

Dear Jai,

    I'm sorry. I know that sentence doesn't go far enough to cover the damage I've done, but it's a start. I never, not in a million years, intended to hurt you or betray your trust the way I did. Yes, I wrote about you. I revealed your most guarded secret, and the information fell into the wrong hands. I consider it the worst mistake I've ever made.

    I value you so much as a friend. I can't imagine not having you in my life. Is there any way you can forgive me?

Becca

Maybe it's too soon to give him this, but the very thought of Jai not knowing how terrible I feel is worse than any potential rant he might throw at me. And I know Jai; he's not prone to acts of rage and bitterness. Once at A&W, I accidentally overturned a fresh basket of ketchup-smothered onion rings onto his lap. He happened to be wearing his favorite vintage gray wool pants that had buttons on the waistband expressly for suspender attachment. The ketchup stains came out, but the grease splotches were permanent. I offered to buy Jai another pair of pants, but he just told me that it was no big deal and never mentioned it again.

This time, it might be harder for Jai to forgive. I messed up more than his pants.

After play practice, I rub my sweaty palms against my backpack and pull the apology letter out. I don't want to make myself too conspicuous, particularly if Jai makes a scene, so I follow him out to the parking lot. Although it's not very cold out today, the wind whips my hair into my face so hard that it actually stings.

"Jai! Got a second?" I call.

Jai is standing at the door of his car, key poised to unlock it. He slowly raises his head and stares at me. There is no fire in his eyes, just a cold hardness.

"No."

"But I just want to give you something," I say, stepping forward with the letter in my outstretched hand.

"What is it?"

"A letter. Of apology. Please read it." I extend the letter toward him, but Jai turns back to his car and unlocks the door, shaking his head.

"You should have learned after Evan dumped you that pathetic letters of apology don't make everything all better!"

"But I just—"

"You just what? I can't *wait* to hear how you're planning to screw up my life next." Jai folds his arms across his parka and stomps his feet. I start to shiver. It's colder out here than I thought.

I squint. "I wanted to—"

"You don't need to do jackshit. You've already done enough. You gave out too much information and totally screwed me. Did you hear that? TMI, Becca. *TMI!*"

I blink back tears. "You told me you'd never say that to me."

"Well, you told me that you'd never reveal my secret. Now leave me alone!" Jai slides into the driver's seat. In a matter of seconds, he has peeled out of the parking lot and is driving down the street. A gust of wind rushes by me, and my hair smacks me in the face again.

"Hey," says a voice behind me. I jump and turn around to see Matt pulling his ski cap on. Oh, no. I so don't need this right now. My former friend has just basically told me to go to hell, and here's Matt.

I clap my hand on my chest. "Jesus. You scared me."

"I can't possibly be as scary as Jai just was," Matt remarks, gesturing toward his car. "Need a ride?"

"Did you just hear all of that?" I ask. I mean, Matt probably already knows what a piece-of-crap friend I am, but if he over-heard Jai telling me off, it will only confirm it for him.

"No, not really." Matt unlocks the passenger door and opens it. "Hop in."

"Thanks," I manage to say, remembering my first time getting into his car with Evan. At the time, I thought that it was one of the most awkward experiences of my life. But compared with what just happened between Jai and me, I'd gladly repeat the Matt-and-Evan sandwich experience.

Matt starts the car and pulls out of the parking lot. We ride along silently for a minute. I wish I knew what he was thinking. It can't be anything good. I'm sure that Matt has heard all about the blog, and he knows how I feel about him, and he's just trying not to laugh at me. I look over at him for any signs of amusement on his face. He's just looking at the road calmly.

"So how's it going?" Matt asks.

"Oh, you know, rehearsal was kind of tough today. I mean, I can't believe I forgot my line in the drive-in scene, and then I practically took your toe off again during the hand jive. I'm really sorry about that," I say. I probably sound pitiful.

"No biggie," replies Matt casually. "Don't forget that I almost chipped your tooth during the stage kiss last week."

Wow, I'd already forgotten about that. I guess I've been just a bit distracted by the problems that have cropped up since then.

I can't think of anything else to say, and Matt is quiet, too. He clears his throat when he reaches my driveway. Then Matt puts the LeSabre in park and looks over at me.

"Becca, I need to tell you something. I think you have a right to know."

The seriousness of Matt's voice makes my heart do a flip turn in my chest. I wonder how many fifteen-year-olds die of cardiac arrest every year. I'm not sure how much more strain my heart can take, given all of the recent heart pounding/sinking/cartwheeling moments I've been having lately.

"Um, I've read your blog."

"You have?" I whisper.

"Yeah."

Crap. I figured that word would get to Matt eventually about my panting, lustful fantasies, but I wasn't sure if he'd actually say anything to me about them. I guessed, even hoped, that he would be too embarrassed to bring it up. I was wrong. This is so horrible. Matt, Mr. Wonderful, Mr. Totally-Out-Of-My-League, knows it all: the tongues, the feeling up, the Preparation H he gave to my mother. Ugh, I should just go stick my head in the snow heap at the end of the driveway and put myself out of my misery.

I timidly look over at Matt, certain that he's going to either start laughing uncontrollably or practically push me out of his car. "Go on, git!" he'll shout. "I can't believe a loser like you even dared to think such things about me! Leave now, you waste of human space!"

Matt doesn't actually look like he's about to do or say either of those things. He takes off his mittens and rubs his thumb against the stubble on his chin. I study his face. He doesn't seem embarrassed or mad, nor does he look thrilled, like he's about to tell me he feels exactly the same way about me.

And suddenly I don't care that Matt knows I like him. After what happened to Jai, this is small potatoes. It's a perfectly normal thing to like a boy, and it's not like I have anything to be ashamed of. In fact, it's about the *only* thing in my life that I'm not ashamed of right now.

"Becca?" Matt asks. He's obviously waiting for me to say something.

"Well, that's that, I guess," I say as I reach for the door handle.

"Please don't go yet, Becca."

I stare into his eyes. His pupils appear almost black in the fading afternoon light. What's going on?

"I was flattered by what you wrote," Matt says.

"You were?" Not totally freaked out that someone who barely knew you at the time was majorly obsessing over you?

"Sure." Matt nods. "I mean, reading your blog was a strange way to find out how you felt about me. But hey, feelings are feelings. They have to come out one way or another."

I think about this for a moment. I was trying so hard to hide my feelings, but they came out anyway. Just like Jai came out anyway. I wonder if there's any point in trying to hide what I feel anymore. I thought I was so clever, tucking away my feelings in a blog, but it turns out that I created an even more public spectacle than I had when I was just telling people stuff. Maybe I just need to face facts: I can't keep things to myself. Even when I try, the thoughts and secrets have a way of getting out. Maybe I just need to accept that this is who I am.

"When did you read my blog?" I ask.

"Monday. Someone, um, gave me a copy of one of the entries you wrote about me."

"Would that someone be Jamie?" I ask.

"Yeah," Matt admits. I wonder if Matt would drive me over to Jamie's house right now. I have a few things I'd like to say to that girl.

"Anyway," continues Matt, "I'm sorry if I was acting a little weird at rehearsal that day, but it just caught me by surprise."

It starts to make sense now. Matt did seem a bit uneasy, and then we had the tooth clash. I got so distracted by what happened with Jai after rehearsal, though, that I hadn't really given Matt's behavior much thought.

"So, um," I stammer, "I'm sorry if, you know—"

"You don't need to apologize for anything. It's cool."

I suppose Matt's right, although I feel like I need to apologize for just about everything lately.

"Has anybody teased you about the blog?" I ask. I'm pretty curious about what people are saying about the blog when I'm not around. Aside from overhearing Haley in study hall, the puny freshman, and a few comments from the Rod and Gun Club, no one else has actually approached me directly about it.

"A little," he admits. "But I don't mind. I can handle it."

"Oh. Good." I say.

Matt takes a deep breath and looks at me.

"It's been a lot of fun doing the musical with you. You're a very talented singer and actress. I think you're really great. But—"

Here it comes. Reality is about to crash down on me once again. This time, I'm prepared for it. I know what Matt's going to say.

Matt inhales again as he pauses.

"I just want to be friends."

While this sentence is so old and loaded it's practically a cliché, I hear the sincerity ringing through Matt's voice.

"I'd like to be your friend," I say, my eyes meeting his. I

could use another friend right now, anyway. And if that friend just happens to be a fine physical specimen and one of the nicest guys in school, then those are just added bonuses.

"I'd like it, too," Matt says. "As I read your blog, I found myself more intrigued with who you are. Sometimes I feel like people at school can be so shallow, and your blog shows that you're a person of depth."

Wow. I don't know what to say to this. A person of depth? I've never really thought about myself that way. Not like I see myself as some superficial airhead, but I usually just feel so bad about myself that I don't take much time to reflect on the good stuff.

"That's really nice to hear," I answer. I look over at the steamed kitchen window of my house and see Dale chopping something. I'm suddenly very hungry, but I can't go yet. As long as I've got Matt here opening up like this, I need to set the record straight about something.

"Um, Matt, can I ask you a question?"

"Okay."

"Well, you know how people at school talk a lot of crap about each other? Normally, I don't believe it, but I heard something about you, and I want to know the truth."

"What did you hear?" Matt still looks completely relaxed, like he couldn't care less that people have talked about him behind his back. Now that we're going to be friends, I'll have to find out how he does this.

"Well, someone said that you were at one of Darren Nelson's parties and that you, like, grabbed a girl or something. Is it true?"

"I was at one of Darren's parties this fall. I wasn't invited or anything, but Lance called me at like midnight and said that he'd had too many beers and needed a ride home. So I showed up to get him, and Haley Matheson was there and she was clearly plowed, too. She actually grabbed me, um, somewhere very personal."

Matt looks down at his lap. Yikes, Haley grabbed his crotch? That is *so* sleazy. I can't imagine ever doing that. Then again, I've never been drunk either.

"What did you do?" I ask. This is fascinating. I've always wanted to know what goes on at Darren's parties and if they're really as wild as the rumors. I guess so.

"Well, um, I removed her hand from the, uh, place it was resting and told her not to touch me again. Then she got all freaked out and started shouting to the entire room that I'd just tried to cop a feel. She started to cry, too. The problem was that no one at the party actually saw who touched who, so they all believed Haley. I guess they just assumed that because I'm a guy, I was the one who did the grabbing. A few of Darren's old football buddies got up in my face about it, and I tried to explain the whole thing, but they wouldn't listen. One of them pulled me outside and pounded on me a little. He gave me a few bumps and bruises, but it could have been a lot worse."

"That's horrible!" I exclaim. "I can't believe Haley did that. She basically got you beaten up."

"Yeah, pretty much. Lance and I got out of there after that. I've tried not to dwell on it, but sometimes when I see Haley and her friends, they just give me this look of death, like *I* was the one who did something wrong. And then they go talking about it and spreading rumors that I'm some sort of perv. That bothers me a lot."

"Of course it would," I agree. I feel really bad for Matt but also relieved that the rumors aren't true. He is a unicorn among high school boys after all. I think about calling Jai to tell him, until I remember he's not speaking to me. But then I think about Matt again and realize that, in a way, his situation is worse than mine. I mean, people know that I betrayed my friend, got dumped by a freshman, and have a rabid crush on a guy I can never have, but at least it's all true. Nobody's accusing me of doing things I haven't actually done.

"So that's what happened there," Matt says. "Is there anything else you want to know?"

"Well, I think that's it for now. And just so you know, I didn't think that that rumor could be true, but I wanted to make sure. I mean, this town is so small and people think that they know each other. I'm finding out that a lot of the time, we don't know each other at all."

"You're right. And we should. I'm glad I'm getting to know you."

I can't help but blush as Matt says this. I hope that I'll be able to put aside my romantic feelings so that we can have a real friendship, because it seems so worth it.

"Me, too," I respond. "I mean, with you. I'm glad I'm getting to know you, too."

Matt looks over at the kitchen window, where Dale is still working away.

"Say, would you like to join me and my family for dinner?" I ask. I don't think anyone would mind.

"I'd love that," Matt answers. "My folks are at bowling league tonight, so I was just going to have frozen pizza. I'm sure that whatever your dad's making will be much nicer."

"Definitely. Dale's an awesome cook. Come on, let's go inside."

Matt turns off the engine, and we get out of his car. We crunch across my backyard, and I prepare to introduce my family to the unicorn. I just hope Nathan doesn't ask about his peanut.

26

On Friday, I excuse myself to the bathroom during study hall. When I walk into the girls' room, Ashli Berg is standing at the sink brushing her hair. Seeing her here makes me a bit apprehensive. She and Jai have eaten lunch together for the past couple of days, and I have a hard time imagining that she thinks highly of me, especially after seeing how thinly I veiled her identity on my blog. Not that I wrote anything really mean about her, but I made it obvious that she has a huge crush on Jai. I wouldn't blame her for being mad at me. And she *has* to be disappointed knowing that Jai is gay.

"Hi, Ashli," I say, smiling. I want to show her that I'm not a completely terrible person, despite what she read and what Jai may be telling her.

"Oh, hi," she says, like she almost didn't notice me walk in. I'm sure she noticed.

"How are you?" I ask.

"Fine."

I'm not sure what to do next. I came in here to pee, but I also feel like this is a prime opportunity to try to smooth things over with Ashli if she is, in fact, angry with me. She puts down her hairbrush, pulls some lip gloss out of her bag, and starts applying it.

"Can you believe it's only a week till opening night?" I ask.

"I know," Ashli agrees. Her voice is devoid of its usual cheer.

I shuffle my feet and stare at the floor. I have to say something, even though I'm not sure what the outcome will be.

"Um, Ashli? Can I say something?"

"It's a free country."

Yes, she's pissed, but I can't imagine that Ashli will go all überbitch on me. She could just walk out while I'm in the middle of talking. She could tell Jai at lunch that I tried to apologize, and they could commiserate about how lame I am. They probably already do that anyway. I don't see how I have anything more to lose at this point.

"Ashli, I just want you to know how sorry I am for the whole blog thing. I'm sorry I wrote about you. It wasn't nice."

Ashli puts down her lip gloss and turns to me. "No, it really wasn't."

I'm not sure what to say next. Should I apologize again? Just leave? Volunteer my services at the next German Club fundraiser?

Ashli takes a deep breath. She doesn't look angry, exactly, but she does look serious. It's one of the first times I think I've seen her without a smile on her face.

"You know," Ashli begins, "I never made my feelings for Jai a secret, and I was already getting teased for liking him. Now it's just gone up a notch. People keep asking me if I'm devastated that Jai is gay."

"Are you?" I ask, my curiosity getting the better of me.

Ashli leans against the sink and contemplates this. "I wouldn't say devastated. A little embarrassed, maybe. But I still get to be friends with him. I'm not sure that would have happened if all of this stuff hadn't, um, come out. Excuse the pun."

I just nod. Now I *know* Ashli can't be mad if she's making jokes. Still, I don't think it would be appropriate to start laughing. Not just yet.

"I'm glad that you guys are friends now," I say, thinking that it's just a shame that their friendship had to come at the expense of *my* friendship with Jai.

"I should get back to class," Ashli says, stuffing her lip gloss and brush into her bag and pulling it over her shoulder.

"Yeah, me, too," I agree.

Ashli starts toward the bathroom door. My heart flutters. I can't let this go.

"Um, Ashli?"

"Yeah." She turns and looks at me.

"Do you think Jai will forgive me? I mean, do you think it's possible?"

Ashli purses her lips thoughtfully. "I don't really want to get in the middle of it. But I hope he does. I think he could."

"I hope you're right," I say.

"See you." Ashli turns and walks out.

I wish I had her optimism.

Later that day at lunch, I can see that Katie is brooding about something.

"What's wrong?" I ask her.

Katie glances over at Jai and Ashli, who are talking animatedly a few tables away.

"I miss Jai," she says. "I mean, he's still giving me rides home from play practice, but I hate the fact that we're all divided like this at lunch. I feel so in the middle."

Hearing Katie say this makes me feel guilty. It's my fault that things are like this, and it isn't right that Katie should have to go back and forth between Jai and me like a kid in a custody battle. Plus, I worry that she'll start to resent me and maybe even resent Jai and get frustrated that we can't patch things up. Not that I wouldn't love to. Not that I haven't tried. At this point, it's all on Jai's shoulders to change things.

"I'm sorry, Katie," I say. "I don't know what else I can do. But if you want to go over there and join Jai and Ashli, you should. I'll be okay."

Of course this is a lie. I would be so ashamed to sit at a table by myself, and I know that the Rod and Gun Club would have some choice words about my pathetic social status. The whole thing would be so humiliating that I'd probably just leave the cafeteria and each lunch in the hallway or the lobby. That is such a depressing thought.

It suddenly occurs to me that I could sit with Matt and his friends. Then again, I don't know Matt's friends at all, and they'd probably think that I was just sitting with them because they know about my blog and know how I feel about Matt. And what would we talk about? How great Matt is? Football stats? Ugh, it would be too weird.

"I'm not going to leave you here all alone," Katie says. "You know I wouldn't. But I will talk to Jai and see if we can work something out. This is ridiculous."

"Thanks," I say. "You've been so awesome about all of this."

"Well, you and Jai both mean a lot to me. And honestly, I think this is going to blow over. I don't think Jai will stay mad forever."

It's a huge relief to hear Katie say this, and she makes the second person today who's told me that there might be hope of reconciling with Jai.

✳✳✳

On Saturday, I help my mom sand the woodwork in the bathroom. On Sunday, I babysit Nathan while my parents make a trip to St. Cloud to shop and run errands. Not exactly a raucous party weekend, but I'm busy enough that I don't continuously dwell on the hellish week that I just had, or the fact that Katie, Jai, and Ashli got together on Saturday at Jai's house. Katie told me about their plans, and although it made me a little sad to hear about them, I was thankful that she was honest with me. Katie's not a sneaky girl, and I know she's doing her best not to take sides. Still, I know how hard all of this is on her.

Back at school on Monday, people are still buzzing about Jai and the blog, but they seem to have calmed down a little. I don't hear any reports of rooms going silent when Jai walks into them, and except for a few smug looks from Jamie and her friends, people basically leave me alone. It didn't occur to me that this drama would die down as quickly as it started, but that seems to be the case. In fact, a new scandal has broken out: one of the basketball cheerleaders just announced she's pregnant, so everyone's talking about that.

It's funny how people around here seem to hang on to the negative stuff, like how Jamie and the Rod and Gun Club remember some of my past overshares. Yet, if there's something new to talk about, they temporarily forget the old stuff. I don't think I'll ever understand how the teenage mind works, even though I've got one of my own.

We're in the last week of rehearsals, so Ms. Miller has us staying a little later to work on some of the problem scenes. Matt gives me a ride home every day, and I find myself getting more comfortable around him. Sure, I still think about licking his neck sometimes, and I enjoy looking at his butt whenever I get a chance, but I think he really is becoming a friend.

Things are the same at lunch. Katie and I sit together, and Jai and Ashli sit together, and it seems like a pattern has been established. I wonder if we'll ever be able to break out of it. Ashli is friendly to me at rehearsals, but I can tell that she's still a bit guarded. I think our conversation in the girls' room helped, but it didn't cure everything. I know her loyalties rest with Jai, and that's the way it should be. After all, I'm the one who screwed up.

Mostly, I just feel lonely. Sure, I have Katie and Matt, but things just aren't the same without Jai. It's hard to believe that I met him such a short time ago, and now I'm struggling to get through my days without him. His arrival in Pine Prairie shook up my existence a little. I'd never met anyone like him before. And now I've lost him.

Just like I lost Evan.

I start to wonder if I'm just doomed to repeat my failures. I thought I'd learned from my mistakes when Evan dumped me, but apparently not. Instead, I just went on to do something even dumber, and the consequences were even more severe. What will I do next? I can't imagine doing something worse, but I thought the same thing after Evan and I were through. Is my future full of even bigger screwups? Like, will I get kicked out of college or fired from my dream job for doing stupid things? Or what if I get married, and my husband divorces me because I'm always messing up? And will I have any friends to turn to if this happens?

I don't know.

Maybe I'm the kind of person who's just not meant to have many friends. It's not that I wouldn't like more friends, but perhaps I need to accept the fact that I handle relationships badly. Katie is obviously the exception, and her tolerant and sweet personality is the main reason she has stuck by me. Over the years, everyone else has rolled their eyes and told me to shut up. At the time, I thought those people were just shallow and uptight, but now I see that maybe I should have listened.

27

I don't even consider the possibility of being nervous about performing until I start smoothing pancake makeup over my forehead.

I pass a tube of foundation over to Ashli. "Now don't be scared just because people called this stuff 'grease stick,'" I say.

"Grease stick? How appropriate," Ashli remarks.

"Huh? How so?"

"'Cause we're in *Grease*, silly."

I let out a sound that's a cross between a laugh and a groan. Ashli's eyes twinkle with amusement. Her sense of humor is a bit cornball, but I realize that it's nice to be around someone who doesn't take everything so seriously. There's a lot I could learn from Ashli.

"So how do I use this stuff?" Ashli asks.

"Just watch how I do it," I say, my hand guiding the tube shakily over my face. I'm sure Ashli notices this.

"You're going to be awesome, Becca. You and Matt totally play off each other."

I glance over at Ashli. "That's sweet of you to say."

Just then, Haley Matheson elbows her way between Ashli and me, nearly causing me to smear my eye with the grease stick.

"You guys are totally hogging the mirror," she says.

"Watch it, Haley!" I answer.

Haley ignores the fact that she almost blinded me and scowls at us. Ashli mouths the word *nice* to me, and we exchange a knowing look and continue applying our makeup in silence. It's so not worth it to get into this any further with Haley right now. Better to save the drama for the stage.

A few minutes later, Ashli and I are walking upstairs to the stage. My worries get the better of me, and I whisper, "Do you think Jai is going to be okay tonight?"

Ashli looks at me like I just announced my desire to pluck out my own toenails with a pair of needle-nose pliers. "Becca, this is totally his thing. He's going to be amazing."

"Yeah, I know that. I guess I'm just worried that maybe somebody might, you know, harass him during the performance. Like throw something at him? A shoe, maybe?"

"A shoe?" Ashli raises an eyebrow.

"Maybe I'm overly paranoid," I say, "but you never know."

"I don't think anything bad is going to happen, and if it does, there will be plenty of witnesses."

Nobody throws any shoes.

And the applause is deafening. The cast splits in two, and from the back of the crowd, the people with bit parts come forward and take their bows. The shouts and clapping grow louder when Jai walks to the middle of the stage to bask in his Teen

Angel glory. The audience turns up the volume even more when Ashli emerges on the arm of Derrick Hansen, who plays Doody, her onstage boyfriend.

As Matt and I step forward to take a final bow, he grins at me, reaches for my hand, and raises it high, something he never did when we rehearsed curtain calls. It's like he's proud of me or something.

I line up outside the auditorium with the rest of the cast, and we take in the compliments that the audience members shower on us. Almost everyone, from teachers to little kids to grandparents, stops to praise me.

"You have a beautiful singing voice, Becca."

"Great dancing, Becca!"

"You stole the show!"

For a few shimmering moments, I'm able to forget that I ruined Jai's life. I forget that Jai won't speak to me, that the entire student body knows about my wildest fantasies and insecurities. I'm just Becca, without all of the history and baggage, if for only a moment.

My mom bombards me with a hug.

"Oh, I couldn't be more proud of you!" she gushes. "Your voice was so beautiful, and you danced so well! I kept wanting to stand up and shout, 'That's my baby up there!' I can't wait to see the show again on Sunday. And I know Dale and Nathan will love it, too. You were brilliant, baby girl." Then the tears start flowing for real. I know my mom loves me, but it's a rare occasion when she lavishes so many compliments on me at once.

"Oh, Mom," is all I can say, leaning in for another hug. Dale will attend the show tomorrow night, and they'll both bring Nathan to the Sunday matinee, which is the only performance that doesn't interfere with his bedtime.

My mom looks over at Jai. "I should go congratulate your friend."

My friend. Maybe there's still a chance that Jai will be my friend again.

"Okay," I say, trying not to get too overwhelmed by the crazy mixture of love and sadness coursing through me at this moment.

After the last of the crowd trickles out of the theater, Matt turns to me. "So what are your plans for the evening?"

"Nothing much."

Before Matt can respond, Katie skips up to us. "Oh my God, you guys. That was so good! You were both amazing." Her eyes are shining so brightly, they practically have sparks flying out of them.

"Your sets are amazing, Katie," says Matt. "Really great." And then he leans into her for a hug, which Katie awkwardly accepts.

"Yeah, you did an awesome job!" I say, reaching for Katie's shoulder.

"Oh." Katie turns from Matt and gives *me* a hug.

"So," begins Matt, clapping his hands together. "Would you guys like to go get some pie at the Big 12?" The Big 12 is a truck stop at the edge of town. "My treat."

Katie locks widened eyes with me. "Um, sure."

"Yeah, great," I add, smiling.

"Oh, wait, what about Jai?" Katie's smile melts into a puddle of concern. "Should we invite him?"

Matt shuffles his feet uneasily. "It's up to you guys."

"I guess we can try, although I think I know what his answer will be," I say.

"I'll just go and check quick." Katie walks away.

I turn toward Matt, whose hands are shoved deep into his tight black jeans. He has really sexy, muscular thighs. I think he senses how tense I am. "Take it easy. I don't think Jai can stay mad at you forever."

"That's a nice thought," I reply. "I hope you're right."

Katie comes waltzing back to Matt and me a second later. "No go. Jai says he has plans to hang out at Ashli Berg's house, eat frosting, and watch some movie called *Strictly Ballroom*."

Was it absolutely necessary for Katie to include those details? It makes me jealous and a little sad to think that Ashli might be replacing me, even if she is nice and deserves Jai's friendship.

"So," begins Matt, " you two up for some pie?"

"I am," I say.

"Yeah, me, too," Katie adds.

"Good. Then let's all go get changed and I'll meet you in the lobby." Matt turns and heads back into the auditorium. I look around for a second and spot my mom talking with Ms. Miller in the lobby. I walk up to them.

"I just can't tell you how lucky I feel to have Becca in the lead role. She's been fantastic," Ms. Miller says, offering me a warm smile.

"Thanks, Ms. M," I say. I turn to my mom. "Is it okay if I go with Matt and Katie to the Big 12 for pie?"

"Sure. Do you need some money?"

Suddenly I'm delighted that Katie is part of this excursion. If it were just Matt and me, the Spanish Inquisition would be starting right here in front of the pop machine. After Matt had dinner with my family and me the other night, my mom grilled me about him, wanting to know if we were dating and what was going on. I'm not sure if she'd read my blog, but she at least knew that I had a crush on him, which made him automatically dangerous in her eyes. I had to reassure my mom like a thousand times that he only wants to be friends. She seemed relieved but still a bit skeptical.

"Maybe a little. Like five dollars?"

Matt said he'd pay, but I want to be able to offer. I mean, it's not like we're going on a date or anything.

My mother opens her purse and pulls a bill out of her wallet. "Here you go. Have fun."

"Thanks, Mom."

I run back into the theater and frantically begin to scrape makeup off my face. Ten minutes later, Katie and I meet Matt in the lobby.

"Ready to go, ladies?" Matt asks. He's leaning against one of the lobby walls, looking more gorgeous and lanky than ever. He's rinsed the gel out of his hair, and it hangs in damp strands around his face. Those strands are going to freeze solid once we get to the parking lot.

Pie at the Big 12 ends up being a lot of fun. We laugh a lot and do shots of half-and-half, and everything is just like it's supposed to be. Matt picks up the tab as promised.

Matt drops off Katie first, leaving me alone with him in the LeSabre for a few minutes.

"I had a good time tonight," Matt says. "You and Katie are a lot of fun to hang out with."

"Thanks," I answer. "You're fun, too."

We don't say anything for a few blocks, and Matt clears his throat.

"Katie's a really cool girl. I can see why the two of you are such good friends," Matt says.

"I'm lucky to have such a good friend," I admit. "Katie's always been there for me."

There's another pause.

"Does she have a boyfriend?" Matt asks.

"No," I answer. "She doesn't."

"Hmm."

Oh my God, does Matt have a thing for Katie? How weird would that be if they started dating? I feel a trickle of disappointment wash over me as I realize that Matt meant it when he said he didn't have romantic feelings for me. I mean, I didn't think he was lying when he told me that, but I had kind of hoped that if we continued hanging out, maybe he'd change his mind. I don't think that's going to happen, though, and I'm realizing it's because of my personality. I'm excitable and emotional and I have a tendency to say the wrong things. Now that I've gotten to know Matt a bit better, I can see that he would want to be with someone who's more laid-back and sweet-natured. That's Katie.

Matt and Katie. They'd make a great couple. I'd be jealous, of course, but I'd also be happy for them. Katie deserves to have a boyfriend, and I doubt she'd turn Matt down if he asked her out. Well, maybe she would if she were worried about my feelings. Which would be just like Katie.

"Well, see you tomorrow," Matt says, his arm resting on the back of my seat.

"Yeah, see you. Thanks for the pie, Matt." I unbuckle my seat belt.

"You're most welcome. Good night."

I step out of Matt's car and into the frigid air. I inhale deeply, and the air hits my lungs with a clean crispness. I crunch through the snow to my back door, and as I open it, I turn to wave at Matt, who is waiting to see that I get inside safely.

On Saturday afternoon, I look after Nathan while my mom and Dale go into Prairie Perks to do some bookkeeping and repairs on the espresso machine. After we build block castles, I sit Nathan down on the couch and read to him about tractors until he drifts off into his afternoon nap. I fix myself some cinnamon toast and a root-beer float and go to the computer room.

For the first time in several weeks, I check in on "Bex and the City" for the latest report on her crantini-soaked evenings of sexy scandal. Instead, I find a shocking entry about how Bex was recently fired from her job. Apparently, one of Bex's evil coworkers left her boss a printout of the blog entry in which Bex describes getting it on after hours in her cubicle with Pablo, a copier sales rep from Trenton, New Jersey.

How very interesting. So I guess I'm not the only one who's been experiencing a little TMI comeuppance.

***

The second performance of *Grease* is even better than opening night. The audience is on its feet before we've finished the final number. Dale hugs me so hard after the show that I fear he'll crush me. Once again, Jai keeps his distance from me. I notice Matt go up to Katie after the receiving line ends, and he's grinning from ear to ear as he talks to her. Yep, he's definitely smitten, and why wouldn't he be? Still, if this blooms into a full-on romance, I'm going to have to find a way to deal with it, and it won't be easy.

I ask Dale to wait for me, and I quickly run to the dressing room and change out of my costume. I can take my makeup off at home. When I get back to the hallway, Matt is still talking to Katie, and I don't want to interrupt their conversation by asking Katie if she needs a ride home, which she obviously doesn't. A twinge of jealousy rushes through me as I head out the door with Dale. Still, after all of the crap I've dealt with lately, I know I can handle this.

✳✳✳

My parents must have strapped Nathan to his seat during the Sunday matinee to keep him from running onstage and treating everyone to the impromptu performance he so badly wanted to give. They have obviously removed his shackles by the time curtain call rolls around, because Nathan scampers down the aisle and yells my name repeatedly from the front row as he jumps up and down. As the curtain closes, Matt gives me a friendly nudge and says, "Looks like he's your biggest fan."

It's true. He is. And more affection is forthcoming when I see Nathan outside the auditorium.

"Becca, you're the best singer in the world! Wow!" He jumps into my arms, and I twirl him around.

"Thanks, little dude," I say as he wriggles free from my embrace. Nathan sprints a figure eight through the lobby, yelling,

"Hopelessly we voted for you!" We'll have to buy the *Grease* sound track and work on those lyrics at home.

I'm not embarrassed by Nathan's behavior. Instead, I sigh and wish that I felt as free to express myself as he does, but I know that those days are over. It's time to grow up. And as much as it sucks to be fifteen, I imagine that full-on adult life is even worse. It seems like a very repressed existence.

After my family departs, I head down to the dressing room and change out of my costume for the last time. We all immediately get to work striking the set, which only takes about an hour and a half thanks to Ms. Miller's brilliant delegation skills.

When we finish, a party awaits us in the cafeteria. It's a potluck. Spread out on the table are Midwestern delicacies such as ham on margarine-smeared buns, a half-dozen types of bars, a baked-bean casserole, barbecue-flavor potato chips, and at least three varieties of Jell-O salad. Yep, the usual suspects are here. I'm totally proud that my mom donated four dozen of Prairie Perks' famous cupcakes, which are all topped with about a cup of buttercream frosting each. I note with satisfaction that those cupcakes are first to fly off the table.

After we've all gorged ourselves, Melissa Stromwell steps forward with Ms. Miller's gifts, for which we all chipped in a dollar: a huge bouquet of Gerbera daisies and a blank book that everyone signed with a message.

Ms. Miller gets a bit choked up when Melissa presents her with the gifts, and we all applaud our beloved teacher.

"Ms. M, you effing rule!" shouts Derrick Hansen.

Ms. Miller clamps her fist to her chest and throws her head back in a mock swoon. "Oh, thank you, Derrick. Right back at you." She must be in too good a mood to scold Derrick for his semi-swear.

I sit down with a glass of punch and survey the scene. Jamie is sitting on Lance's lap, and they're whispering in each other's ear. Melissa and Haley sit nearby comparing split ends. Josh is sitting alone at a table reading a comic book and eating what appears to be an entire bag of Doritos. That's fine. At least he's staying out of trouble.

Matt and Katie are both leaning against a table, deep in conversation. I haven't had a chance to ask her yet how she feels about Matt, but based on her body language, it's pretty obvious. She has her hands clasped behind her back, and her shoulders keep scrunching up and down with nervous energy. It's actually very sweet to watch. I will definitely be calling her tonight to find out what's up with her and Mr. Wooderson.

I'm constantly aware of Jai's presence. At one point, I see him talking with Evan, and I wonder if they're discussing all of the ways in which I'm an awful, bigmouthed backstabber. They're both smiling and laughing, so maybe not. Ashli walks up and joins in their conversation, and Jai looks in my direction for a moment. Our eyes meet from across the cafeteria at one point, and he quickly looks away.

Suddenly I feel like crying. Every glance from Jai is a reminder of my mistake, and I wonder how long this is going to go on. Then I remember that just a short time ago, Evan was acting the same way. But he was able to be civil with me on the ride home with Matt, and then he voluntarily talked to me a couple of weeks after that. So maybe there's hope with Jai. Then again, the Evan situation is probably way more forgivable than what happened with Jai.

I feel a little weird sitting here by myself, so I get up to help myself to another glass of punch. I pass the table that Jamie, Lance, Melissa, and Haley are sitting at as I walk toward the punch bowl. Jamie is talking, and the other three are laughing.

"—like we all didn't know Jai was gay anyway. I mean, *duh!* I suppose she thinks that everyone around here was too stupid to figure that out, but she's the stupid one. And it's not like he's the only fag at this school."

I turn around. I don't care that Jamie just called me stupid, but I will not tolerate her talking about Jai that way.

"Don't do that, Jamie," I say.

Jamie looks over at me in surprise. "Don't what? Tell the truth? Get used it, *chica.*"

I stiffen and take a few steps toward her.

"Don't call Jai—or anyone else—a fag. It's hateful."

"It's the truth."

This is maddening. I know I'm not going to convince Jamie that she should be nicer or more sensitive, but she should at least learn to keep her ugly little opinions to herself. I need to take a different tack.

"Jai never did anything to you."

"The fact that he even exists is disturbing in itself."

Now Jamie's got me steamed. My heart is pounding and my hands are sweating. I'd like nothing more than to run out of the cafeteria and go have a good cry, but I can't let Jamie get away with saying the things she's said.

"I would say the same thing about you. You're petty and nasty and pick on people just to make yourself feel better."

Jamie leans back on Lance's chest, and he strokes her hair. Melissa and Haley look like they're going to burst out laughing at any moment. I'm so glad that this is providing them with some entertainment.

"I don't know what you're talking about," Jamie says. "I already feel pretty good about myself."

"I'm sure you do," I reply, my voice cracking slightly. Damn, I *am* going to cry. "But you just might want to consider being nice once in a while. You know, as an experiment or something. Staying out of other people's business wouldn't hurt either."

Jamie's eyes narrow. "If you're referring to that stupid little blog of yours, well, you can only blame yourself for that. I just thought Jai would like to know what his *friend*"—Jamie puts air quotes around *friend*—"was writing about him. So if you want to talk about petty and nasty, you should go look in the mirror, dork."

Lance, Melissa, and Haley all laugh when Jamie says this, and Haley high-fives Jamie.

"Nice," Haley says. "Totally classic."

Tears well up in my eyes. I've said and done enough, and now it's time to get out of here. I whirl around and practically bump heads with Jai. He must have been standing right behind me. Great. I'm sure he loved hearing that confrontation. I wonder if he heard Jamie use the F-word. If he did, he no doubt blames me.

"Sorry," I mutter as I rush past him.

When I get out into the hallway, I'm not sure where to go next. I should probably just call Dale and ask him for a ride home. Or I could walk. It's really not that cold out today. I head toward the theater to fetch my coat from the dressing room.

And suddenly I see Jai.

"Wait!" he shouts, rushing toward me.

What does Jai want? To tell me off? Box my ears? I just stand in the middle of the hallway, my arms dangling by my sides. I'm totally worn out all of a sudden.

When Jai reaches me, he puts his hand on my shoulder. "Becca, I forgive you. You made a mistake, and this wasn't the way that I wanted to come out, but in a way, it's a relief not to be hiding anymore."

"Oh, Jai," is all I can say before leaning forward and sobbing into my hands.

Jai puts his arm around me and strokes my hair. "I know you never meant to hurt me."

"Never," I wheeze between hiccups. "I love you."

"Oh, I love you, too."

And with that, Jai scoops me into a hug, and we both stand there for a minute, crying and holding each other.

We eventually both pull back, and I grasp Jai's wrists. "I can't even begin to tell you how sorry I am for what happened. I've been so scared and so fricking furious with myself for betraying you like that. I was trying to change, trying to be a better person, and it totally backfired. I failed. And I let you down, too."

Jai leans against the wall. "Well, I'd be lying if I said I wasn't incredibly hurt. And I still haven't made up my mind about transferring schools."

"Oh, please stay. Katie and I would go crazy missing you."

"I know, and I'd miss you guys, too. Right now, I'm just trying to separate out the reality of being out in Pine Prairie with my actual desire to go to the performing arts school. And I'm still not sure what I want to do."

"And who's to say that people won't be weird about your sexuality in Minneapolis? I mean, it's not like teenagers there are so much different than the ones here," I add. I'm not sure if this is the most helpful thing I could be saying at this moment, but I'm sick of holding everything inside. And I think Jai would appreciate my point of view.

Jai nods. "You're probably right. And not to dwell on it right now, but I'm not sure that I'd come out if I went to that school. At least not right away. But you know what? Aside from a little teasing from the Rod and Gun Club, most people have been pretty cool about things. I mean, people have stared or laughed at me a little, but I've also gotten a few notes and e-mails from people telling me that they don't think it's a big deal and that I shouldn't worry about what everyone thinks."

"Really?" I ask. "Like from who?"

"Well, for starters, from Matt. And Evan, too."

"They did? That's great."

I must have good taste in guys.

"And of course Ashli's been wonderful. She's a really great girl, and now that she knows I'm gay, well, let's just say that I'm a lot more comfortable around her. When we were watching

Strictly Ballroom the other night, Ashli said she still wanted to go to the prom with me, too. Can you believe that?"

I burst out laughing. "Yes, I totally can, Jai. People think you're great, and they admire your strength, too. They like you just the way you are."

"Funny," remarks Jai, "I was just thinking the same thing about you."

Becca's diary:
NO ELECTRONIC VERSION AVAILABLE

Saturday, February 21

My birthday was a rock-star day full of wonderful surprises. Things got off to a great start when I woke up to the heavenly scent of bacon, onions, and green peppers. Dale made me an incredible omelet along with one of his sour-cream coffee cakes and freshly squeezed orange juice.

For his part, my brother ran around the house serenading me like a broken record. Dale had taught him "Birthday" by the Beatles, and as he repeated the opening strains of "na-na-na-na-na-na, you say it's your birthday," I couldn't help but think of the Geek from *Sixteen Candles*. However, I predict Nathan will be much more socially successful than Anthony Michael Hall ever was. Nathan doesn't go around sniffing girls' necks all the time or declaring himself the King of the Dipshits. He prefers the title of Captain Fix-It.

During lunch at school, Jai, Katie, and Ashli totally embarrassed me by singing "Happy Birthday" as loudly as they could in front of the entire cafeteria. I quickly forgave them when Katie broke out a tinful of my mom's cupcakes.

I felt supernervous when my mom picked me up after school

for my driving test. I mean, I'd taken driver's ed and driving lessons last summer but hadn't practiced much since it started snowing in November. Dale took me out a couple of times earlier in the week, but I was still feeling pretty rusty. Although I kind of screwed up the parallel-parking part, I passed!

My mom let me drive the minivan home after my test, and as I pulled in to the driveway, I saw my aunt Susan's 1995 Honda Civic parked next to Dale's pickup. My mom pulled some keys out of her purse and pointed at the Civic. I looked questioningly back at her, and she told me Aunt Susan got a minivan of her own earlier this week, and Dale worked out a deal. She could see how stunned I was, but the only other thing she said was, "Happy birthday, honey." Then she told me to buckle up and enjoy my newfound independence.

Enjoy I did. I drove myself over to Jai's house that evening, where he was waiting with Katie, Ashli, Matt, and Evan. We feasted on pizza and this ridiculously chocolaty cake that Jai and Katie had baked. Then we settled in for a viewing of *Heathers*, which Evan and Ashli admitted they'd never seen before. It might have been my imagination, but I think Ashli and Evan sat next to each other on purpose.

And I *know* that Matt and Katie sat next to each other on purpose. In fact, I totally saw him reach for Katie's hand halfway through the movie.

For a minute, I felt a little depressed. I mean, there I was, boyfriendless on my sweet sixteen. I never imagined that I'd be sitting in a room with my ex-boyfriend, former crush, two best friends, a new friend . . .

Then I realized how silly I was being. These people are *all* my friends. They like and care about me, and they've all proven that in their own ways lately. I've come a long way in just a couple of months, and it's no longer just Katie and me sitting by ourselves while I babble about something stupid and inappropriate.

I leaned back on Jai's sofa and let out a breath of relief. I'm no longer the Overshare Queen, the girl everyone can count on for too much information.

I'm just Becca, and it feels good.